WHO'S LOVING YOU

Sareeta Domingo is the creator and editor of *Who's Loving You*, as well as a contributor writer. She is also the author of *If I Don't Have You* and *The Nearness of You*. She has written numerous erotic short stories and an erotic novella. Her books for Young Adults are published under S.A. Domingo, including *Love, Secret Santa*. She has contributed to publications including *gal-dem*, *Black Ballad*, *Stylist* and *TOKEN Magazine*, and has taken part in events for Hachette Books, Winchester Writers' Festival, Black Girls Book Club and Bare Lit Festival among others. She lives in southeast London.

sareetadomingo.com // @SareetaDomingo

WHO'S LOVING YOU

Love Stories by Women of Colour

Edited by Sareeta Domingo

First published in Great Britain in 2021 by Trapeze
an imprint of The Orion Publishing Group Ltd
Carmelite House, 50 Victoria Embankment
London EC4Y 0DZ

An Hachette UK Company

1 3 5 7 9 10 8 6 4 2

A CIP catalogue record for this book is
available from the British Library.

ISBN (Hardback) 978-1-4091-9372-2
ISBN (Trade Paperback) 978-1-4091-9373-9
ISBN (eBook) 978-1-4091-9375-3

Typeset by Born Group
Printed and bound in Great Britain by Clays Ltd, Elcograf S.p.A.

www.orionbooks.co.uk

For my husband – he's the answer to the question.
And for everyone in my life whose love fuels me.

Contents

Introduction

'Who's loving you?' I never really considered this spirited demand sung by '90s R'n'B group En Vogue while I tried to emulate their sweet harmonies as a teenager – or even the bygone, innocent clarity of Michael Jackson, backed by his brothers, when they initially asked it decades earlier. The answer was, of course, nobody much at that age, for all my interest in the idea of romance.

But between the pages of my beloved books, it soon became apparent that neither the tales of high school romantic woe, nor the sexy bonkbusters I'd eye curiously on the shelves (OK, and sneakily read), nor even those sophisticated, classically revered literary tales of love and honour, featured any people who looked like me. What did that mean? How did that condition young Black girls like me, or any people of colour at that impressionable age, to think about who society deemed 'deserving' of that elusive, fizzy feeling, those butterflies, that heartache? Was love and desire not for us?

The first time I can remember seeing protagonists that I could truly relate to, and who were engaging in that coveted act of falling in love, it wasn't in the pages of a book at all. It was in a film – and an American film, at that. As I grew into adulthood, it almost became expected. Finding fiction that portrayed the most essential of all human emotions – love – or that most intimate of human interactions – sex – featuring characters whose experiences reflected my own as a Black British woman, was going to be nigh on impossible.

As these narratives didn't seem readily available, I started to consider putting finger to keyboard myself. They began as stories for nobody in particular, then I progressed to writing short fictions for university professors to praise or critique and later, stop-start attempts at larger projects. But suddenly, there it was: I was given the opportunity to become a published author. Commissioned to write a number of erotic shorts, and then a novella in the same genre, I was finally on my way to establishing myself as an author. My main brief was to make the stories appeal to women aged 18–35, but, if I'm truly honest, my initial concern was that this audience wouldn't want to see people like myself portrayed within them. Through the fiction I'd consumed up until then, I'd been conditioned to think of the readers of romantic or sexy stories as a certain demographic, and wanting only to consume a homogeneous, singular representation. Would they want to read what I wanted to write?

Of course, as time has gone on, I've shaken off the shackles of such concerns. I portray love and desire between a variety of characters in my writing – people who look like me, and whose world view is similar to my own, or in some cases not. However – and this should be obvious, *but* – human beings *of all kinds* fall in love, and have desire, and heartache, and heartbreak. It's vital that we get to see one another in this sometimes fire-hot, sometimes soul-warming, sometimes icily-devastating light. It is vital that we see *ourselves* portrayed in this way. Seeing love of all kinds represented fully, in art as in life, allows us to relate on a level that can be dangerous when lacking.

Romantic stories work on a special alchemy. They tap into something that is totally outside of any other human experience. Experiencing love and heartache vicariously through the pages of a story, over and over again, is a feeling like no other. We may not know what it's like to fly a spaceship, or commit a murder, or hike across the wilderness when we read about such things – but we understand love and desire, whether we've actually experienced it or not. The feeling of craving it, of being in it, of having lost it; these feelings are inherent to our humanity. Love is inside us – *all of us.*

I conceived this anthology as a way to create space for British women of colour to write about romantic love in its many guises, for all of us to read, experience and relish. I've chosen this group of incredible authors, some of the very best working today, for their unique ability to delve into the emotional landscapes of their characters. It is my honour to be among them, and to create a showcase for a collection of stories imbued with love and romance. Who's loving us? Let us show you . . .

Sareeta Domingo

THE WATCHERS

Kelechi Okafor

PROLOGUE

In the sliver of space between this world and the next, we the Watchers reside. Our purpose is simple: to guide the souls we are assigned in the task they chose when they were formless orbs of light.

There are many times we have looked on as you humans (or, as we know you, 'the Watched') have described an experience as a mere coincidence, instead of accepting that there is a particular path you are on. Those gentle nudges are our way of reminding you of that which you never wanted to forget.

We can only help so much, because ultimately whether Watcher or Watched, we are all an aspect of the divine and must be allowed to express that divinity in the way we choose. We slip between time and galaxies, simultaneously observing all that has been, all that is and all that will be. Time is only a suggestion and yet I have watched as so many of you enter a world only to obsess over this measure of your own making. The Watched return eventually and are reminded that what seemed like a lifetime barely amounted to a moment here.

Returning to this place that is really no place while being every place, is a chance to reflect on the lessons garnered on the earth, and to plan which lessons still need exploration until the time comes when all the lessons have been mastered.

The Watched tell themselves that 'Time is the best healer' but what they truly mean is that *love* is the best healer. Time cowers in the face of love's many manifestations. In this realm, the Watched decide on a theme of love they want to explore in various lifetimes. The soul remembers the task, but once the Watched enter into a human form, they go through the forgetting which is necessary at the beginning of each lifetime. The Watched are always aware that they will forget once they enter the earthly realm, so they chart reminders in their human lives just in case they were to ever lose their way. It sounds simple enough, until the Watched enter into a world where so many obstacles have been put in place, some by those higher than us and some by those who are not, to test their will and power to love against all odds.

Many of the Watched tire quickly when they feel that they have very little control over the life they chose – but then there are others, like Chinonso and Ndidi, who persevere lifetime after lifetime.

They meet in each human stint having no memory of the other meetings, only a vague yet visceral sense of having met before. I must make it known to you at this point, dear honorary Watcher, that this isn't a love story of the sort the Watched seem to spend an amusing amount of their lives chasing. This love is not propelled by flimsy romance. Instead it is spurred on by the unwavering desire to evolve into one's highest self while in human form. In other pairings between two beings of light – or twin flames, as they are commonly known – there is an alternation between who remembers something of the task both beings agreed to complete. The being who remembers will usually be the chaser, the one tasked with helping the other to acknowledge something greater than the human flesh they now inhabit. The other, being the runner, will avoid the intensity of the calling for a number of earthly reasons. Between these two, though, it seems that Chinonso has taken on the role of chaser for many lifetimes, which isn't to indicate Ndidi loves less, because in fact her devotion to being human helps them both to grow in their understanding of humanity . . .

CHINONSO AND NDIDI

Today I watch Ndidi teeter in the heels she debated over wearing, while cocooned in her sanitation pod and navigating it on a cobbled pavement by Albert Docks. The pods were interesting inventions and still needed a lot of work, but in a world where the fear of pandemics had taken hold, government-issued sanitation pods had become the norm when out in public. Made from self-sterilising thin plastic, the pods would enclose the individual, allowing for normal range of movement while limiting contact with others.

I catch the 'fucking hell' Ndidi mutters under her breath as her ankles momentarily wobble in the pod because of the uneven ground, and maybe the weight of her expectations of the evening ahead. 'Who the fuck chooses a slavery museum for a first date?' I hear her think to herself. Chinonso is the who.

Chinonso loads his phone screen onto his pod to see if an 'almost there!' text has been sent by Ndidi. Nothing. He would usually be annoyed by this lack of an update but on this occasion it makes him smile. He likes that this woman he is about to meet seems to care very little about explaining herself and just seems to dance to her own tune.

'Nonso?' is what he hears that causes him to turn around and look straight into the face of Ndidi.

'Ah! Didi, hey!'

A thick Liverpudlian accent cascades out of Ndidi's mouth as she smilingly says,

'I told you not to call me that, professor boy, it means nowt. You of all people should know that you don't fuck around with Igbo names – they have meanings, you know. I noticed in the app that you shortened your name, but I won't be joining you in such rebellious behaviour.'

I look on at them meeting for the first time again and notice as always the way time bends to allow a brief instant of knowing. They both feel it but laugh it off as first-date jitters.

'I'm very happy for you to still call me Nonso . . .' he teases. They both laugh, while taking each other in. They've sent so many messages to each other on the dating app that they mistake the pre-existing deep connection with one another for merely feeling comfortable from such long conversations. Swiping on a person's picture on a dating app had become mechanical for the two of them, so it is a relief they cherish to have found someone that feels different to all the other dates they have been on. A brief silence is Ndidi's prompt to say what has been on her mind.

'Not being rude or nothin', but a slavery museum for the first date? I know I agreed but fucking hell, it's intense, innit?'

Chinonso worries for a moment that he might sound weird for admitting how he had come to decide on the venue of their date, but decides to be brave, as something tells him that he will be safe here.

'I actually had a dream about you before—'

Ndidi interjects, 'Oh come off it! A dream! About me! Do you use that line on all the girls then?!'

Chinonso continues, sensing that somewhere in her tone Ndidi believes him.

'Before seeing you on the app, I had a dream where you turned to say something to me and it was in front of one of the displays at this museum.'

Curious, Ndidi asks, 'What did I say? And was I dressed like this?'

With the courage fleeting now, Chinonso smirks, 'I'll let you know when you say it. As for what you were wearing, I can't remember. But the shoes looked more comfortable.'

Ndidi is surprised by her own laughter at the cheeky joke.

'The museum will close soon, so why don't we go in and I can show you the things I find most fascinating here, then dinner after?' Chinonso feigns confidence as he states this because it is unlike any other date he has been on. Usually it would be a coffee and a chat or drinks mixed with a fun night and mundane texts thereafter.

Chinonso's decision to move to Liverpool from London so he could teach Postcolonial Studies seemed very random to everyone who knew him, but, as he explained to them all, once he had seen the job vacancy, a gut feeling led him to apply. As you, honorary Watcher, are beginning to learn, nothing is really by chance. From Chinonso's father in Nigeria being an avid Liverpool FC supporter, to the 'visit Liverpool' billboards Chinonso kept noticing when he was out and about. Everything delicately placed and carefully planned so this moment could happen. This moment where they would both make the choice to pursue their task in this life or not. It would seem rather peculiar to someone unfamiliar with fate and free will as to how these seemingly opposing systems could coexist, but the truth is that they were and always will be one. Chinonso and Ndidi haven't always decided to exist in the same lifetime as each other. It has happened in a few lives where one of these flames has decided to rest and simply ruminate on every lived experience or has chosen a different galaxy completely. What usually happens is that they spend these lives learning something unique to them about the nature of humans and love while feeling a lifelong yearning for another soul that they can't quite place. That isn't to say that they aren't happy in these lifetimes, because they are, sometimes even happier than the lives where they do meet. The only defining factor is that desire for another, yet not knowing who exactly it is.

'She's cute!' Ndidi points at a projected painting.

'That is Queen Nzinga. She ruled in the seventeenth century and actively resisted the transatlantic slave trade,' Chinonso shares almost automatically.

In the aftermath of the virus, all museums were forced to store artefacts in airtight vaults, and present the public with holograms of these artefacts instead, but despite this, Chinonso still knew of these African histories so deeply and couldn't quite fathom why he was so attached to learning and feeling as much as he was.

'I would've been like her, I think,' Ndidi says as she looks at the painting intently. 'I would've told 'em, "You want to enslave somebody, do you?! Well come and enslave this, you knobheads!" And I would've cut their balls off.'

It is maybe her matter-of-fact way of saying what she would've done that makes Chinonso laugh – the type of laughter that breaks one's heart open.

'That is extremely graphic! Should I be scared?!' Chinonso says as he wipes the tears of laughter from the corners of his eyes.

Ndidi chides, 'You're making people look at us weird because we're laughing in a slavery museum!' But secretly she is happy that her no-nonsense manner of talking seems to enamour Chinonso. She is used to men being rather wary of her fire and trying their best to dampen her spirits by encouraging her to be more 'ladylike'; hence the heels on the first date.

'This was the moment, by the way,' Chinonso mutters shyly. This was indeed the moment he had seen in his dream, almost like déjà vu. Ndidi saying she would've been like Queen Nzinga and not realising just how much she had shared that spirit in another life.

Our role as Watchers requires an extensive knowledge of our Watched, so I remember the time well when Ndidi and

Chinonso met as the slave ships arrived more frequently on the shores of Bonny, Nigeria.

It was 1756 and Ndidi's father, Chief Damieibi, saw it fitting to ensure the Portuguese traders knew of his daughter's beauty. He would've been elated that she marry someone capable of strengthening the family's reputation in the kingdom. Chinonso's family were newly converted Christians who had departed from their indigenous religion of Ijaw.

Their meeting in this lifetime was in a bustling marketplace where Chinonso sold his woodcarvings of ancient deities, much to the disapproval of his mother, who desperately wanted him to be more enthusiastic about their new Christian way of life.

Ndidi had been ordered by her father to show Pedro, one of the highly regarded new merchants, their beautiful town. Ndidi very much enjoyed the attention of this exotic-looking man, but couldn't help being repulsed by the trading of people who looked like herself. She understood, though, that her family's reputation and affluence couldn't rely on hereditary chieftaincies alone.

'This is very fine wood. It reminds me of your skin.' Pedro smiled as he looked at Chinonso's sculptures. Glad to have some interest in his work but understanding very little of what Pedro was saying, Chinonso began to explain to Ndidi about the deity known as Egbesu, who oversaw warfare. Chinonso didn't get much further, though, as Ndidi's eyes caught his and time waned and twisted.

In that split second, I saw them both forget Pedro's presence as well as the noise of the marketplace.

It wasn't about beauty here, dear honorary Watcher. What they both felt was the burning of meeting a kindred soul whom they had been searching for without ever realising that they were doing so.

Pedro asked how much for the mini carved god, and before Chinonso could answer, Ndidi stated a price four times more than Chinonso would've asked for. In that gesture he decided that he loved her and would spend his life doing so, regardless of their differing status within the kingdom. A trivial reason to decide to love someone, you might say, but these two souls never needed much of a reason to love. Watching the different moments when either of the two decide in each lifetime to love the other is always endearing to witness. It takes a brave soul to choose love, which is why so many of your kind prefer to believe that they merely fall into love as a shield from all the other sometimes painful choices that come along with it.

It was a surprise to Chinonso when, the next week, Ndidi appeared at his stall again as he was packing up for the day. Her father, Damieibi, would usually ensure that she was accompanied by a guard, but on this day she had fabricated a vague friend whom she needed to meet for ceremonial dance performance practice. Damieibi had chosen not to remarry after Ndidi's mother passed away when giving birth to Ndidi's younger brother, so he was perfectly oblivious to the fact that generally ceremonial dance practices only began three months prior to the event, not seven months before!

'Hello, woodcarver.'

'Hello, chief's daughter.'

They both smiled at the feigned formality and began walking alongside each other without a destination in mind.

'I hope you haven't spent all the money I negotiated for you last week. Maybe you will buy me an orange from this seller.' Ndidi was teasing but was touched at Chinonso's instant indignation at being in any way irresponsible with money.

'I would love to buy you an orange but I gave the money to my parents. They still see it as dirty spirit money, but even dirty spirit money can pay for our home, so they accepted.' Chinonso was quite unsure as to why he was explaining all of this to somebody he had only said a few words to the week before, but of course, we know that his soul understood Ndidi's soul and would always remember her.

'It is funny, isn't it? Since they brought us this god of theirs, who is meant to give us so much when we die, we keep having less and less while we are alive.' Ndidi surprised herself with this observation as she wouldn't have dared to say anything similar if her father were nearby.

'I'm surprised you feel that way, as you seemed rather enthusiastic when you were showing the foreigner around last time.'

'So I shouldn't have shown him around and my father should lose business, and I should end up having to join you in selling pieces of wood in the marketplace?' Ndidi was curter in her response than she had hoped to be, but looking over at Chinonso as they walked to nowhere in particular, she was comforted by the fact that he didn't seem offended by her comment. Chinonso indeed wasn't offended because he was too engrossed in this new feeling that he was experiencing because of her presence, which he could only describe to himself as a sweet pain.

I hovered by them as they chose a bench to sit on where the roadside met some woodland. Ndidi looked up at the majesty of the trees and recognised deep within herself that, without saying much, they had both decided to be like this together always.

Ndidi continued to meet Chinonso as he closed his stall every week even after the annual town ceremony had passed and thus the ceremonial dance practice should've ceased. Damieibi had gotten wind of Ndidi's meetings through one of his guards, and saw no real harm in them since Chinonso and Ndidi only ever seemed to sit on a rickety bench and talk until sunset.

Unfortunately, he had failed to remember that love doesn't require grand outings and such in order to grow. It is the very reason he had chosen to not take another wife after Ndidi's mother: when he was a boisterous aspiring businessman carrying yam around for his father, his wife had believed in him always. His love for her continued for his entire life and he wouldn't have had it any other way.

Pedro had taken a strong liking to Ndidi and had attempted a few times to talk to Damieibi about what a great business opportunity it would be for them both if he were to marry Ndidi. Of course, Ndidi's father saw this opportunity too, but couldn't ignore the ever so slight way Ndidi would recoil whenever Pedro made any gesture in her direction.

Damieibi had hardened himself over time to the selling of people because, as his father had told him, 'Yam is something we can only sell with the season. These devils will continue coming and taking our people. The sooner we have some control of the situation, the easier it will be to keep the devils at bay.' Somehow the ever-looming prospect of his own daughter marrying into such an industry softened the hardness he thought he had done well to build over the years. If these merchants were in fact devils, would that make Ndidi a sacrifice if he were to allow a marriage to go ahead? These were questions that plagued Damieibi and they wouldn't cease until his last earthly breath.

As they sat on the rickety bench under the majestic trees as they had done many times before, not realising it would be the last time they would ever see each other in this lifetime, Ndidi told Chinonso of the plans her father and Pedro were making for marriage. I felt the pain in Chinonso's heart as he realised that he would need to do something lest he lose Ndidi forever.

'We can leave.'

'What?'

'We can leave here together. I can find a way to send my parents money that I make from my sculptures and I will take on other work to provide for us both. I know you will not have all the wonderful materials and jewellery you are used to now, but I will do my best to give you something.'

Ndidi wanted to think the idea was ridiculous and to believe that she couldn't live without the fine world her father had provided for her, but Chinonso's face gave her every reassurance that they would have more than enough, because they had each other.

'Maybe we don't have to run away. Maybe I can tell my father about us and he can find some extra employment for you.' The two flames hugged tightly and the celestial sparks that they could not see, but felt, danced around the two of them and ascended past me and into the heavens to mark their place in that lifetime.

And so it was that Ndidi told her father of the love she felt for Chinonso and her hope that her father might allow for them to be together. Ndidi's father was so taken aback by the courage of his daughter's request that he, too, felt bold enough to approach Pedro about calling off plans they had been making regarding Ndidi's hand in marriage.

One of the lessons we Watchers learn about humankind in every time's timeline is that their capacity for good far exceeds their capacity to do unkind things, yet, oftentimes it is the unkind things that people seem to focus on the most.

Pedro was a businessman first and foremost, and he considered the months of conversations he'd had with Ndidi's father as a negotiating of terms for an otherwise done deal.

He had arrived from Portugal pleasantly surprised at the beauty of this West African land and the intelligence of its people, but that did not mean he thought them equal to himself in the slightest. He was well aware of the intricate systems they had in place and the knowledge they possessed that far exceeded his own, but nothing could shift his perception that they were savage and that he had done well to engage with them amicably for this long. Pedro had already written ahead to King José to tell him of the pretty African girl he had secured to strengthen his trades deals with the locals.

I tell you all of this, honorary Watcher, so you understand that when Ndidi's father explained to Pedro that they could not go ahead with their deal because his daughter had already chosen a lover, he was met with rage.

It confirmed everything that Pedro had heard of these people, that they would be underhanded and sly in their business dealings. He had been told by other merchants that the best thing to do was to move with a firm and unrelenting hand, so the locals would understand where the power truly resided.

Pedro scoffed at the nonsensical love that was being positioned as an obstacle to his plans and so made it clear to Damieibi that if Ndidi did not accompany him on the ship and leave with him for the New World, he would take her woodcarving wretch of a lover instead. When Ndidi heard of this ultimatum and her father's insistence that he would find some way to fight back and call upon the other chiefs in Bonny, she knew she had to do something to save her father, Chinonso and her home. For Damieibi to enter into a battle with this merchant would mean many of the Bonny people suffering in the process.

Ndidi decided that she would leave with Pedro, and she prayed deep down that some day she would return to Bonny to finally be with Chinonso.

Damieibi felt great sorrow at having to accept his daughter's wish to go ahead with the marriage and to prepare to leave with Pedro within a couple of days. The great wedding ceremony he had imagined that would set him apart from all the other chiefs didn't go ahead, and he wouldn't have wanted it to, as the shame he felt at betraying his daughter was too much for him to bear.

Ndidi was beside herself that she could not find a way to let Chinonso know that she would have to leave at such short notice, but somehow she believed that she would one day return. She did return, many years later when the town she had known had changed into something quite different and her father had passed away and the trading of humans was even more aggressive with mounting British influence.

Pedro had gotten his way, yet the unkindness I spoke of can only be apparent to you, dear honorary Watcher, when you learn that he ordered his men to go in search of Chinonso and to find a way to abduct him. To think that a lowly woodcarver could've posed a potential hindrance to Pedro getting what he wanted in marrying Ndidi was enough to rouse the spiteful snake coiled within his soul. Pedro's men found Chinonso in the nighttime, carving outside in his parents' small compound while the rest of the family sang praise and songs of worship inside. Chinonso was loaded onto the ship that would take all those men who were bought and stolen from their homes across the Atlantic Ocean to be sold off into the unknown.

As Ndidi stepped on the ship with her heart in pieces, waving goodbye to her father, who was forever broken by the work of his own hands, she thought of Chinonso and his beautiful woodcarvings. Ndidi would only learn after departing Barbados, where Chinonso had been sold, that they had in fact been on the same ship for weeks, with Chinonso packed among many who had only just started the journey towards their misery and suffering.

Ndidi made no indication that she would seek revenge for what Pedro had done to Chinonso, but I would be with them both as Chinonso prayed to his deities and carved their images from bits of sugarcane shavings that he kept, and Ndidi prayed to the same deities for the strength to appear favourable to Pedro until the time was right to exact her vengeance. The deities looked upon them, as did I, and we all watched silently, knowing that the two were beings of light who would find a way to be together in another lifetime.

Years passed and Ndidi had become somewhat accustomed to the ways in Portugal, although many refused to grow accustomed to her. She tolerated Pedro's affection, which was only dressed-up ownership. Eventually, she knew the day would come when he would venture back to Bonny again for more 'stock'. Pedro had made quite an impression on the previous king of Portugal before his death because of Pedro's initiative at having returned home with the daughter of one of the main tradesmen, thus keeping business thriving. Pedro relied on his company men to travel to Africa in his place, but having received news of Chief Damieibi's passing, he had to return to Bonny to foster new relationships with the up-and-coming traders. For this reason alone, he allowed Ndidi to accompany him; not because it would mean so much to her to see her father's grave, but simply because it would ease communication with the locals.

Chinonso, meanwhile, thousands of miles away in Barbados, being treated as less than human on the best days, still held onto a capacity for love. Eventually he married Ebiere. Chinonso had chosen Ebiere because she was a kind and funny woman who originated from a town not too far from his own in Nigeria. Although he cared for Ebiere very much, he would often think of Ndidi, praying that, wherever she was, she was being loved as much as he loved her.

Ndidi waited until the second night of her and Pedro's arrival in Bonny to add poison to Pedro's food. I looked on as Ndidi calmly placed the woodcarving of Egbesu, made by Chinonso all those years ago, over Pedro's body as his life-force left him and she thanked the deities for bringing her this far, back to her own land, to rebalance the unfairness of fate. Ndidi gathered her belongings and we left in the dead of night, never to return to Bonny.

This is the reason that now, in the Museum of Slavery, Ndidi could recognise the bravery of Queen Nzinga – because, in another life, she too had fought in her own way against the tyranny of those who wanted to own those they could not be.

'I have to say I've enjoyed walking around this museum with you, Nonso. You've mixed education with flirtation and I kinda dig it!'

Chinonso smiles broadly at the compliment. Time has passed by the two of them effortlessly in the museum and they both relish each other's company. They walk closer together, at times their pods brush past each other and, although the pods feel rather clinical, they both still feel the sparks that I see dance between them and ascend into the heavens, marking their place in this lifetime.

'Can I ask you something?'

Ndidi laughs. 'You had better not be bloody asking me why I'm single, I hate that damn question!'

'No! I wouldn't dare ask that – it's clear that it's because you've been kicking men in their balls.'

They both laugh and Chinonso continues despite his nervousness at the intensity of the imminent question.

'What do you think happens to love when people die?'

Surprisingly, Ndidi doesn't resort to a witty deflection like she usually would. 'I dunno, to be honest, I'm still waiting to really feel what love truly is, but my guess is that the love carries on. Kinda like a frequency, the energy just stays there for all of time. My grandma says she still feels my grandpa's love and he isn't here any more, so yeah, I guess the love stays because it doesn't need a body to do so.'

Chinonso is stunned by the answer. 'Maybe you should become a professor.'

'Oh feck off!!!'

They continue to chat cheerily as they leave the museum and both look out over the docks.

'Your turn: what do you think happens?'

Chinonso pauses before responding, 'I think it's similar to what you were saying, but I think the love keeps moving. It can't really stay in one place because it has to find you in every lifetime.'

'Wow, deep.'

Neither of them laughs this time, as an unexpected seriousness befalls the pair of them. It isn't surprising to me, you understand, because this moment like many others has happened before. What both Chinonso and Ndidi are experiencing is a soul decision. It is that space in a human's existence where they must make a choice while subconsciously remembering every time they have made a similar choice in other lives.

Whether Ndidi and Chinonso realise it or not, all the times they have loved and felt great pain as well as great joy is being remembered by their higher knowing, and they are making the decision whether to pursue a love in this lifetime or not. They are not to know what will happen and what they will face. Chinonso always seems to choose to love Ndidi no matter where they find themselves. Maybe since Bonny, Ndidi has carried the weight of that life and fears a heartbreak and a loss that great happening again.

'Shall we get something to eat as planned, or have I bored you to the point of no hunger?' asks Chinonso, in a way that he hopes sounds casual enough to not appear too forward.

'Yeah sure, there's a Nigerian restaurant near Bold Street, I think?'

'With your strong accent I thought you might want something more European . . .' Chinonso teases.

'It's clear that you want me to show you just how African I am, and that might require the sending of an AirSlap!'

People who pass by them see a cute couple happily navigating their pods down cobbled streets, but if only they could see what I see, dear honorary Watcher; two melding lights made from stars and lives gone before and yet to come.

The entire evening they tell each other stories of their childhoods and hint at their own hopes and dreams, while they share quick glances deep into each other's eyes almost as a way of reassuring themselves that the one felt what the other was feeling too.

'You know what made me laugh when I saw your profile on the app? It was your answer to what three things you would need to have with you in social isolation to stay sane . . .'

Ndidi laughs, remembering her answers. 'Malt drinks, a fridge and seasoning!'

'So would you season the malt drink? Because you didn't specify having any food.'

'Look, professor boy, you've got to read in between the lines!'

'You sound like a politician!'

Ndidi hadn't put too much thought into her answer, as the weird time of social isolation was something she would've preferred not to dwell on, especially since it had changed the trajectory of the entire world. One minute you could meet up and party with friends, the next minute the entire country was assigned sanitation pods, among other stringent new ways of living. During the early stages of the social isolation rules, Ndidi spent what seemed like endless time in her apartment attempting to get on with her graphic design commissions, but losing hours in her day creating images of beings made of all the elements in nature. Ndidi found the desire to create these images rather disconcerting, as she had never considered herself to be someone very in tune with nature, yet with all that time alone, she dreamt of places and faces and events which seemed far beyond what she had seen in her waking life. A persistent feeling of there being more to everything that she had ever known refused to leave her be and as soon as the government relaxed the rules on virus precautions, she pushed all the dreams and drawings somewhere far away inside herself. In Ndidi's mind, whatever could've been waiting there to be explored felt too soul-taxing, and she felt too weary even in her late twenties to follow this exploration through.

'Where did you go? Did I say something wrong?' Chinonso worries that he might've offended Ndidi by making fun of her dating profile. On other dates he has found it rather odd how some women seem oddly embarrassed to have their profiles mentioned, as if they would rather pretend that's not how they had ended up on the date.

'No, not at all. I guess I just got a bit lost in my thoughts about how so many things have changed since the virus. Even the fact that you have to upload your monthly virus scans in order to be approved for dating capabilities on the app.'

They both smile wanly at each other, as they both wish to think of something lighter.

'There's an online Beyoncé concert next week. I had bought tickets for my sister, but she won't be able to go with me, so would you like to come along?' Ndidi feels uncharacteristically shy at making the first insinuation at another date. In the past she would've left it to the guy to initiate, but there is something about the fact that she doesn't want this date to end that reassures her of her choice.

'How is she not able to go with you – she could log in from anywhere?! Only humans could find a way to flake on an event they can attend from anywhere in the world . . .'

'Hey! Is that a "no" or what?!'

'Oh sorry! No. I mean yes! I would love to go with you. It's actually a cool way to get past the "waiting fourteen days before we can meet up again" legislation. Only takes one no-pod fool to cause an infection uptick.'

'Exactly, professor boy. I'm smart, me!'

With their next date agreed, Ndidi insists on paying for the meal and they leave the restaurant. Outside they stand silently, not knowing quite how to end a date that they wish wouldn't end. Ndidi inputs her location into her pod to initiate the city-wide curfew sequence, and looks over at Chinonso. 'So, guess that's it for tonight then. My oxygen supply in this thing needs charging anyway. Best get to practising your Beyoncé moves for next week.'

Chinonso playfully scoffs. 'I'm offended that you think I even have to practise! It has been really nice hanging with you, Di— I mean Ndidi.'

'It's been fun hanging out with you, prof— I mean Nonso.'

Their pods head in opposite directions into the night, and that is where you leave them, dear honorary Watcher. What happens next, you wonder? Well, both Chinonso and Ndidi will decide. I had warned that this would be unlike the romance stories you are accustomed to, where you are mostly gifted with an ending to ease your own anxieties about the fate of your experiences of love. We, the Watchers, look on from a space where endings don't actually exist. We see you without your constraints of time, thus we see you more clearly than you see yourselves. Rather than existing for answers, we are always hopeful that you might enjoy living in the questions. Breathe in and out of the unknown, because that is where the eternal wisdom you desire truly resides.

Chinonso and Ndidi have lived so many lives and yet somehow their story has only just begun. I will continue to leave the clues as they have requested, and watch them find each other again and again, each time their understanding of love growing so that when they meet once more in this sliver of space between this world and the next, they get that much closer to divinity.

LONG DISTANCE

Varaidzo

I had watched her cry for three days before asking if she was OK.

'Oh,' she said, a millisecond sooner than her mouth, the pixels jerking awkwardly as she wiped her blue-lit cheeks. 'Sorry, I thought I was the only one here.'

The air con in my office whirred. Outside, the lights in the corridor were off as nobody had walked past for hours.

i think it's just you and me, I told her honestly. *wanna talk about it?*

It was against the rules to talk to her while I was at work, but at this hour there was no witness to discipline me. Her gaze moved to the bottom right where my chat bubbles popped up. The computer glare reflected off her wet eyes, making shiny umber pools out of her irises.

She shook her head no and sniffed, wiped her nose with the back of her hand and slumped into her desk chair. I waited until I'd seen her stuttered breaths peter out into an even rhythm. Half an hour, perhaps longer. She looked ahead at nothing, her lip quivering. At some point I yawned and, though she couldn't see me, she caught it, her mouth opening wide as she stretched out her arms.

'Actually, I've had trouble sleeping lately,' she said. 'Are you still there?'

still here, I typed.

'I know this is strange,' she said, her voice uncertain. 'But could you stay with me? Until I fall asleep?'

I hesitated before replying. She blinked anxiously at the corner of the screen, anticipating my response.

'I like the thought of someone watching over me,' she said, quietly this time. 'It makes me feel safe.'

sure, I typed eventually, and she nodded gratefully at the words as they appeared. I watched her get into bed and click off her bedside lamp, so that the only thing lighting up the room was her monitor. It cast an alien glow across her face.

Mine was as repetitive a job as any, same routine, same motions. I showered and dressed, picked up coffee from the 24-hour gas station en route. I said hi to Samson or Joe – whoever was on security – and clocked in with my key fob. The only slight deviation from the norm was that my workday started at 2 a.m. and ended at 10 a.m., so it was hard to meet anyone on the job.

For the most part, the schedule suited me. I had opted to do the night shift at Journl after Jack broke up with me, to save myself from the particular torment of sharing an open-plan office with an ex. Seeing him every day had felt like pulling on a hangnail, and the more time that passed the more I'd felt myself peeling away until it seemed that half my skin had unravelled, just raw wound and broken heart bleeding over the coffee filters in view of everyone.

When the opportunity presented itself, I opted to become the sole night technician, fixing bugs that might occur when the day team was sleeping. I was glad to be alone. Mostly, the job entailed running systems updates that could take hours at a time, watching the percentages creep up slowly, silently . . . 45 per cent finished, 46 per cent done. Nothing to keep me company but my desk cacti and the fuzzing hum of the computer fan. Not usually.

Not until the glitch.

It first appeared during routine testing. An account had been flagged for having an issue with its timestamps, which in itself wasn't uncommon. Journl was meant to have revolutionised social networking, its unique MO being that each user could stream or update daily, but once those twenty-four hours were up every single post was wiped from the network. Follower counts: reset to zero. Likes and favourites: gone, along with the posts. The impermanence was intended to mimic real life, all posts living on only as memories, presenting a new blank sheet to fill in each morning with the turning of the clock. It boasted of being a platform for growth and forgiveness. An opportunity to start over, to do things differently today.

Part of my job involved making sure every user really did start over. Sometimes, say when a user travelled from one time zone to another, the system might get confused and think a post hadn't been fully wiped from the day before. It would flag the account as having a time discrepancy and I'd have to investigate, to make sure there weren't any remnants of yesterday's posts left over, relics from the past that should've decayed overnight.

But this glitch was different. An isolated account was persistently showing up as being live four years ahead of time, not a simple time zone confusion by a few hours but rather *years* into the future. An impossibility and thus a problem. I ran every test I could think of that first night, inspected the problem for three long hours and nothing, not a single thing, was operating out of the ordinary.

My guidelines were explicit: any account with suspicious activity should be suspended until the day team could look into it too, but this was more bizarre than it was suspicious. And, as my pride had been left to stew in the loneliness of the office, I refused to be stumped so easily. Clueless and frustrated, I dug my chin into the top of my desk and tuned into the live stream that had bested me.

There, I found her crying.

The room was relatively small. Bed behind her, beneath a window, and covered by wine-red sheets. She sat in a large black swivel chair which dwarfed her, and her knees were curled up towards her chest. Her dark brown skin was engulfed by the blue of her monitor, painting her navy, and as I watched the tears roll from her eyes I felt for a moment that she was underwater, drowning, the computer screen a barrier like aquarium glass, and a rush of panic coursed up my back realising that she was too far away and I wouldn't be able to save her.

I clutched my throat with my hand and shook away the vision, scolding my imagination. In its place entered a strong compulsion to watch, a curiosity that seemed outside of my control. I observed her anonymously, watching her crying at her monitor, not speaking, not saying a word. Occasionally, she'd sniff or wipe her nose, tuck her hair behind her ears so no flyaways would stick to her dampened face. So small and vulnerable, she seemed to be. In need, I felt, of a cuddle. I passed half my shift with this watching. Until eventually, she logged off, gone, and I went back to work.

The next day it was the same. Timestamp reading four years ahead, and there she was again, crying right into my office. At this point, I knew for certain that I should have suspended her account. But I was fixated, that voyeuristic tug rooting me to her live stream. She needed this, clearly. Nobody would cry on the internet if they weren't looking for someone to reach out to them. Perhaps this account was her only outlet – just waiting for someone, anyone, to notice her pain. So on the third day, I did the thing we were strictly forbidden from doing. I left a comment on her stream.

hey, I typed. *are you ok?*

When I came into work the following shift, I had the long-forgotten feeling of looking forward to something. It was the first time since Jack had broken up with me that I'd hurried through the building with a spring in my step, keen to reach my desk and start the day. With him, it had been the hot coffee and soft butter croissants waiting next to my Post-its which had coaxed me out of bed, the illicit shoulder squeezes whenever he swanned past me, and the lunches we spent walking around the nearby park together, watching pigeons eat artisanal sandwiches out of bins. They were simple comforts, but I looked forward to them nevertheless.

Now, it was the promise of an unsolved mystery that had me eager to start my shift. It wasn't just the glitch that intrigued me, it was this weeping woman, this stranger I knew nothing about, let alone what might be causing her upset. Yet, at her request, I found myself quietly observing as she tried to soothe herself enough to sleep. And I was happy to do it. Each day that I came to work and saw her account had been flagged by the system, I felt compelled to tune in, to look for answers in the low light of her bedroom and the captivating canvas of her tear-bitten face. To check in. To see if she was doing OK.

you look like i feel, I said to her, as snot bubbled from one of her nostrils.

'I fucking bet,' she said, sniffing it away but smiling now, at least. 'You've got to be a loser to still be haunting Journl, right?'

haha, I typed, straight-faced and hunched over at my desk, knowing that our site had grown by hundreds of thousands this quarter alone. I couldn't say this without telling her I worked here, of course, and then I'd have to explain that I needed to suspend her account. I wasn't ready to do that, not yet. I wanted to unravel more of the mystery first.

Instead, we chit-chatted. We exchanged pleasantries – me typing, her talking, and we'd tell each other about the day we'd had, what we ate for breakfast; anything simple to distract from her crying. We even exchanged names.

'My name is May,' she told me.

weird, I typed back, *i'm june*. Her expression faltered for a second, her eyes narrowing as if she was suspicious.

no, seriously, I typed back. *june and may. bizarre right?*

For a millisecond she looked stunned, as if she had seen a ghost, then her shoulders relaxed and she sank backwards into her chair.

'June comes after May,' she smiled, the first honest smile I had seen from her yet, as if pleased to find out this much about me. 'Of all the coincidences on the internet.'

The more we spoke, the more her personality revealed itself. Despite the troubled states I often found her in, her manner was naturally playful. She couldn't sit still properly, nearly always sat lopsided in her chair, legs hanging over the armrests, spinning around as she spoke. I took to teasing her to cheer her up – sarcastic comments and light ribbing here and there – and found that she responded to this well, that this distraction could sometimes stop her from weeping altogether. She couldn't help herself, it seemed like. May could give just as good as she could take, her eyes glinting mischievously through the camera despite not being able to see my reaction on the other side. She loved to play with hypotheticals, and we could waste hours on them, mocking each other for our differences. Often, they were light and silly.

'If you had to give up tea or coffee for the rest of your life, which would you choose?'

tea, easy, I said.

'Coffee, naturally,' May replied. Other times the topics veered darker; life, death and the universe.

'If there was an oracle that told you exactly when and how you were going to die, would you go to her?'

i'd always be curious, I typed, but remembered my late mother in the hospital, and the six months diagnosis she had received which had given her no comfort at all. *but*

33

what would it serve me? no, only worth knowing if you could
change it, i think.

'Right, too much pressure to know,' said May. Then a
beat later, 'Though, I wonder, is it more or less pressure
to know only about your own death, than for the poor
oracle who must know everyone else's?'

On this point neither of us could decide.

May lived in Manchester, had found herself back in her
childhood bedroom at her parents' home, but had done
'that whole London thing' for some years previously. She
knew of some of the cafés, pubs I'd frequented before I
took the night shift, and all at once seemed less like a
stranger because of this. We established that we were
the same age, both twenty-five, but the way May dressed
and did her make-up was far more fun and youthful than
anything I could achieve. It was otherworldly and experi-
mental, all patterns and asymmetric cuts. She seemed to
have an ever-rotating wardrobe of wigs, different colours,
cuts, lengths. And as the nights went on and I began to
find her crying less, I learned that she could do make-up
like a stage artist too, would appear in front of the camera
looking so immaculate it was as if each live stream was
a performance itself, as if she anticipated that one day
she might log on to an audience of thousands more than
just my one as it currently stood. I wished I had even a
smidgen of her cosmetic prowess, but knew little more
than mascara and edge control myself, wore the same
uniform of blue jeans and beige jumper nearly every day
and had the same black box braids as I did at age twelve.

But it was May's nighttime routine that fascinated me
most. As I watched her wipe down her face and take

down her hair, revealing the neat cane-rows underneath, it seemed so intimate, the transformation. I felt strangely honoured that she would share these moments with me. When all was done, she would check that I was still there and ask, cautiously, like she was afraid I might say no, if I would stay until she fell asleep. Every night I said yes. Every night I kept my word.

At 9 a.m. on Mondays and Thursdays, a full team meeting was held across our floor. It was the last hour of my shift and the first hour of everybody else's, so nobody was at their most switched on. These were also the moments when it was hardest to avoid Jack, as often he would lead. I'd begun working at Journl before him, not long after graduating, and suggested Jack apply for a vacancy within the company. My position hadn't changed much since I'd joined – I was part of the IT crowd, once a technician that worked during the daytime, and now a technician that worked during the night. But Jack had quickly risen up the ranks. He'd joined as a designer, initially responsible for bits and bobs on the site's design, but he was now the total overseer of Journl's brand management and engagement. This meant he was essentially one of my bosses, and I had to deliver reports to him every week. Working alongside an ex is one thing, but working beneath him was a specific kind of hell.

He knew this, too – I could tell by the way he averted his gaze, focused on anything in the room other than me whenever he delivered, but I figured his guilt was something I could take advantage of.

After the morning meeting, I pulled him aside to explain my dilemma.

'There's an account I need the day team to look at,' I said. 'Her timestamps are glitching, but I don't think it's anything she's doing. I'm hoping we can resolve it without suspending her account. I think Journl's her lifeline at the minute.'

Jack seemed flustered, pushed his glasses up to the bridge of his nose.

'If you can't work it out, I'm not sure the day team will fare any better. Best to follow the guidelines.'

He nodded at me and turned to leave, but I reached out and grabbed his hand, a knee-jerk response out of desperation.

'No, please,' I said, imagining May's crestfallen face were she to find her account suspended, the drop at the corners of her mouth when she realised she was alone again.

Jack looked at where our fingers touched like a deer in headlights. 'Just this once.'

'OK, Junie—' he faltered and corrected himself, 'sorry. June. I'll have the day team look into it.' I grinned amicably enough, satisfied by this offer. But when I let go of his hand I was surprised to feel that, for a split second before my fingers loosened from his, he had clung a little harder, as if trying to resist.

It was a Monday when May finally asked to see me.

'Don't you have a camera? Microphone? Anything?' she said. I had it all, but the thought made me nervous.

i'm at work, I typed. *it's probably best if i don't.*

'Come on, dude!' she said, exasperated. 'I'm not asking for much. I just wanna check you're not, I don't know, some weirdo teen who likes perving on crying women or whatever.'

I looked around at the grey emptiness of my office, everything in shadow except my yellow desk chair and the computer screen. Nobody would catch me if I turned the camera on – I'd only be reported to myself. But I felt self-conscious. I rarely made an effort for work, making do with washing my face and oiling my braids – who was there to see me, after all? Now, as it turned out, there was May.

'I want to see who I'm speaking to,' she said. 'Please.'

I nodded, not for her benefit, but to encourage myself. I requested to join her stream. Seeing my face pop up below hers startled me, and I began to preen automatically, straightening my top and tucking any loose braids back into their bun.

May looked delighted, stared at me with the bambi-eyed joy of a child who has just seen snow for the first time.

'Hello, June.' She smiled.

'Hi, May,' I said awkwardly, crossing my arms protectively over as much of my body as I could. 'As you can see – not some perv.'

'Oh, I don't know about *that*,' May said, smirking, her gaze lazily taking me in. I felt my cheeks go hot, and was rattled to feel my stomach flutter nervously as I watched her watching me. 'So, this is your office?' she said.

'Yup.'

'It's bigger than I imagined.'

'You were imagining my office?' I pondered aloud.

'I really like your braids,' she said, ignoring me. I put a hand up tentatively towards my hair.

'Thanks. I can never decide if they suit me.'

'They definitely—' May began, but interrupted herself by yawning.

'You should sleep,' I told her. 'This is late even for you.'

'Worth it, to see your face, though,' she said dozily. 'Will you watch me?'

'I always do,' I told her.

'Keep your camera on this time?'

'Of course.'

Face-to-face discussions opened us up to each other. May, the mystery, became my perfect confidante, and I hers. Finally, I found out what had caused her to cry so, revealing another thing we had in common.

'If you must know,' she said, resting her head against her hand and gazing up at me. 'I'm going through a heartbreak.'

She looked at me expectantly, one eyebrow raised, and I felt as though I was being tested, that whatever I said next would determine whether or not our communications continued beyond this point.

'At least you're going *through* it,' I said sympathetically. 'I'm confident that I'll be stuck in mine permanently.'

She smirked and swigged from a green-striped mug on her desk.

'It got you too, hey?' She plonked the mug down like a gavel. 'What's your story?'

She leaned back in her chair as if settling in for the ride, but the truth was there was nothing much for me to tell. No scandal. Even mine and Jack's origin story was bland and typical.

We had lived in the same halls at uni and skirted around each other awkwardly in the shared common spaces: fumbling around the stovetop as we boiled our separate pots of pasta, or waiting our turns on table football in winner-stays-on. I'd recently lost my mother to cancer, and the grief had made me hard and shy. The most we spoke was during communal pre-drinks, and even then it was mostly small talk. I did Computer Science, he Design, and so fairly often we found ourselves shoved together as the square techy outliers on a floor of ostentatious humanities students. We might raise the odd eyebrow at one another in solidarity, or nod as we passed in the corridor.

Likely, our relationship may never have progressed beyond this, were it not for the toilets flooding at the SU one evening, cancelling our entire hall's evening plans and leaving us boozed up and restless in the common rooms playing childish drinking games. Truth or dare was the people's favourite.

'Jack, if you could sleep with anyone in this room, who it would it be?'

A nervous look around before his eyes finally settled on me. He meekly pushed his glasses up the tip of his nose.

'June. No contest.'

When it was my turn, I picked dare, and we spent the rest of the night cuddled up in each other's arms, kissing and sharing rum and cola from an old litre bottle of Pepsi. From then on, without fuss or much discussion, it was understood that we were together. And as far as I was concerned, it had worked perfectly.

Recalling this to May, I found my voice catching in my throat, a lump forming. Since the break-up, I hadn't spoken to anyone about our relationship, scared they'd accuse me of not being over it and not trying to move on. But May looked at me sincerely, mmming and ahhing in the right places, and smiling politely during the moments of sweetness where the story called for such a response.

'We never argued,' I told her earnestly. 'Not even once. It was so easy, *comfortable*,' I explained. 'And then . . .'

'And then?' said May.

'Then it was done. It was a Tuesday, I remember, and he'd sat me down at a park bench around the corner from where we worked, and told me it was over. One day, he'd been snuggling his nose into my ear and whispering sweet nothings about our future together. The next he'd fallen out of love. Just like that, said he couldn't be with me any longer.'

'Fuck,' May breathed out on a whisper. 'That's a punch to the gut.'

I groaned and hugged my knees into my chest, cringing at the brevity of my own rejection.

'Right?' I said into my hands. 'I'm sorry. I really wasn't expecting to get this emotional.'

'No, let it out. It's good,' May said encouragingly. 'I would know.'

I peeked through my hands and saw that she had pulled herself closer to the camera and was grinning at me now. She chuckled and pretended to tap the screen. 'Oi, come on, come outta there. No need to hide your pretty face.'

I lifted my head a fraction, exposing one eye to her.

'That's it . . . now a little more,' May coaxed. I lifted my whole head up and looked at her sheepishly. May began to beam.

'There she is,' she said gently. '*Beautiful*.'

I laughed, embarrassed, and tried to discreetly wipe

away a tear that had been pooling in the corner of my eye before it exposed itself by dribbling down my cheek.

'Yeah, well,' I said. 'These things happen. What about your break-up story? What did your partner do?'

May stiffened and stared into her camera, suddenly serious. She sat up straight in her chair, something I'd never seen her do before. Even through a screen, the intensity of her gaze was so strong I swore I could almost feel her breathing, imagine her heavy, even breaths tickling the hairs on my cheek.

'She died,' May said, the weight of her words filling up every corner of my office. 'And now I'm alone.'

That weekend, as I binged on daytime television and Kettle Chips, I chastised myself for getting so emotional about Jack to May. From the beginning, I had envisioned myself as a white knight in this strange scenario, concerned about the welfare of this woman who cried for the world every night – and yet I could barely hold my tongue as soon as there was an opportunity to discuss myself.

Our heartbreaks were not comparable, and I'd felt foolish instantly, crumpling up into my chair.

'I'm so sorry,' were the only words I found to make it better. May shrugged and began to fiddle with the draw-strings of her hoodie.

'Hey, it's not your fault, right?' she said. 'Cancer's a bitch. You catch it early enough or you don't.'

'Wanna talk about it?' I asked.

'Not really,' she shrugged. 'If that's all right.'

I nodded, understanding her wholly. I had struggled to speak about my mother when I first got together with

Jack and— Shit, there he was again in my thoughts. In the pause that followed, I felt embarrassment slip its way between May and me.

'I can't believe I whined on and on about my nothing boyfriend drama when you're legitimately in mourning.' I shook my head at myself. 'Forgive me for not reading the room, OK?'

'You weren't to know,' May said kindly.

We both smiled sadly at each other, and suddenly I felt the weight of the distance between my screen and hers, yearned to be sharing this moment in person so that I could give her the cuddle that she deserved. I wanted to find the words to let May know I was here for her, that I'd been where she was and understood why it could be easier to cry to a stranger than to anybody else. Instead, I confused myself by feeling shy about it. I kept looking at her, a sloppy smile in place of the words that should have been forming. And in the moment just before eye contact becomes uncomfortable, May flopped down in her chair and sighed, deflating fully.

'In some ways, I think your situation's worse,' she said gently. I raised my eyebrows incredulously.

'No way is it—'

'I'm serious,' she interjected. 'Before my girlfriend . . . before she *left* me, and I moved back in with my parents, I was still so full of love. I'd miss her even when she was in the same room, talking on the telephone or watching TV. Sometimes, when we were drifting off to sleep, I'd imagine myself shrinking so, so small that I could crawl into her ear and sit there, my feet swinging against her earlobe, because that's how close I wanted to be with her.'

I wrinkled my nose, surprised by this admission. May laughed.

'I know it sounds strange, but that's how I felt. So then when she passed, when suddenly she wasn't there any more, I knew: this is the worst pain I will ever go through. The grief feels like a parasite crawling through every vein in my body. But there's other times where somewhere deep, deep inside my belly, at the very core of my being, it also feels like warmth.'

She looked up to the sky then, her eyes glistening wistfully.

'Warmth?' I asked, curious.

'Yep. How funny is that? And I realised it means that the grief must be nothing more than smoke and ash, by-products of the fire that is our love. Love that will never fade or burn out, because it'll never get the chance to. The love still burns, and so the grief smokes.'

She stretched then, rolling her neck back and pointing out every limb like a starfish. When she released and looked at me once again, the wistfulness had been replaced with a juicy wickedness, that mischievous glint in her eye that made my pulse quicken.

'You, on the other hand,' May said, very matter-of-fact. 'Got told to your face that the love was done. Fuck going through that. What a dick. What a bellend. What a bloody—'

And then, to my surprise, she blew a long, drawn-out raspberry, her pink tongue sending speckles of spit onto her camera, making me jump as if there was a risk it might land on me too. It shocked us both into rapturous, glorious laughter.

*

'Junie – June, sorry, can I bother you for a second?'

Less than an hour left of my shift and there was Jack, recently showered and freshly caffeinated while I'd had a night's worth of being huddled over a screen to bruise the bags under my eyes. I nodded defeatedly.

'The day team tried to check out the username you sent me yesterday, but the account doesn't exist,' he said. He handed me back the paper I'd given him with May's details. Seeing her name in the morning light, folded up neatly in Jack's palms, I felt strangely exposed, like two separate worlds colliding, and I wished that I had kept the glitch my secret. I snatched back the paper protectively.

'Not possible,' I whispered, reading her name to myself. May, May, May. We had spoken just hours ago.

'Nobody's signed up with this account name. They spent a significant portion of their afternoon on this, June, it's not productive for staff to waste time on this stuff.'

I frowned at Jack. If our system had an unfixable glitch, surely that would damage the brand's integrity. But if he and the day team weren't bothered, then maybe I could still keep May my secret. If nobody was going to notice that I hadn't suspended her account, perhaps I wouldn't have to. I would never even have to admit to her that I worked at Journl at all.

'Doesn't it concern you?' I queried further. 'We've never had an account flagged as posting four years ahead of time before, Jack. It's odd.'

He held his hands up as if it didn't concern him much, and then ran his fingers through his hair.

'What do you want me to say? That someone's magically posting from the future? In which case, as long as her posts are still being wiped at the end of her day, I don't care. There's no problem for us to worry about.'

'Well, that's not possible,' I half-laughed. Jack didn't. He stared at me curiously over the rim of his glasses. 'That's not *possible*,' I repeated again.

'Well, there we go,' Jack said, shrugging. 'If anyone knows what is and isn't possible, it would be you,' he said.

On his way back towards his desk, he patted me patronisingly on the shoulder.

When I began my next shift, I still felt heated from this interaction with Jack, and sat down with the hot energy to moan about him to May for a good slice of my workday. When I joined her, she was in a short pink wig, eating from a packet of chocolate-covered raisins. As soon as my face appeared on her screen, she shook them at me, smiling.

'Watch, watch . . . you ready?'

She jumped up from her chair and sat on the edge of her bed facing me, one foot tucked under her thigh. She delved into the pack and retrieved a raisin, presenting it to me like a magician beginning a trick.

'Count for me,' she said. I nodded. She threw back her long, gliding neck, and one by one began to throw the raisins in the air, catching them expertly in her wide-open mouth. Her body swayed this side and that, judging with playful precision each little fruit as it fell down, down to be greeted by her tongue. Every time she leaned back, her vest would rise up, revealing the soft plump skin of her lower belly. With each successful catch, my mood lifted, my smile widened, I willed the streak to continue until I clocked out at 10 a.m. How could May's account not exist? I was right there, watching her, keeping count.

'Twenty-eight,' I finished for her, as a raisin bounced off the tip of her nose.

She laughed, falling backwards onto her bed, arms splayed out like an angel, breathing deeply. 'Not bad, hey?' she called over to me.

'No,' I replied, smiling. 'Not bad at all.'

That day was the first time since the break-up that I hadn't dreamt about Jack. When I woke up and realised this, I felt elated, good enough to punch the air – until the sombre realisation that I was, once again, letting him squat rent-free in my thoughts swiftly ruined the novelty.

When I spoke to May that night, I was fidgety and jarred, biting the skin of my finger and talking a mile a minute.

'I hate this,' I complained. 'I wish real life was like Journl and I could just wake up tomorrow with a clean slate, no memories of my ex any more.'

May flopped her legs over the side of her desk chair, exposing her boy shorts and thick, round thighs.

'Been there before,' she said, all knowingly. 'I went old-school with it and cut all my hair off.'

My eyes widened, incredulous.

'My advice?' May said. 'Shave it. Don't do it with scissors.'

'Did you regret it?' I asked.

'Uh, yes!' She practically squealed, flipping the long brown curly hair she'd chosen for herself that day. 'It was necessary though. I never would have met my girlfriend otherwise.'

I had never asked about the girlfriend much. I saw how it upset her so, how she brushed off the subject because it made her eyes water and how, to my shame, it made me feel uncomfortable. Jealous, even, watching how soft her face became whenever she spoke of their love. It seemed so pure and honest, a reflection of emotions that I had never seen coming from Jack. I wanted such looks for myself.

Today, though, May was particularly chipper, and wanted to talk. I was curious too. She walked me through their meet-cute, far more romantic than the one I had shared with her.

'So, originally, I'd moved to London with an ex. She'd started a postgrad down there,' May explained, swivelling in her chair. 'But the relationship soured a few months in.'

It sounded to me like the relationship had always been sour. The ex was overprotective, jealous. Wouldn't let May go out and meet people, so she spent most of her days cooped up in the flat alone, watching sitcom reruns and comfort-eating.

'She didn't even want me in a job,' May shook her head, 'just . . . awful woman. So, I took to practising my make-up while she was out – I was bored, right? Needed something to fill up the day. But all it took was one bad mood.'

The ex came home to her, shouting, effing and blinding. She swore the only reason May was doing herself up was that she must be cheating, chatting to people online or something. May's phone ended up in two pieces halfway across the room, her make-up landed in the bottom of the bin.

'Man, I had to get out of there!' May said, slapping her thigh, downplaying the seriousness. After this incident, she found herself a waitressing job at a little café and slept on a co-worker's pull-out sofa for a few months.

'It took me ages to wear make-up again,' she admitted. 'Felt like I was doing something wrong still. Eventually I thought, fuck it, what I need is a clean slate. So, I went at my hair with scissors in the bathroom.'

The hair was discarded unceremoniously on the bathroom tiles, and the task felt so momentous and overwhelming that she barely even looked at the end result in the mirror. It wasn't until the day after, passing her reflection in a shop window on the way to work, that she established the awful reality. Sides wonky, tufts and curls sticking out at odd angles – something out of a horror show.

'I was stuck . . . couldn't stop gaping at the shit show I'd created on top of my own head. Probably would have been outside that window all day had my girlfriend – well, she was a stranger then – not walked past that very same shop at the very same time.'

'And what did she do?' I asked, gripped.

'She said, "Miss, I'm sorry to interrupt. I just had to tell you, you have the most gorgeous bone structure I've ever seen," and it was like the most perfect thing she could have told me in that moment, because all I could see was my hair, but she had seen *me*, seen everything that was underneath. When I turned to look at her, I began weeping. You've seen it: snot dribbling and everything,' May said, shaking her head fondly. 'She took it well though, bless her. Gave me a tissue and bought me a chocolate bar from the corner shop. She had a shaved head too, see, and that afternoon she took me round her barber's to get my disaster sorted. I grew it back instantly, of course, but . . . me and her . . .' May trailed off and stared into the sky. 'We became inseparable,' she told the ceiling, softly. 'As comfortable with one another as we were with our shadows.'

When she looked back at the camera, I could tell from the shine on her eyes that she'd been trying to hold back tears.

'It's funny,' May said, returning to her cheerful self as if I hadn't noticed, 'that memory still feels clear as day. Like it only just happened.'

'How long has it been?' I asked.

'God, about four years ago now.'

'And what year was that?' I said, probing at the impossible theory that had started to twirl around my head.

May blinked at me. She furrowed her eyebrows, opened her mouth to reply and then reclined back into her chair. She looked at me quizzically, as if the question was lost on her.

'Are we in the same year, May?' I asked, so quiet I was almost whispering. I cocked my head to the side and waited for her to confess. She shook her head lightly and allowed a smile to creep into one corner of her mouth.

'You're a strange one, June,' she said. 'Very strange indeed.'

She excused herself to go to the bathroom then, and when she returned, she was bubbly with chatter and digressions. The conversation had moved on, and so a confession never came.

*

In bed, in the minutes before sleep took hold, I mulled over all the impossibilities my work brain would never let me fully indulge in. What if I *could* time-travel, took myself four years forward and ended up finding May sitting in that same bedroom, chatting away to me as if all was normal? I'd be pushing thirty, she wouldn't have aged a day. Could that be right?

If she really was four years ahead, if this was some bizarre glitch in time, where would this mean May was now? Had she moved to London yet or was she still in Manchester? And she would be twenty-one, of course. No longer the same age as me. Perhaps we wouldn't get on. What if I bumped into her in one of my locals and she had no idea who I was, this person I had spent hours sharing my innermost thoughts with? What if she looked at me from the shoes up and when her eyes locked with mine I saw the vacant stare of a stranger? My chest lurched at the thought. Would I say something? What would there even be to say?

It was an unlikely risk, however, as I rarely left the house these days beyond going to work – even my groceries were delivered. Socialising was a struggle at the best of times, but my work made it mission impossible. When most wanted to go for after-work drinks, I was still under my covers getting my eight hours in. When they were pooling out of clubs, I was strolling into the office. Eventually my social circles accepted that they should cross my name off the invite lists. I would tell them thanks but no thanks, knowing it was better to leave them to it, and they knew better than to press. I still wasn't up for being surrounded by lovesick couples, and was too glum to be good company myself. Before, I had felt mild disappointment at missing out, seeing the social media playback of my friends' wine-soaked evenings when I woke for work. But since meeting May, I felt that I wasn't missing anything at all. Whenever I wasn't talking to her, I was thinking about talking to her, banking anecdotes for when we would speak again.

The familiar, almost teenage fun she and I had together – catching raisins and playing would-you-rather – outweighed any night out. Eventually, I'd watch her go to sleep, her live stream still open on my desktop as I worked around her. Watching her snuggle up inside her duvet. Watching how serene her face looked, how I'd learned to tell when she'd started dreaming because the middle of her brow relaxed, the corner of her mouth turned upwards, and she had a face on her as peaceful and free as a newborn.

Truly, I felt that I was missing out on nothing. Not with May. Not until, one day, she reminded me that I was.

She brushed her newly painted black nails across her collarbone.

'Mmm,' she sighed, her eyes closing. 'June, do you ever miss it? You know, *with him*?'

I crossed my legs and played ignorant. Her fingertips slid into the v of her cleavage, her palm brushed over the print of her nipples under the vest.

'I miss it,' she said, 'I miss there being another person.'

She sighed dreamily, and her hand wandered beneath the waistband of her shorts.

'Would you watch me?' she said, opening her eyes and her legs.

I swallowed. I wasn't sure how to admit to her what I'd not yet admitted to myself. I took a deep breath and nodded.

'No, tell me,' she said. 'I need to hear you say yes.'

'Yes,' I said. 'I'll watch.'

Under her shorts, the shape of her fingers began to move in slow circles. She kneaded at her chest with the other hand.

'You like looking at me, don't you, June?'

My thighs began to throb with how tightly my legs were crossed. I glanced into the corridor, paranoid that someone else might be around. It was 4 a.m. The cleaners didn't get in until 6. It was just May and me.

'Yes,' I whispered. My mouth was wet.

She took off her shorts and pushed her underwear to the side. Her fingers disappeared and came out glistening.

'June,' she said, her voice breathless, her body open. 'June,' my name unfurled from her mouth on a moan. 'Would you join me?'

'I've never been with a girl before,' I said, the computer screen a poor substitute for pillow talk.

'Could I be considered your first?' May's eye twinkled. 'Did you like it?'

'Stop,' I giggled, red from the shame and the excitement simultaneously. 'I'm literally at my work desk, remember.'

'I like you, June,' she said. 'I wish I could fucking . . .' She reached her hand out towards me, but it didn't break through my screen like I wanted it to. 'I wish I could just touch you.'

'Let's meet each other,' I said, the words gushing out before I could properly think them through. She stared at me a little sadly.

'If only it was that easy,' she said.

'I know we're on opposite sides of the country,' I said. 'But I can get a train.'

'Really?' She sounded sceptical. I was sceptical too. If the impossible was true, and we met tomorrow, it wouldn't be May I saw, not my May. She'd be with somebody else, have some other girlfriend. She'd be four years younger and not know who I was. But the impossible was impossible, so I banished the thoughts as instantly as I'd had them. Instead, I focused my attention on realising these plans to meet May.

I would tell her often that I would visit whenever it suited, she just needed to give me the word, but every time I pressed for a specific date she would get vague and distant, something would always come up. At first I worried that she was going off me, that she didn't need me any more. But our conversations told a different story. In the following weeks, we devoured each other, shared secrets, shared fears, shared desires. I wanted to soak her up, know everything, know what she smelled like, know what her skin felt like beneath my fingertips. I tried to imagine her street, her front door.

'Come on, give me a date,' I told her.

'One day,' May said. 'Soon.'

Then came the day that May appeared in front of her camera looking solemn and serious, her natural hair in small twists framing her face. When we said our hellos and how are yous she addressed me rigidly, as if she had rehearsed the words before she said them.

'I'm coming down to London next week,' she told me. 'I can't hide in my grief forever. I think it's time for me to go back now. I think I'm ready.'

I clapped my hands and beamed.

'So we can meet?' I said, giddy. 'When does your train arrive?'

She looked straight down the lens, her eyes piercing mine, our locked gaze threaded across the cosmos. When she told me the date I gasped. Just fourteen days in time for her. But almost fifteen hundred for me.

Of course, I had my doubts about our meeting. Perhaps this was an elaborate hoax that she was playing on me, that she'd got what she wanted and now this was her plan to leave me hanging, have me waiting around forever. But I was too scared to ask if this was the case and find it out to be true, and so we didn't discuss it. If it *was* a hoax, it was one I was committed to now. I marked a reminder in my calendar, for four years ahead of time. And I swore to myself that I wouldn't forget.

I thought about what I would look like in four years' time. Would I be the same, or would I have aged dramatically? I worried how the world might have changed me in that time. What if I was different, and what if she was put off by me? In the two weeks leading up to her trip to London, we found ourselves speaking for most of my shift, my work performance slipping towards nothingness and her sleep pattern altering so greatly that she was almost as nocturnal as I.

On the night before she was due to get her train, it got so late that the cleaners had been and gone before we'd said our goodbyes. I urged May to sleep and she refused.

'Do you think I've helped you get over Jack?' she said sleepily, her eyes large as she looked up at the camera. I wasn't sure how to answer.

'I . . . I've never felt about Jack, or anyone, how I feel with you,' I said honestly. She nodded, and we gazed at each other longingly.

'And I . . . have *I* helped?' I asked.

'You help the fire,' she said, 'you help keep me warm.'

I wasn't sure what to make of this so I said nothing, just tried to take in the beauty of her face until May's eyes began to close again and she fought with herself to keep them open. At that point I ordered her to sleep.

'It's OK,' I told her. 'You're seeing me tomorrow anyway.'

'Please, June,' she said. 'Stay with me until I fall asleep.'

'I always do,' I said.

'Promise me this time. I don't want to be awake and you're not there.'

'I promise,' I nodded, and blew her a kiss. May tucked herself into bed, and, with her head turned at an angle, slightly upwards, I thought how odd it was; it almost looked like she was crying again, the way her skin seemed shiny under the light of the lamp. My screen went dark when she turned it off.

The next day, I rushed into work, giddy to see how our date went. If my suspicions were true, May would have gotten off a train in four years' time and found me at the station waiting for her. I was intrigued what she might say about it now, having met each other, finally, in her timeline – to see if between us she and I could piece together this time warp, this glitch, now I'd been on both sides of it.

But nothing was active when I first got online, no accounts flagged on the system. Perhaps I was still with her, I reasoned; perhaps we were having too much fun and enjoying our first moments together in the flesh, our first moments in awe of this strange glitch that had led us to one another. I began to whistle, imagining us together at last, how good it would feel to watch her as she fell asleep with my arms curled tightly around her.

But the next day was the same. May wasn't there. And then I felt annoyed at my future self – she too must have lived through this very same waiting. Surely she would know how agonising it was? The least she could do was tell May to check in and let me know all was fine.

Then a week passed. What if I'd forgotten about our arrangement, stood May up? Four years was a long time – what if I'd got the date wrong? What if May was pissed?

A month went by. What if the glitch had fixed itself? What if May couldn't make contact with me again?

And then I grew desperate. I toyed with our systems to see if I could recreate the glitch myself – to see if there was any way I could send a post from the future back to the past. But I wasn't a developer and I couldn't make any real changes to how the site worked, so the avenues were dead ends. I tried to make an account with May's username, to see if there were any clues there, but all that got me was an email from the day team.

'Just got a notification that the user account you were

concerned about is now live. IP address suggests you made it. Playing the long game with us, June? Haha, very funny.'

But I wasn't playing a game. I thought of the words Jack had said to me that day when he'd squeezed my shoulder, '*the account doesn't exist*', and started to doubt my own memories. Had I created her? A coping mechanism, perhaps, to get through the heartbreak and the long shifts – a collaboration between my fragile mental state and my disrupted circadian rhythm. I'd spent so long on my own recently. I'd spent so long on my own.

When six months passed, I had half convinced myself that this was the case, the relationship seemed so surreal, so impossible, so perfect. For my sanity, I knew I had to let her go, take a leaf out of Journl's book and start things afresh. Create a blank sheet to rewrite my story.

I honoured what memories I had of May and took out my braids. I remembered her advice and found a local barber to shave my head, to shave off the heartbreaks I'd been holding onto, to do things differently today.

That Monday, I called Jack for a private meeting, and was surprised to find I felt nothing at all when he walked in. Just tired from another long shift.

'I'd like to work for the day team again,' I said. 'We both know I'm not doing my best work in this position.'

'I thought you preferred working on your own?' he said.

'So did I,' I admitted. 'But I was wrong.'

He pledged to pass on my desires, and when the company reshuffled not long after, I found myself offered a role on the development team instead. It was the promotion I had been waiting for for years, came with triple my previous salary and a brand-new desk on a whole new floor, away from Jack. It was also essentially playtime. I had free rein to design fun quirks for the website, and was encouraged, even, to make these quirks as outlandish and as out-of-the-box as possible – to consider the limits of social networking and go beyond it. If ever an idea didn't work, was too nonsensical to be executed properly, it was no big deal on our side. It was simply seen as a necessary . . . *glitch*.

With my work now solidly confined to a 9-to-5, the social invitations began to make their way into my inbox again. Takeaways and beer on a Sunday at my flat. Drinks at the local when a match was on. And I began, once again, on my own terms now, to get small pleasures from the workday. I woke up grateful and awed by the infinite beauty of the world, even in its ugliest iterations; the patterns gum spots make on the pavements, the cacophony of city traffic, or that familiar coo-cooing of pigeons eating artisanal sandwiches out of the bins as I walked through the park, alone, on my lunch break. My simple comforts, my favourite parts of the day. Truly, I felt that I was missing out on nothing.

Not until there, a little further down the street, I saw a woman staring at herself in a shop window, her fingertips pressed against the glass, cherry mouth open, her hair short but sticking out at awkward angles. I pushed past the pedestrians to greet her, my body moving on instinct as if it knew what was going to happen before I realised myself, as if we had already done this once before.

'Miss, I'm sorry to interrupt,' I called out, breathless, heart pounding as if I had been running through sand to get here. She turned to look at me, eyes agape. 'I just had to tell you, you have the most gorgeous bone structure I've ever seen.'

THE WAVES WILL CARRY US BACK

Sareeta Domingo

Andre

It was quiet, that's what I remember. Only the soft rush of the waves, and that early amber light spreading away across the sand. It was smooth where the water met the shore, but the dunes further up the beach cast shadows. My body clock was still dodgy from the flight over the Atlantic, so I'd taken advantage. I'd have been up with the sun anyway, though, because those waves were calling to me from the minute I'd landed.

This was nothing like the familiar swells of Fresh'West that I'd drive out to at the weekends back home, and definitely nothing like Rockaway, where I'd just been – even the salt in the air tasted different. Here, there were no whispers as I carried a surfboard onto the subway. There were no laughs, no 'ay, ay, nigga, we don't do that shit, man . . . ay, you see this guy?' echoing behind me on the pavements of New York before my headphones masked the words. My cousin Shawn had warned me as much – a London accent coming out of my mouth blew most of their minds to begin with, let alone a Black Brit with a board. But now my summer sofa-and-wave surfing tour had taken me to my final stop in Spain. My toes twitched eagerly, ready to grip the rough surface of the vessel I'd carried thousands of miles from the UK, to NYC, to Tarifa. Ready to ride, to see what the water at this particular spot on the planet had to tell me.

I dumped my stuff on the sand, letting a shiver shake me more awake as I stared out to that line of horizon that felt like it was always part of my vision. But there was a shape on it that morning – moving. A boat. I looked left and right. Not another soul on the beach. I pulled up my wetsuit, still watching. Then I glanced down to pick up my board, but looked back up because I heard a rumble – just a burst of one, from a motor – before it cut off into silence again. The boat was closer, a dinghy I reckon you'd call it. Nothing more than that.

It was full, though. Completely full of tall, dark bodies so similar to mine, but theirs bowed in dishevelled exhaustion.

I stood staring as it coasted in, sneaking with a *shhh* up to the shoreline. The people – men mainly, a couple of women – spoke to each other in hushed voices, but I could feel weary euphoria coming off of them as they spilled out into the shallows, pulling the boat up with them. None of them seemed to see me. Their gazes were fixed over that rise in the beach, and they ran to it, fast and urgent in one mass. Out of the water, onto the land and gone.

All of them except for her.

She was the last one, and as she took a few steps on foal-like legs, she stumbled and folded silently onto the sand, her face pressed into it, turned towards me. She was stunning. Her hair was cropped close so that the rest of her features could triumph. The smoothest skin stretched over her cheekbones, contoured by the morning light. Her lips were shaped like my most precious wave, full like a pillow and pale against their surrounding dark. And her eyes. Massive and brown and so staggeringly beautiful there was no way I would ever forget them.

They blinked at me . . . once, twice, three times . . . then air sank from her and she closed them.

'Hang o—'

My voice was low, but the sound of it jolted through the stillness. She was still, too, for a couple of seconds, and for those seconds fear swept over me. Then she started to tremble, her long dark brown limbs quaking gently against the damp grains of sand, and finally I felt my legs engage. I let my board fall and grabbed my bag, my steps sounding like the rustle of brushes on a cymbal as I raced over the beach towards her and dropped to my knees. I was almost scared to touch her. I looked around for a minute, not entirely sure this was my place. I had no idea what the hell had just happened, but those people she had been with were gone and I was all she had now.

I flipped my locs out of my eyes and shook my worn-thin, oversized towel out of my bag, settling it over her as she shivered, her eyes still closed. The trembles of her body didn't cease, and so I did all I could think to do. Dropped down behind her and reached my arms over her, cradling her into whatever warmth I could offer. She smelled deeply human, and I lay flat on the sand, one of her shoulders shielded under my chin, her arm tucked in the crook of my elbow, my other hand gently supporting her forehead. I absorbed each tremor until she finally settled, and I released a breath I hadn't realised I was holding. Instead, I continued to hold her, whispering low rumbles of comfort even though I wasn't sure if she could hear or even understand me. I stared down at her beautiful face, and the tense gathering of her eyebrows finally relaxed. In exhaustion or peace, I wasn't certain, but I held her.

Then I heard voices coming closer, arguing in bursts of Spanish. A white-haired couple with matching pot bellies, and a little white mutt yapping between them, adding its twopence as they splashed along the shoreline for a morning stroll. They didn't seem too interested in us yet, but I knew it was time to get a move on.

'Oi . . . can you stand?' She stirred beneath me, her eyelids fluttering then blinking open, looking up at me and devastating me all over again. 'W-we should get you away from here.'

The darkness at the centre of her eyes was surrounded by bloodshot whites: wide, stunned, stunning. She was drinking me in like I was some kind of dream – or that might have just been wishful thinking. It was as if there was a flicker of recognition, but it turned into confusion, probably when she realised I wasn't one of her fellow passengers.

The couple had come to a stop a few feet from the boat that had carried this woman and the others, hands on their hips, baffled. I turned her slowly towards me, onto her back.

'We should get a move on,' I said again, sort of like I was trying to convince myself that we shouldn't just lie here, me holding her and ignoring the rest of the world. Gently, I pulled her up to sitting and she shrank away from me, glancing around her. She tried to say something, but her voice was barely a croak. She coughed, and I quickly rummaged in my bag again, pulling out a bottle of water – half-drunk and forgotten, but she took it and drained it quickly. She didn't try to talk again, but she pulled my towel up around her shoulders, gripping it over her stained T-shirt and shorts. I stood up and then reached down a hand to pull her up, too. She looked at me before she took it, getting to her feet shakily. We were almost eye to eye, she was that tall, and it seemed to take her a moment to remember she was still holding onto me. She dropped my hand, eyeing me up like she was trying to work out how much trust she could allow. I held up my palms, hoping to reassure. Her eyes still trained on me, she patted her hands urgently around her waist. It was only then I noticed she had a bag tied to it, bulging with what I guessed were the few belongings she had with her.

'It's all right, no worries, yeah? I want to help,' I said to her. She looked at me, and then around her again – toward the boat and then urgently around the beach, taking in the couple, who were now looking over at us as well. 'Hey . . . Hey . . .' I pointed up over the rise where the others had disappeared, and she seemed to understand. She took a faltering step over there, then another, and I went to support her elbow, but—

'Bollocks . . . !'

I hesitated; it felt wrong to leave her side even for the time it took to run back for my board. I heaved it under one arm and returned to her, grabbing my bag and slinging it onto my back. She said something, her voice light like a feather on the wind, and then she tried to head away.

'Let me help you?' I asked. She locked her eyes onto mine again, but didn't protest as I moved to her side. We began a slow procession up the beach and over the rise to where I knew the main road ran, mimicking the folds of the shoreline. I could hear every breath she took, and subconsciously synced mine with hers, feeling her skin against my fingertips as I held onto her. Thoughts jammed up against each other in my head, trying to work out how the hell I *was* going to help her, trying to imagine how I was going to let her go.

A few cars rushed by us when we reached the side of the road, making her jolt. Her hand tightened in mine like a reflex, rattling my pulse.

'It's fine, it's all right,' I said to her. She glanced down to our interlinked hands and slowly released her grip. Her eyes went to the ground, looking at our matching bare brown feet on the tarmac, which was heating in the sun, then came back up to me. I had no idea what emotion was passing between us, but it felt important. Like nothing I'd felt before. Not like the eager possibility of link-ups back at home, not like any meet-my-mum hopeful I'd known. It was so completely outside of anything I'd ever experienced.

A man's voice reached us, a shout. One of the guys from the boat, I realised. I didn't understand what he'd said, but we both turned, and I saw her shoulders sag. She tried to call something back but her voice was too weak, so she just raised a long, thin arm to wave over at the two blokes and one small woman who were huddled a little way ahead of us. It looked like they had flagged down a cab, which seemed surreal given what they'd been through, but I was glad too. All I wanted was for her to be safe. The banger of a motor idled at the dusty side of the road with a door open, and her people beckoned to her.

'You've got to get going, yeah?' I said, stupidly. I went to help her over to them, but she shook her head, and then made to pull my towel from around her shoulders and give it back to me, so I shook my head harder. Her eyes watched my locs fly around my face. 'No, please . . . keep it.' I reached over, picking up the fabric to settle it more firmly back around her. Her eyes drank in my face, and mine hers. She said something that I knew was a thank you, and then turned. Her back was straight like a catwalk model's, her steps faster now, heading away to some life I could hardly comprehend. When she got to the others, she turned, giving me a silent wave before they all disappeared into the car and it sped away, leaving a trail of dust.

I wanted to go with her. Foolish to even think it, but I wanted just to know her name. I stood, watching as she disappeared.

THREE YEARS LATER

Amina

The money itches against my breast, but I ignore it. Drawing attention to it would be foolish, because there is more there than I need to cover my rent. Not a lot more, but some. Señora Rosalia shouts down at me from her balcony, and I quicken my pace.

'Si, vengo. Lo siento,' I murmur. Those words, and others, were among the first I had to learn.

The relief I feel as I open the door to the flat does not last long. The stench of the dustbin that has gathered heat in the summer sun reaches me across the living room from the small kitchen. I step over Mena's mattress on the floor. She is snoring softly. I am not sure if she even left to go to work today. At least Fatima and the new girl, whose name I cannot yet recall, are not in the bedroom we share. I tiptoe between our beds laid out on the dusty tiles, and sink gratefully down onto my own. I spring up again, not wishing to crease my uniform too much – I have three more days before I can wash it. I unzip the stiff pale pink cotton dress and hang it up on the back of the door, straightening my name badge still attached to it. *Amna.* I did not correct them. It does not matter to them anyway, our names, and I try to just be 'Amna', a girl who doesn't belong anywhere but here, with a mop in her hand.

I slip my green housedress over my head, and then reach into my bra, glancing towards the door before I pull out the few notes. I tuck ten euros into my hiding place, deep inside the folds of the worn blue towel I have kept all this time, which I press back into the corner underneath my clothes. Then I stand again, groaning like my grandmother.

This is what you hoped for, Amina? I ignore the question in my mind, and shuffle back out of the flat and up the stairs in the sunset to pay Señora Rosalia her rent.

*

'Keep watch for me, OK?'

I shake my head, gathering replacement coffee pods from the cleaning cart.

'Please, Amina? The water was cut off at my place three days ago. I am seeing Emilio tonight, I smell like an ox!'

I sigh, because I understand – and because she isn't wrong. As it is, I have slipped one of the tiny bottles of soap into the pocket of my dress for myself, already dreaming of the shower tonight. Buchra's green-brown eyes shine earnestly out at me.

'OK. Two minutes. If you are not done when I have changed the bedclothes—'

She is already picking up one of the used towels the guest had discarded on the floor of the bathroom. 'I will be like lightning, my sister!' she says with a giggle, and I can't help allowing one to slip out as well. I never wanted to ask her why, with her Spanish boyfriend (even if he does work in the kitchens) and the country she is from, her lighter skin, that she does not try to live outside of our shadows. I know if she is with us, she has a reason. I am grateful to her, not least for the additional English she has taught me, along with the help of the CNN channel. We leave the televisions on in the rooms when we clean. I look away if they ever show what is happening at home, that's all.

I'm tucking the last fold of the bedspread when I hear the shower cut off, and a minute later Buchra appears back in the room, knotting her dark, wet hair on top of her head with a grateful smile. We double-time with the next two rooms so that we hit the correct timing for our break.

'Amna, ven aquí por favor,' the chief says loudly. He always picks me. I can hear the tone of a chore that is outside of my work in his voice. 'Take these to the kitchens, OK?' He huffs each of his words because of his large frame, packed with the meals he is 'entitled to' as 'part of his job'. He gestures down from the clipboard he is holding, at two large parcels of white napkins with the hotel's new logo. I am not a pack mule, but he seems to believe I am one, and has no care about my break, as usual. I fix daggers into my eyes, but do not argue. Instead I turn to Buchra with my eyebrow arched, and she sighs. I smile secretly as she grudgingly takes one of the parcels from my arms when we round the corner.

In the service elevator to the kitchens we are not alone. I try to edge further back against the cool metal wall, away from Hassan, the handyman who is always trying to gain favour with me. He's reaching the edge of making me uncomfortable, but I feel my invisible wall of armour surround me, striding wordlessly around him when Buchra and I reach our floor. He smirks, and I ignore him. So much I have to ignore. I feel sometimes like I just live in a world inside myself.

We drop off the parcels, and from the way Buchra adjusts her dress, I can tell Emilio must have begun his shift in the heat of the kitchens. I leave her to seek him and flirt, and decide to try to capture the last ten minutes of my break in the outdoors. I sigh as the sun hits my face. I never let myself think of home now. I am my home. But still, sometimes I remember this same feeling from a time before . . .

Ignoring that now, I step lightly around the side of the building, looking at the rows of sugar cane swaying on either side of the path that leads down to the hotel's own stretch of the beach. Glancing at the small plastic watch on my wrist, I see I have only six or seven minutes left of my break, but I am here now. Before I know it, my plimsolls shuffle quietly and quickly along the sand-sprinkled path towards the sound of the waves.

The ocean should hold my fears, but instead it holds my memories. As does this sand between my toes while I hold my shoes for a moment and feel its warmth . . . remember *his* warmth. I crouch, letting the fine grains run through my fingers as I stare out to the wide blue horizon. Like I do every time, I scan the men in their tight black suits, carrying boards, some with sails, towards the surf. None of them are him. I know because even with the sun darkening them, all these men are pale. They always are. But I look.

Andre

I can tell the bloke beside me is at the end of his rope with me shuffling in my seat, but it's been four hours since I finished my presentation, and I'm still here, all buttoned up, looking at the backs of people's heads in rows of identical chairs. I straighten with a sigh as the host finally wraps things up.

'OK, I think with that we have come to the end! Thank you all so much for being here, and my thanks as well to Ronan Technologies and the city of Seville for hosting this year's ArtTech Conference 2004 . . .'

My clapping along with the rest of the audience is a bit

overloud, but I'm just so glad the bloody thing is over. It's only a two-hour drive down to the coast, but I thought I'd be on the road by now. I remind myself I'm lucky I get paid to do this. Lucky that music tech pays my bills and more, and leaves me free enough to still keep my feet in the waves every now and then.

I've got my hotel key card gripped between my fingers before I even hit the lift, making sure I avoid eye contact with anyone as I eat the lobby up with long strides. Arriving at my floor, the beep of the hotel room door opening gives me even more relief, and as soon as it closes behind me, I'm pulling off my shirt, stuffing it inside my holdall and pulling on a T-shirt. Shorts and sliders instead of trousers and lace-ups, and I finally feel more like me. The only thing taking my mood down a bit is the message sitting on my phone's answering service. Should never have taken the girl out again after that first date, but I could be reading too much into her tone. Maybe she honestly did just want to say that she had a nice time. I did, too, but . . .

'*The shit doesn't happen in an instant, cuz. That's a fuckin' fantasy. You gotta work at it.*' That's what Shawn keeps telling me. Thing is, I've *felt* instant. I know it's real. Maybe all that's on my mind because of coming back here. I thought I'd never have a decent excuse to be in this area again, but the international conference gods were smiling on me. It's probably sentimental, or nostalgic or something – I know she's got to be long gone from here; she was the minute she got into that taxi all those years ago. But I want to feel that particular wind, taste that particular salt, and bathe in those fleeting memories along with the waves . . .

I grab my stuff and exit the room. It's weird without my board, but I'll hire one, it's fine. I feel anonymous as I check out. These same geezers that were asking me details about modulation and input jacks a few hours ago don't seem to even see me now I have a different uniform on. I'll take that blindness as a privilege, in this case at least.

A few hours later, and despite the new TomTom satnav in my rental car being set up en Español, I round a corner and feel every muscle relax as the coast unravels into view. The sky around me glows orange, but I have a bit of time before dark I reckon. Enough for a quick set. I try not to seem anxious as the brunette behind the desk meticulously explains breakfast hours and checkout times in heavily accented English.

'Perfect, nice one,' I say quickly as she finishes, and shake my head to her enquiry about needing help with luggage. 'Err, where can I hire a board? Um . . . tabla de surf?'

She smiles indulgently. 'There is a surfing school, sir, it is maybe five or ten minutes' walk along the beach from our property?'

'They hire out, too, yeah?' I don't have time to get indignant about the need for lessons, so instead I wave my hand. 'Listen, thanks a lot for your help.' I slide yet another hotel key off the counter, eager to get to my room and then out. I head up, dump my bag and pull out the shorty wetsuit I'd packed optimistically, barely taking in the view of the sea through the balcony doors of my room.

I'm feeling naked without my board, but the woman at the desk was right. A quick walk down the beach, and I'm sorted with a three-day hire. The fibres of my muscles relax as I stride towards the water, which is still kicking up foam in the dying sunlight. Then I'm into the waves and away . . .

It's only when I realise I'm seeing twinkling lights begin to dot the shoreline that I think I should probably head back in. I coast in to the shore, nodding at the few other surfers calling it a day, and inevitably my mind drifts back to that morning three years ago. How *she* must have felt then, as land approached. Scared, certainly. Not expecting me, that's for sure. I was the same way. Wistfully, I head back towards my stuff balled up a few feet from the edge of the water, hoisting the unfamiliar board under my arm.

As I see the little wooden signs pointing the way back to my hotel, I walk up the path and round the side of the building, missing a turning somewhere in the gathering darkness and trying to work out how to get inside from the beach. A guy in a white kitchen porter's jacket is standing under a light, with insects darting around above him as he flicks a cigarette away and pulls a dark-haired woman in a pink uniform closer to him. It's an intimate moment, and they spring apart as I shuffle past them.

'Sorry, you're all right . . . Carry on,' I say. Just then, a side-entrance door opens, and a tall, dark-skinned woman wearing the same pink uniform steps through it and into the halo of light.

'I will see you tomorrow, Buchra,' she calls, smiling towards the couple I'd interrupted.

I freeze. Her face is illuminated into planes and contours in the weak light, her hair still short, now cropped closer at the sides and longer on top. But it's unmistakable. I'm completely certain, and completely unsure. Then she turns to look at me, staring as droplets of water patter softly from my locs onto my shoulders. I can feel the impact of her eyes hitting mine and sweeping down my torso, bare to the waist as I'd rolled down my wetsuit. She's not moving either, and I'm dimly aware of the other two people in this tableau looking between us.

'I . . . Oh my god,' I stutter. 'Are . . . are you . . . ?'

But the moment I speak, she seems to reanimate, looking straight down at the floor. She adjusts a small bag on her shoulder, then glances towards the friend she had spoken to, turning away from me. She mutters a goodbye to her, then folds her arms around herself, walking quickly away then breaking into a slight jog.

'No, uh . . . Wait,' I try, but my voice is dried to dust, and I can't make my legs move, and before I know it, she's disappeared around the corner and into the night. I look helplessly at the other two. The man is already opening the side door to head back inside.

'Are you OK, sir?' the woman asks. 'The entrance, it is, uh . . .' She makes a gesture in the air, waiting for words to come to her. 'Around . . . to the right?'

I nod, hardly knowing if my head is even moving. 'Thanks,' I murmur, and then look at her properly. 'Do you know that woman?' My voice is louder now, urgent. 'The woman who just said goodbye, do you know her? Does she work here?'

The dark-haired woman frowns. 'Amina?' she asks, and I sink into the beauty of actually *knowing her name*. At last. It's hard to keep up with the surrealism unfolding, but for confirmation the woman jerks a thumb in the direction she went. I nod again, more emphatically.

'Does she work here?' I repeat.

Her friend is warier now, assessing me. 'Yes,' she says cautiously.

I hold up my free hand. 'OK, uh . . . I met her once before.' It sounds so bloody ridiculous, but then this whole thing feels like some creation from the depths of my mind. 'It's OK,' I say again, stupidly. 'Thank you.'

What do I do? Head out into the darkness, try to run after her? No. God. She saw me, though, I know she did. I know she's somewhere close to me now, and I know her name.

And I know, somehow, that the universe has given us another chance.

Amina

The breathing of Fatima and the new girl surrounds me in the darkness, calm and soft. Nothing like my own. Every breath I draw in as I stare up at the ceiling sounds ragged. How could this be? Was it truly him? It must have been. The way he stood, the way he stared at me . . . How has he been brought back to me? *Stupid, Amina, stupid. Why did you run from him?*

I reach underneath my thin pillow until I feel the worn fibres of the towel he gave me that day. I pull it up to touch my cheek, and my body enlivens, picturing again his deep brown skin, the tight muscles of his chest, stomach, his arm as it bent to grip that board. It was *him*. But what does it mean, or matter? Fear and desire and confusion dance together in my mind until I drift into a fitful sleep.

The next morning as I walk the familiar streets towards the hotel, the day is already warm, although my shift begins not far past dawn. My thoughts churn on. He must be a guest. Will he be in one of my rooms? If I am cleaning it, will I be able to sense which is his, even if he is not there? I sigh, looking around like a thief as I go in through the service entrance, like he might be waiting there again. Already people are making their way from the hotel towards the ocean to use their boards on the waves. He could be among them.

I had debated with myself about calling the chief to say I am ill, but I cannot afford to lose the day's wages. How long will he be staying here? I am pulled left and right in my mind – overwhelmed with a desire to see the man who helped me, and frightened to my core that I will.

'Amna . . . Llegas tarde,' the chief's stern voice drones as I place my bag in my locker that is temperamental about locking. A check of my watch shows he is right, but only by five minutes. I gather my supplies and cart, and pick up my room assignments for the day. I will be alone this morning at least – Buchra is on a late shift.

As I take the service elevator to the fifth floor, my mind suddenly jumps to a memory that assails my heart. Ada, my sister, smiling so wide as she told us about the computer they would all gather around in class to learn the book-keeping program. Her telling me how much easier it will be for me to manage my salon once she has finished her studies and can help me. All her potential beaming out of that smile. How could it ever be gone? Snuffed out and snatched away before her time? This was why I had to leave. To try for better. For her. I knew it would be hard, but I made it. She always told me that pure will would carry me, but I think it was her. In my heart, I think she sent *him* to pick me up when I fell. Did she send him to me again, now?

I turn my head and brush my cheeks against my shoulder to dry the tears that have fallen, then knock on the first door.

'Limpieza . . .'

I knock. I wait. I enter, and I clean. Over and again. Trying not to take personally the disgusting state of some rooms, feeling the relief of the *No molestar* signs hanging on the doors of others. Trying not to determine if I am in a space that he has been . . . Before I know it, I am done on this floor and check my chart. Next I am to go to floor eight – the larger rooms with the balconies. I sigh, as these of course require longer to clean, though they do not seem to assign us more time for them.

Heading up there, I knock at the first room I come to and call out. No reply – but then a shout of something rude as I open the door and see a couple in a crumpled heap on the bed, and minibar bottles on the floor next to it.

'Oh! I am sorry . . . Lo siento.' I back out, hoping they won't complain to the front desk. I move on to the next door, cautiously knocking and calling, 'Limpieza . . .'

'No, thank you,' comes a reply. At least I will have more time to clean the others. I am about to knock on the third door when I hear someone emerge from one of the rooms towards the end of the corridor. I sense they have not moved – and then I know immediately that it is him. I turn slowly, and my desire and my fear smash into one another as our eyes connect. He is dressed in a white T-shirt and dark shorts, legs strong and seeming hairless, like I had noticed all those years ago. His long toes grip his slide-on sandals like fingers, and in spite of myself I feel a smile touch my lips at that. The shape of his eyes radiates their kindness. It is them that I had remembered the most each night since I left him. They are like upended half-moons, dark and shining. His lips are equal in their thickness, sensual and solid. His hair hangs to his shoulders in dreadlocks with sun-bleached ends. His hands reach up to push them back, a reflex I had also observed and banked in my memory from our first encounter. Now, he holds both palms out to me, like he feels he may need to plead with me.

'I was waiting, sort of hoping I'd hear when someone came to— Hoping it would be you. I . . .' he begins, now walking quickly down the corridor's length. I have nowhere I can escape to, so I just watch as he strides closer to me. 'Amina,' he breathes as he finally stands before me, and I feel my eyes widen in shock, even as the sound of his deep voice saying my name melts into me. My name badge has my name wrong, so how does he—

'Your . . . your friend, last night . . .' He answers my thought. 'Don't worry, she wouldn't tell me where . . .' He draws in a long breath, unable to finish sentences, shaking his head as he stares at me, still incredulous, I think. I, too, marvel at the sight of him. 'Wait, I should start again,' he says. I need only to tilt my chin slightly to meet his eye. I was always tall, skinny, but the way his eyes drink me in now, I feel maybe . . . beautiful.

'I can't *believe* I found you,' he says, more quietly. I realise I have not spoken. For a heartbeat, I think about pretending not to know him, or what he is saying. But I cannot.

'Yes,' I whisper.

He presses a large hand to his chest. 'I . . . I'm Andre.'

'Andre,' I repeat, holding his name in my mouth at last.

'Yeah.'

He smiles broadly and I have to look away from its beauty. 'I . . . I must work . . .' I begin, then tail off as I return to his gaze.

'I know, yeah, of course. Er, when's your break? Could we maybe talk then?'

I grip the handle of my cart tighter. 'I do not think they would like to see me speaking with you,' I begin. But as I look at the folded towels on the cart, my mouth speaks before my mind can think. 'We . . . we can talk while I clean your room?' I venture, then bite my lip as though it could take back the suggestion. *How, Amina? Alone in the room with him?*

He watches me, waiting, but somehow I do not take it back. 'OK,' he says cautiously then points back down the corridor. 'I'm at the end there. Obviously we can leave the door propped open and . . . Yeah, I mean, if that's OK?'

I nod silently, and begin to push the cart. He moves to one side and I feel him following behind me. I pause, unsure which room exactly it is, or even why I am leading the way. He brushes past me, holding his hands up towards his shoulders as though he is afraid to touch me, then points to one of the doors. 'This one,' he says, smiling slightly, then rubs his key card against the reader. He pushes the door open then holds it, waiting for me to enter first. Again it is awkward, but I inhale as I move under his outstretched arm, and he smells like burnt butter and spices. I fight not to close my eyes and savour the scent.

I leave the cart outside as always while I head towards the bin in the room and begin to remove the lining. There is very little inside it, but it is habit and I feel I must do something to keep busy.

'Oh,' he says, remaining by the door. 'You don't have to actually . . . Or I suppose it's better if you do clean a bit?' He softly adds, 'Whatever you want.'

I don't reply, but go to the bathroom to empty that bin, too, pulling replacement liners out of the pocket in the front of my dress where I keep them for ease. *Say something, Amina!* The room is so clean. He has even straightened the bedclothes. I return to the bedroom, and my eyes linger on the bed as I hold the balled-up plastic trash bags in my hand.

'I will . . . um . . .' I gesture towards my cart through the still-open door, head out to push the bags into the waste compartment, then turn back to see Andre standing in his room's doorway. I glance down the corridor, unsure who I think would be monitoring us, but still a bit concerned. I pick up some fresh towels, although I noticed he had hung up the one he had used. 'I will give you these.' I hold the towels up with a tiny smile at him. He backs away as I return to the room, pausing to push a stopper under the door so it is only slightly ajar now. 'In case, I don't know, my boss or anybody checks . . .' I say.

He nods quickly. 'Course, course.'

I move further inside, and he reaches out to remove the towels from my hands. I suck in a small breath as his fingers brush mine.

'I can—' I begin.

'No, no, it's fine. I'll take them.' He puts them down on the bed and then looks around like he's unsure what to do next. His eyes move to the balcony. 'Can we sit out there for a minute?'

I nod, and he bends down to open the minibar, pulling out two bottles of water. He slides open the balcony door and I follow, welcoming the fresh air even though the day is now undeniably hot. At least for the moment, the space on the balcony is in the shade. He pulls out one of the chairs under the table and gestures for me to sit. Ahead, the ocean stretches out before us. Andre sits beside me, holding out one of the bottles. Even in the day's heat, I feel his unique warmth radiating towards me. My body remembers it, still.

'Are you thirsty?' he asks, and I am reminded of his same offer that day. I smile, remembering, and I think he does, too. 'Déjà vu hardly covers this, eh?' He laughs lightly as I take the bottle and undo its lid slowly. 'Amina,' he says again, almost reverently, and our eyes meet. 'I'm so glad I've found you. I can't tell you how many times I've thought about you over the years, how much I've wondered . . . what happened to you, if you were OK. Oh, uh . . . you've learned some English, yeah?' he adds, as though he has suddenly realised I may not understand him.

I smile. 'I knew a little,' I begin, my voice sounding strange. I take a sip of the water. 'Before. But I was afraid, so . . . And I have learned more now. And some Spanish, too.'

'Better than me.' He returns my smile, and we sit like that for a moment.

I draw a breath. 'I have thought of you, too. Often.' I swallow, because of the way he looks at me as I say that. 'I . . . I was not able to properly thank you, and I wished that I could. Now, I have my wish.'

He nods. 'Me too. And, you're welcome. I mean, bloody hell. I wish I could have done more. What did you—? How—? I mean . . . Are things are OK?'

I shrug, and nod, chuckling at his hesitant speech.

'Told you I barely had a grip on English myself.' He grins, and I notice a slight dimple in one of his cheeks.

'I found work,' I tell him. 'I did not have to go far, as you see. They take on staff here with not too many questions. Little money, but enough for me. Some to send home, too.' I feel pride in my chest at that, in spite of my loneliness. But although he smiles, I worry that I see pity in his eyes.

'They're good to you though, yeah? They treat you all right? Where are you living?'

I feel more guarded now. 'I have an apartment,' I tell him. We are always careful to whom we reveal specifics, to protect one another. It is one of the first things we learn.

'Good. Good.' He does not press. My heart swells once more at the thought of his kindness. He stares at me, and my expression must be quizzical because he apologises. 'Sorry, I . . . You're just so . . . so beautiful.' He whispers the final words so softly I can hardly hear them over the distant rush of the waves.

I know the word for this is *desire* – because I feel it, too.

'I should go.' I begin to stand, and it is then that he reaches for my hand. Electricity shoots up my arm as he holds it for a moment, looking up at me, and then he releases it.

'Sorry,' he repeats reluctantly. But I am not. *Touch me again. Touch me more.*

'It's OK,' I reply faintly.

'Can I . . . can I buy you dinner? Tonight, away from here, somewhere else, where we can . . . God, I don't know what I'm trying to say. Can I see you? Tonight?'

His question burns in his eyes, and I know I cannot deny him.

'Yes,' I say quietly. I step back inside the room, anxious already that I have been here too long.

'Why don't we meet at the surf school,' he says, following behind me. 'Down the beach? I'll find somewhere we can go from there. Would that be all right? Say eight o'clock this evening?' He stays a respectful distance, waiting for the answers to his questions as I move around past the bed and towards the door.

'I think that is OK. Yes. I . . . I would like that. Thank you.' I blink down at the floor. 'Thank you . . . Andre.' My eyes meet his once more, and he looks rewarded simply by me saying his name.

Each footstep I take back to my cart pounds along with my heartbeat.

Andre

I'm early, keen like a teen, and my mind is choppier than the waves were this afternoon. It's still warm although the sun's set, and I undo my cuffs and roll back the sleeves of my denim shirt, staring up and down the wooden walkway at the far edge of the sand. I'm not sure where she'll approach from. *If she turns up at all.* I have to ask myself if I would. It's a risk for her. She doesn't know me, not really. I could upset things for her, and to what end? But something about the connection I felt between us gives me hope that she might trust me.

Hoping is all I can do, until . . .

My jaw actually drops open as I see her coming towards me. She's wearing a calf-length lace dress, yellow like the brightest sun against her smooth dark skin. Sunshine at nightfall. Her cheekbones gleam, and she tugs at the cap sleeves of her dress and holds onto the small bag that hangs from her shoulder.

'Hello,' she says to me softly as she comes to a halt, looking up at me through her eyelashes as though she's unsure of herself.

'Hi,' I say, blinking a few times trying not to stare. 'You look stunning.' I can't help saying it, even as I see her flush.

'It is OK?' she says, looking down at her dress. 'I do not have many . . . many things to wear.'

I reach out a hand, my heart pounding the moment my palm reaches the soft skin of her arm. Her eyes return to mine. 'It . . . you . . . are perfect.' I suck in a breath and reluctantly move my hand away again.

Her smile spreads slowly across her face and she giggles, white teeth glinting. 'Where will we eat?'

We walk in a silence that feels both content and sparking with tension. Feeling her beside me is like being beside a moving flame – warm and dangerous. The restaurant is only five minutes from where we met, on the oceanfront. The smell of fish grilling when we arrive makes Amina turn to me, smiling again. Each smile she gives me feels like winning a trophy.

I'd already been by here earlier when I was trying to work out where to eat, and I'd requested a table outside on the porch next to the beach. I get a stupid territorial rush as the waiter, casually dressed in a T-shirt and jeans, eyes Amina appreciatively while he pulls the chair out for her. He passes us each a laminated menu, and I notice Amina's jaw clench as her eyes scan it.

'So, we have some specials tonight,' the waiter begins in practised English, but then he calls out in urgent Spanish as one of the other staff trips and spills a small tray of drinks. He holds up an apologetic hand as he goes to help sort things out, and I take the opportunity to lean towards Amina.

'Get whatever you like, yeah?' I say, sounding like a prick in my head, but my heart rate spikes when I realise there are tears balanced in her large eyes.

'I have not been to a meal . . . To sit down . . .'

'A restaurant?' I supply.

She nods. 'A restaurant. I have not been to one since I left . . .'

'Oh.' One of her hands rests on the small table, while the other still grips the menu. I reach forward, brushing her fingertips.

'So!' the waiter says, suddenly appearing back at our table. 'My apologies. Yes. We have specials for the fish . . .' Her fingers retract as the waiter begins listing the delicious-sounding options. I look to Amina, who softly indicates she'll have whatever I'm having. I order us the hake, and a beer, glancing at her again. She nods with a half-smile.

'You like beer?' I ask as the waiter leaves.

Her eyes still shine wistfully. 'My friend, she used to run a bar out by the water back home. It was where we would go to, uh . . . hang out?'

I nod a confirmation of the phrase, and then draw in a breath, taking my opportunity to ask, 'Where is home?'

Immediately, Amina looks away, down to her hands in her lap, then flicks her eyes back up to me. 'I don't want to talk about home. I am sorry. I know it is my fault . . .'

'No worries, that's all right,' I say quickly, but she shifts restlessly in her chair, and makes a noise like she's not quite finished speaking.

'Actually, it is not all right,' she says. Her lashes bat as she studies me, tilting her head to one side a bit, and suddenly amusement spreads on her features. 'You are afraid of me, Andre?'

I let out a short laugh, slightly wrong-footed. 'No?'

She chuckles quietly. 'You are afraid of insulting me. I can tell. It is . . . sweet.' She presses those beautiful lips together contemplatively for a moment. 'I . . . I try not to let my mind sail back over that ocean,' she says, looking across the beach to the water. Then back to me. 'I am from Dakar,' she tells me, and I see it's hard for her to even say the word.

'Right.' I give her a little time, and she looks up gratefully as another waiter quickly sets down our beers on the table, bottles sweating already in the warm night air. We reach for them simultaneously, smiling as we drink. 'I'm West African, too. My family's from Sierra Leone,' I tell her.

She assesses me. 'But they have left there. You have not been there?' Her tone seems to negate any common ground. It's fair enough, I suppose.

I flip my locs out of my face. 'No, you're right. I live in London, and so do my parents and brother and a load of other family. Some of my cousins, aunties and uncles are over in the States, in New York. I don't have much family left in Salone.'

She studies the beer bottle in her hand for a moment, and then wrinkles the skin between her brows. 'London . . . There is no sea in London, though. A river only, no? You cannot ride on your board in the river?'

I laugh. 'Yeah, definitely no surfing on the Thames.'

'Why do you do it?' she asks, sounding puzzled but curious.

'Surf?' I look out towards the moonlit waves. 'Well, it's fun. It's a challenge, you know what I mean?' I turn back to her, and feel a deeper truth coming to my surface. One I don't often say out loud. 'And . . . I like how small it makes me feel. Closer to . . . God maybe. A higher power.' I draw in a longer breath. 'The ocean always returns you to where you're supposed to be.'

We're quiet for a moment.

'I was afraid of the water,' she says after a while. 'I was often beside it, but the waves, they scared me before.' She swallows more beer, fiddles with the label. 'But I wonder if perhaps you are right about the ocean.' She's silent for a moment as she looks at me. 'I had a salon,' she begins. 'I made effort to make it special. Good-quality, you know? And it was successful. Many women, they came to my salon because it was one of the best in the city.' Again her smile is wistful, until it falls away. 'But then my sister . . . She was going to help me. Ada. She was going to accounting school. She was so smart.' Air leaves her lungs in a shaky sigh. 'But she was struck by a car, and she died.' Her jaw tightens; she looks at me, steely. She has to protect herself from the emotion of it, and I understand. 'I closed the business for a while, because it was too difficult . . .' She takes a moment. 'When I opened again, I had fewer customers, and it was harder. I wanted to assist my parents, but money was scarce . . . Then someone told me about a man who was helping people cross, to come here. I had a little money saved, and I decided to put it towards the cost they asked. Towards a chance to do better.' She nods, almost to herself. 'After the journey here . . .' I know those last few words contain a massive oversimplification. 'After that, I feel I am no longer afraid of much at all.'

I'm totally mesmerised by her, and I only notice we're both leaning towards each other, elbows on the table, when the waiter comes with our food. We spring back, and then pick up our cutlery and begin to eat. She asks about my life in London, and I tell her about my job, about my flat in Streatham. How I drive over to Wales on the weekends to surf, how much I love to travel.

I settle my knife and fork beside the skeleton of my fish with a sigh. 'Honestly . . .' I feel like there's no other way I can be with her. 'That morning, before you came, I remember thinking how glad I was to be alone. But I was lying to myself.'

'Lying?'

'Yeah. Lying.' I think for a moment. 'I spend a lot of time alone and I do enjoy my own company. But some-times . . . most of the time . . . I wish there was someone I connected with. Someone I didn't have to explain anything to.' I feel her eyes on me, and lift mine to meet them. 'And then there was *you*. You just fell onto the sand, practically at my feet. A gift from out of the ocean.'

'And we . . . connected?' she whispers. But it's more a statement than a question.

'Yeah.'

We stare at one another – but as ever, the waiter's timing is top-notch. He swoops by, oblivious to the tension, clearing our plates and asking how the food was.

'Delicious,' I answer truthfully, and Amina nods her assent as well. He hustles away, and I grow still as I feel her soft hand close over my own on the table between us.

'Andre . . . can we take a walk?' she asks.

I can't speak for the feel of her skin against mine, and so I nod. I leave a fan of euros on the table, probably too much but I don't care. We stand and I reach over, feeling her hand settle into mine once more. As we walk down the wooden steps that lead onto the beach from the restaurant, she pauses to remove her sandals using my hand for balance, and I don't want to let go of it again.

Amina

We walk along the water's edge under the night sky. Andre holds onto my hand so carefully, but I squeeze it harder and relish the feeling as he tightens his grip. He pauses for a moment and I look over at him. The restaurant is now in the distance, and it is quieter here. I can almost see stars overhead, but I realise that his eyes are closed.

'Listen,' he whispers, and so I do, watching his face. His expression is so peaceful. Without thinking, I reach up and touch his cheek. His eyes spring open, surprised. He grasps my hand where it touches him, and now both of mine are in his. 'That sound of the waves. I swear, it's in my soul,' he says.

He closes his eyes again. His breaths echo the movement of the water, and my own match it, too. I cannot resist any longer. I move closer, and press my ear to his chest. His muscles tense, and then he releases my hands so that his arms can encircle me. He pulls me close and he holds me. Again, the warmth of his body is a memory, and I cannot help the tears that build and spill even through my tightly closed eyelids. I attempt to stifle a sob, but fail. He sways gently, rocking me.

'I'm coming back for you,' he says. I hear his voice through his chest. 'I promise you, Amina.'

I pull away a little, opening my eyes to look into his. 'I am afraid again. This feeling, here with you, it gives me hope. For the first time in a long time, I am . . . awake. But that makes me afraid, too.'

He shakes his head, his dreadlocks shuffling slightly. 'You are the strongest person I've ever met. And I promise you. I won't let you go.' He moves his mouth towards mine, then hesitates, and so I reach up, pulling his head down until our lips meet. I feel light, spinning, floating. My fingers probe the heat at the nape of his neck, and Andre's hands grip my waist, a low hum moving from him into me. His tongue tangles slowly against mine, igniting heat – but this kiss is so much more. It *is* a promise, like his words. But one that I do still fear has no guarantee.

It brings more of my tears, which mingle between our lips. Saltwater and his sweetness. The taste of the waves, and the sand. Anticipation and fear. The memory of that place from which Andre lifted me those years ago.

I wrench myself away, unable to look at him. 'I want to believe you . . .' I say.

Will I see doubt in his eyes? But when I look up again, all I see is certainty.

He brushes his hands gently down my cheeks, and clasps my face, settling his gaze on me and holding me in it.

'Amina, I believe it enough for the both of us.' He brushes his lips over mine once more, and whispers against them, 'The waves will carry us back.'

BRIEF ENCOUNTERS

Sara Collins

She had decided to try to get some work done, which meant waking up early, packing her bag with laptop, notebook and pens, taking the tube to King's Cross, then a train. Any train. Going anywhere. It didn't matter where, so long as she could go there and back in four hours. If she didn't follow this routine every morning, she wouldn't know what to do with herself. She needed the chatter around her, the feeling of movement. She was terrified of stillness, of being unable to work. Yet that morning, even after she'd clicked along the platform in her distressing new boots, found herself a seat with a table, and flicked her notebook open, she couldn't write. Outside, the light made the city seem warm and beautiful, even where it was not, and she liked watching the way world flees from a departing train. So she turned to gaze out the window, feeling herself slip into a kind of restfulness, a feeling that did not come easily to her these days, which was why when she felt the shadow of someone moving into her space, she looked up, prepared to be annoyed.

But it was him.

'Hey! Oat milk,' he said.

'Oh, my god!' She laughed. It had been so long since she had laughed, for any reason. She found herself wanting to do it again.

He smiled, though he was looking at her warily. 'Seat taken?'

The first thing she noticed was how the light was playing its tricks all over him, too. Making *him* seem warm, beautiful. She could see he wanted to say something more to her, but he did not speak. He was probably thinking she was a nutter, given what had happened in the station.

She watched him settling into his seat, so tall he had to pull his legs in. The woman across the aisle looked up from her Leon takeaway breakfast, gave him an admiring glance. Buildings scrolled past them. Beneath her she felt the small vibrations of the train.

'You must have thought I was a right bitch,' she said.

He smiled. 'Either that or you're having a bitch of a morning.'

'Even so. I stole your coffee. I'm sorry.'

'It's all good. Honestly.' It sounded like *'ah-nes-ly'*. A little tinge of Jamaica that reminded her of her dad, whom death had frozen forever as a bus driver coming off his shift and adding fried bacon and Scotch bonnet peppers to his Sunday rice-and-peas while she rested her head on the table beside him, and his chocolatey baritone shivered through her bones: *My Bonnie lies over the ocean, My Bonnie lies over the sea* . . . Beginning with her dad, she had learned that death is a bit like celebrity in that it fixes you at the age you are when it happens to you.

'So. Were you?'

'Pardon?'

'Having a bitch of a morning?'

'Oh. *All* mornings are bitchy, aren't they? Especially Mondays,' she said. They laughed together. If she were a different, unbroken, woman, this would be considered flirting. This pit-of-the-stomach feeling, the body connecting itself to something electric. A switch flipping, deep inside. Lust. Attraction. Call it what you want, she was surprised she could still feel it, that she still *wanted* to feel it. Across the table he gave her a look. He had that deep seam of cockiness that goes right down the backbone of good-looking men, swooping his locs off his forehead with long fingers. (*M-m-m-assive hands, m-m-m-magnificent penis!* as she and Lucy used to whisper drunkenly to each other during their days rating potential one-night stands in clubs.) He reminded her of the photograph of Fanon she'd pinned on the corkboard above her desk at uni. Intense, watchful. A beautiful, dreadlocked Fanon.

'Anyway,' he said, gesturing towards her notebook. 'Looks like you're hard at work.' He was economical in his movements, as if realising he took up too much space already. 'I'll leave you to it.'

She felt the feeling of flirtation drifting away, and discovered that she wanted to hold onto it. *What harm could it do?* To smile, to flirt. To forget, temporarily.

'I *wish*,' she said. 'I mean – I wish I *could* work. I'm not getting much done, lately. I'm about to miss a deadline. *Whoosh.*' She did a Douglas Adams deadline-flying-over-my-head gesture, instantly regretting how much of a nerd this would make her seem. But he only gave her that ear-to-ear grin again.

'Ah. A *writer*.'

'For two hours every morning on the train. Outside of that, absolutely no writing gets done.'

'Good plan,' he said, chuckling. 'I'm sure it's more than most writers manage?' The train wobbled and caught itself as they passed through a station where trees huddled together like smokers outside an office building.

'Not a plan, as such. Just the result of being unable to get anything done at home.'

'I see.' He nodded. 'Kids?'

'What?' As soon as she said it, she knew she had been too loud, too harsh.

He looked at her strangely. 'You said you couldn't work at home.'

'Oh.' Her heart knocked against her ribs. 'Yes. I have a daughter. Saskia. Sassi, we call her. And sassy she is. She's four. A right little handful.'

The train lurched. Stopped. She was already on the move, straining forward, trying to make out the name of the station, trying to slow her breaths. For a moment, she had felt the pleasure of conversation, of being out in the world, more importantly of being *herself*. But she had forgotten that the trouble with going out into the world was other people. She looked over again at the stranger – *Seb*, had he said his name was Seb? – who was still looking at her thoughtfully, as if he wanted to say something.

'This is me,' she said, pointing, panicking, this second lie scrambling out of her as she scrambled for her things. She had no idea where they were.

'OK,' he said, bemused, rubbing his neck. 'Nice chatting to you.'

*

Making herself get out of bed every morning, pottering around the kitchen washing up and clearing the counters, leaving Jacob asleep, walking down King Street. Through the turnstiles, down to the tube. She was strict with herself about following this routine, about getting her work done. They could live for another two years on the dregs of the advance from her last novel, but she needed to keep publishing. She had never considered herself a selfish person. She had been raised by Jamaican parents, after all – if there'd been one philosophy guiding her life up to that point it had been, *Do not disappoint other people*. So this feeling – wanting something solely for herself and solely for pleasure – was new. If she'd been honest with herself, she would have admitted that she wanted one thing in particular – to run into him again. Although she *didn't* admit this, she did wait for the 8:32 King's Cross to Cambridge every day for the following two weeks. Which is why it wasn't much of a coincidence when she did.

Now that she'd already met him, there was no missing him. He drew the eye: tall, lean, restless. Hovering near the Caffè Nero kiosk, takeaway cup in one hand, in the other a copy of *Between the World and Me*.

'Hey!' he said.

'Hey,' she said. 'Seb, right?'

'Right. And you're . . . ?'

'Evie.'

'Evie. Figured I'd say hi.'

'Oh,' she said. 'Hi.'

A moment of silence. He gave her a serious look, as if he was afraid to scare her off again. She ran her hand over her scalp, suddenly self-conscious. She'd shaved her head on a whim. No more barbershop every two weeks to shape up her afro, no more time or energy wasted breaking and burying combs in her 4c hair. Setting the clippers aside she had felt so *light*, which was how she felt standing there in front of him, as if the raw wind, that had found its way inside her somehow, could just sweep her up and whisk her somewhere better, or at least surprising.

'Nice fade,' he said, like he meant it, even though there was very little fade, mostly scalp. 'Seatmates again?'

She could tell even then that she was sliding out of a groove. Loosening, like a pulled thread. 'Sure,' she said, hoping she sounded more casual than she felt. 'The eight thirty-two?'

She sat slanted towards him. He kept his eyes on her, his long legs filling the space between their seats. She could feel the warmth of them. If she moved, even an inch, she would brush against him. Therefore she was careful to hold still.

One thing she liked about the train was that it was a world of its own, no room for Jacob, or for Sassi. It was a kind of limbo, moving between places and identities, having to be neither mother nor wife. And now she sat across from Seb, savouring the freedom of this mild flirtation, guilt and gladness going hand in hand.

He owned a residential construction company, had recently moved out of Cambridge but went back every Monday lunchtime to review an ongoing project. He showed her the bag in which he carried work clothes, because sometimes he fancied getting his hands dirty while he was there. They discovered they had both done English degrees, both had old-school Jamaican parents. His were still pottering around Shepherd's Bush, where they had moved (straight from Montego Bay) when he was ten, hers had both died before she turned fifteen.

The appeal of strangers is that they allow you to edit yourself into something interesting. Her mum and dad, she told him, had eaten nothing but hard-dough bread and butter for breakfast, lunch and dinner one term to pay her private school fees, yet they would have sworn that hugging was something you only did once a week in church. 'And as for having fun! *When chicken merry, hawk deh near.*'

He laughed. It had been *his* mum's favourite saying too. Talking to him pushed the usual noise out of her head, like time-travelling to a calmer, better version of herself. The space between them was thick with all the things they prevented themselves from saying. It grew warm in the carriage, so he rolled his sleeves up, giving her a glimpse of a tattoo marching down his forearm: *I am not your Negro.*

'You a Baldwin fan?' she asked, thinking about how often she had watched the documentary.

'*Everyone* should be,' he said. 'In a just world, the man would be on the curriculum at least as much as Shakespeare.'

'I couldn't agree more.'

'But also . . .' He laughed. It creased his whole face in a way she found delightful. 'I'm just . . . not anybody's Negro.'

She felt not only attracted, but attractive. She sensed danger even then, the risk of addiction. The train pulled into Cambridge and he asked if she'd like to see his project, a Victorian conversion.

Why not? she thought. Suddenly, the thought of staying on the train, of keeping going, felt exhausting. Cambridge had been his destination, it might as well be hers.

For a moment, she said nothing. And then she said yes.

They waited together at the taxi rank. He opened up his umbrella to shield them when it started to rain.

Later, she let herself into her quiet house, stopped to skim her finger along the silver-framed photo of Sassi that was hung on the wall near the front door. Jacob would have taken it, because he had taken all of their photos. In it, Sassi was marching upstairs, looking back at him over her shoulder. Her hair in four little plaits. Jacob must have done those, too – they were slightly askew. She was holding *The Gruffalo* in one hand and her blue stuffed bunny in the other. Gruffalo and bunny, her favourite bedtime combo. An image came to Evie as she pressed her forefinger against the glass of the photo frame: Jacob putting his new camera together, spreading its spidery parts out across their bed while she kept the baby out of the way. Sassi's first birthday but the camera had been a gift to himself, the same model he'd used as a student. He wanted good photos, he'd said when she had laughed at how much time he'd spent hunting one down second-hand. He wanted to document his daughter's life for her, carefully, artfully, to show her when she was all grown up.

Look at Sassi. Look at her baby girl. The tiny fearless pistons of her knees! Evie could almost hear her. '*Up, Dadda, up!*'

She tore herself away from the photo.

There was no sign of Jacob, but there was vomit in the hallway, so he was around somewhere.

She flicked the kettle on, rooting around in the cupboard for bicarbonate of soda, taking her time with her cup of tea, cleaning up before heading upstairs. She found him fully clothed in the bath, shower running. She flicked it off, slipped her arms around him, tried to stop herself comparing his body to the one she was hankering after. 'All right, honey,' she said, lifting. 'You're all right.'

He raised his arms. She peeled off his sopping shirt. She could see there was no point asking him if he'd left the house, or gotten any work done today.

'So sorry, Evie,' Jacob said. 'Sorry.'

'I know, Jacob, I know.' But anger throttled her. She had to face away from him for a minute, take a deep breath.

Their first Christmas together Jacob gave her a copy of Sontag's journal. He knew his wife, so he knew Sontag was worth more than rubies. And forever afterwards she was always half-remembering that line from it, and quoting it in her head, the one that goes, '*Marriage is based on the principle of inertia,*' especially years later during her phase of wearing the old green velour tracksuit about the house and failing daily to comb her hair, when Jacob had joked with her about her own inertia. 'You better shape up, Evie, I need my woman shipshape.' She'd known he didn't mean it. The joke was that he would never leave her. He loved her too much, plus he was a loyal, decent man. *Plus ça change*, he liked to say, whenever something struck him as foolish in a kind of timeless way.

The very thing she thought she'd like about being married was the fact that nothing was going to change, that it would be a way of stopping the clock on a moment of happiness. But *they* had changed. First, they had multiplied, then divided, and now she had split in two – like a cancer cell, or the nucleus of an atom. One half of her here putting her husband to bed, the other half laughing with a stranger on a train.

The same routine. Cleaning, writing, King's Cross. Time was going to pass anyway, but for the first time in a long time it began to *feel* like it was passing. The next time she met Seb it was by design, having swapped numbers and agreed that they would chat if they were ever again together on the 8:32. 'I like the company,' he'd said. 'If you do too?' It meant getting no work done, but she decided to take a holiday. Talking to him was the only time she didn't feel she had to be in motion. She wanted to memorise him and carry that feeling around with her. Maybe then she could stop, and just be still.

He told her he'd been to visit his daughter, Diana, that weekend up in Bristol where she was at uni. Every time he visited her, he said – healthy, happy, drinking too much – he felt like doing a little dance. 'Hell, sometimes I *do* dance,' he said. 'Right outside her door, hoping she can't see her embarrassing dad!'

Three years earlier, he and his wife had taken her to a residential eating disorder treatment ward. On the way in they'd passed four girls roughly Diana's age huddled around a table, digging into identical tubs of yoghurt as carefully as archaeologists. After he helped with the unpacking he had excused himself to the hallway, and found himself gasping for air. This was how it would feel to drop her at uni, he had thought, *if* she ever made it there. To settle her into halls, to meet her neighbours. He'd wanted nothing more than to see her there, to do that with her. If he had been alone, grief would have slammed him to his knees, but he'd held himself together for Mina, his wife, who had barely eaten for weeks herself before they'd dropped off Diana.

Evie didn't tell him how much she knew about the way that felt. How impossible it is to look after yourself while your child cannot, or while you are unable to look after your child.

'You're not supposed to outlive your children but you're not supposed to have to drop them off at a psych ward either,' he said, and she startled, as if someone had dropped a plate behind her, but this time she did not run.

The very next Monday she awoke to a text. When she lifted her phone, her hand shook. She shielded the tiny light, telling herself it was because she didn't want to wake Jacob.

Can you skive off today?

Maybe, she typed, thinking that lately all she'd been doing was skiving.

As she waited for a reply, she listened to Jacob's breathing, a sound that seemed to come from far away. The air leaving him, coming back. In, out. Waves of breath. She noticed how every few seconds there was a hitch, something mistimed or misfiring. A breath retained.

She turned over and held him from behind. Part of the problem at home was how quiet it was. She wanted to shout, anything to fill the space between them.

She closed her eyes. Counted to ten. Turned back. Lifted her phone again.

Something I really want to show you.

She thought for a moment. Gathering her courage, maybe. But enjoying the feeling also, the anticipation like something flowering, opening up inside her. Like something in bloom.

It was a beautiful afternoon. Clear and dry, but cold. They met at the Tate Modern. He was early, waiting at the top of the ramp. Jeans, navy wax jacket. Dreads tied back, one loc holding the others in place. They didn't touch. He led the way inside, towards the sound of rushing water, which they followed towards the back of the gallery, where he stopped with a flourish, stepping back so she could get a better view. An enormous fountain rose above them. 'Here it is. *Fons Americanus.*'

It was impossible to take in the whole thing at once. Showers of water rippling over pale stone. A ring of sculpted sharks; a proud African sailor at the masthead; a dangling noose. Figures carved in postures of drowning. *There have always been terrible things in the world*, she thought. *But they have been survived.* It was strangely calming to stand there with the sculptures and the noise of water. Hypnotic, almost. She found herself wanting to linger, wondering what it would be like if she and Seb were a proper couple, visiting a gallery together, killing time before going home to a takeaway and sex on the couch.

She looked over at him, imagining it.

'Fucking brilliant, isn't it?' he said, and she jumped, afraid he'd read her thoughts. But, no – he was talking about the installation. They'd stopped at the placard. He read aloud: '*A gift and talisman towards the reconciliation of our respective motherlands.*'

'*This* is the kind of statue that should be everywhere,' she said, watching a man sitting on the lip of the fountain, tugging his little girl onto his lap. 'The kind that tells the truth.'

The little girl wanted to leave. Her father was growing more and more frustrated. Tugging, tugging. Evie wanted to run over. Shake him. Slap him.

'I've been five times already.' *Ahl-redd-i.* His voice at her ear was deep and warm. 'I'd come every weekend if I could. Spent an hour standing here by myself last week. Found myself thinking how much *you* would like it. Wanting to show it to you. Wanting to see it with you.'

She turned and smiled at him, felt the leap of desire. Like a hot taper touched to her face. She didn't answer him. She had to turn away. Leave it all unspoken. Unspoken, but understood. They were heading towards something, navigating their way towards a kind of truth. 'Coffee?' she said. 'Pretty sure I owe you one.'

They found a table in the café, and sat looking at each other. The kind of sudden, off-kilter intimacy that leaps into the space between people who are stranded together: in prison, say, or primary school.

'Tell me how you and Jacob met,' he said.

She took a sip. Perhaps it *was* safest to talk about their spouses, their families. 'At King's. I know, I know, one of *those* couples. It really does feel we've been together forever. I was in the quad, reading—'

'Of course you were.'

'Don't *interrupt*.'

'Reading what?'

'*Anna Karenina*.'

'Ah! Nerdy young Evie, big plaits, big eyes, big track-suit bottoms—'

'Big *backside*, more like.'

'Now don't *you* interrupt. I'm trying to picture you. Clever, beautiful. Dog-eared copy of fat-ass Russian novel. Exactly as I would have imagined. OK. Go ahead.'

'Anyway, I looked up from my book and there was this incredibly *tall* and incredibly awkward-looking guy, badly in need of a haircut, hovering beside my bench, and he said nothing for a minute, so that was even more awkward, but then he asked if I'd pose for him.'

'*Pose?*'

'He had a camera.'

He drained his cup, a hint of teasing in his laughter. 'As if *that* made it any less creepy!'

'I mean, he launched straight into this long explanation about how he was supposed to have models lined up for photography club but everyone he knew was busy and he only had three hours.'

The part about the assignment was true, Jacob had told her later: but when he'd seen her sitting there he'd also known it was a perfect excuse. It was the first time in his life he'd ever approached a woman without being introduced to her first.

'I don't know if I should say this.' Seb's eyes locked on hers. Dark, unwavering, molten. She felt herself unravel.

'Say it.'

'If it had been me?' he said. 'The chance to step to *you*? Well, sis, all I'm saying is I'd have had to gear myself up to come a little better than that.'

She heard trays clattering near the cash register. The words stuck in her throat. I wish, she wanted to say. *I wish.*

The next day she met with her agent. She hadn't seen him for over a year, but now she had news worth calling him up for, and he happened to be both free to meet and eager to hear from her. 'I scrapped the thriller. I'm thinking . . . along the lines of a classic love story,' she said, over gin and tonics at the Delaunay.

'My fave,' he replied.

'Oh god, I am actually so fired up about this, Martin!' She raised her voice above the clamour of people and plates. 'Something like *Casablanca* meets *Brief Encounter* meets *Anna Karenina*, you know? A man smitten by a woman. And she with him. That's it. That's the whole story. Nothing heavy, nothing thematic. Just the kind of love that makes people throw themselves in front of trains. Just like all those classic love stories. They're always, like, this . . . *trifecta* of Caucasian, tragic and adulterous, you know?' She waved a hand. She would write about how falling in love with someone makes you feel you're falling in love with life, as if by doing that she could give herself permission. Or absolution. 'All *that*, minus the Caucasian part.'

'OK.' He paused. Sipped. 'They're going to be Black?'

'And there will be absolutely *zero* sentences like, *she looked down at his smooth brown arm resting against her jet-black skin.* None of that. No one ever describes anybody as white.'

'So . . . Black lovers. But . . . we won't know they're Black?'

She sighed. 'We'll know, Martin. I just won't be spelling it out. I won't be describing anyone's skin.'

A feeling of weightlessness, of being held, or floating. All that energy she'd spent on her good grades, her good husband, her good mothering, seemed so wasted now, as she watched her old self slipping into sin like bathwater, the awful current of pleasure passing through her. She had been reduced to this. Still, all they'd done was talk. There was no sin in that. She didn't look like the picture of an adulterer in her head, put there by books and period films: a woman both idle and white (those were essential ingredients) who blows up her life for nothing more than the bone-marrow goodness of finally getting a good seeing-to. *That* wasn't her. She loved Jacob, she really loved him. Til death did them part. But, then again, maybe it had. And now here she was, a frog kicking her legs in blissful warming water, and she knew, she *knew* with whatever joy she was capable of feeling, that she was going to sink deeper and deeper, shameful as that was.

Since the day she'd gotten married, eight years ago, she had never thought she would say this, but the problem was Jacob. Her husband. The love of her life. She had stood opposite him, in the town hall, watched him duck his head sheepishly, his curls gelled to within an inch of their life, his face creasing into a smile as if he could not believe his good fortune. (A fact he verified later, waving his glass while all their friends laughed at him down at the pub: 'Ladies and gentlemen, I cannot *believe* my motherfucking luck. This woman! The best, brightest, most beautiful woman, and *my* best, brightest, most beautiful friend, is now my wife.')

She could not get Seb out of her head, but he was not the one who was in her life. Jacob was. And to her surprise, when she got home after meeting Martin, he was also *up*, in the kitchen, espresso cup in hand.

'Evie.' He looked at her across the kitchen counter, wet hair twisting into coils. Freshly showered, wearing his favourite tracksuit bottoms. Tired eyes.

'Did you work today?' she said.

He had made proper coffee, on the stove. Jacob was the one who was obsessed with coffee, buying the right beans, finding the right machines, even drinking it in the evening before bed, as he was doing now. He had been obsessed with cooking, too. A new roasting tin recipe every night. Grilling on their little rooftop terrace on weekends. Jerk chicken. American-style barbecue, Sassi's favourite. Declaring that his two queens would eat like queens.

'Could we talk?' he said.

'What, right now?'

'Please, Evie?'

'OK.' She sat on one of the stools. Waited for him to start.

'I've been googling. Reading. That AA stuff is *way* too religious, it's just not me—'

She held up a hand. 'I don't want to hear the excuses any more, J. I'm tired of it.'

'OK. But I was thinking maybe a therapist or a psychologist. Something like that. There has to be something. I don't know. There has to be some other kind of programme. The point is, Evie, I want it to be different. I want to be us. I want to be us again. I'll do anything—'

She shook her head. 'J,' she said. 'We can't go back.' That was the whole problem.

He held out a hand, raised a brow. He wanted to take her upstairs. To bed. He wanted to talk. He wanted to fuck. He wanted her to absorb him, or at least the dark parts of him, somehow. When she took his hand their matching gold bands tapped feebly together. She was afraid he would cry, and then he did.

'Jacob, please,' she said. 'Stop.' She asked if he would take a sleeping pill and then remembered that was probably not a good idea. How glad she was that Sassi couldn't see them behaving like this, that some future version of their daughter wasn't at that very moment keeping watch from the narrow, airless doorway, teenaged and unimpressed. *These are my parents, can you imagine? What losers.*

They were not like this before they had Sassi. This was all because of her.

She stared across the duvet at him. She remembered how she once picked fights in their very early days, before Sassi came along, as a way of trying to find his line in the sand. Marriage was a pretty big risk to take on someone else. How else to do it other than pushing at him and pushing at him so he'd give her signs that he was going to stay? 'I hate the way you *always* empty your pockets on the bed,' she would say. But, also, she hated the way he always left the bins for her to do, and the way he wore socks with sandals. Sometimes she left and waited (in the park, at the pub down the road, wherever) for him to phone, and only then would she come back. *Give me a fucking break*, he'd say. *What if one day I just don't phone? Why does everything have to be* like this *with you?*

Once, she tried to explain: 'I guess I need to figure out how to feel settled.'

'And you figure that out by fighting?'

'I guess I figure it out by making up.'

'Jesus, Evie.'

'I know, I know.'

'No one *knows* anything, that's the point, Evie. Jesus Christ. You figure it out by going along.'

One week later. Gail's, Clapham, 3 p.m.

It was almost warm enough for the sundress she was wearing, warm enough that she felt a prickle of sweat as she waited, squashed between tables, and the smells of coffee and warm sugar, and other people, for Seb to speak. It had been a week since she'd seen him. She was the one who had messaged, asked if he could meet, felt elated when he'd said yes. The sight of him was like a slap, and she couldn't watch his fingers skimming his mug without wishing they were moving, just as smoothly, into her.

He tipped his chair back. 'You look great.'

She smiled, set some tulips she'd bought between them on the table. Afterwards she'd race around Sainsbury's and pick up some cheese and olives and bread, as pathetic excuses for where she's been. Need was making her ruthless. Not to mention a liar.

Until now they'd been careful. The only part of her that had gotten past his clothes was her imagination. She felt hyper, manic. Soft as a bruise, sitting there. And *wet*. Oh my god she had never before been wetter in all her life.

Which is no excuse. But how else to explain reaching under the table for his hand? Nothing but nerves, the feeling just before being sick, knowing that afterwards she would ration all her energy for the next time she could see him, like some drowned, or drowning, girl.

She looked up at him in despair, already giving in. 'Seb,' she said. 'Seb. What are we going to do?'

He looked back at her, steady, sure. Between them were all the things that were still going unspoken. 'Whatever you want.'

What does she want?

There's a game she and Jacob used to play, which they called, *What's their story?* They'd pick other couples, at random, on the street, in restaurants, waiting to board a plane, and guess their stories.

He's fed up of the plump purple cushions strewn all over their bed, and having to lift them one by one like drowsy toddlers, before he can get to sleep.

OK, but *she* wishes he would get rid of that ridiculous beard.

The last time they played it, they were out to dinner. They were trying; they were supposed to recover, everyone wanted them to recover, so they had been devoting all their energy to it. (What was the alternative to recovering? It was a question they were continually asking themselves.) She took a sip of the wine he'd chosen, something that felt thick as ink on her tongue, and agreed that it was good, because she could see he was hoping he had pleased her, like the old times. She set her glass down, moving slowly, as if she was drunk, though she was not. He bent to study the menu.

'What's their story, then?' she asked him, after a minute, nodding towards a couple sitting near the kitchen door. A man and a woman, both in their eighties at least, chewing steadfastly through a shared portion of thick-cut chips.

'Tinder date,' he said, making them both burst into laughter. The laughter surprised them.

She had only pointed out the older couple as a way of getting him to look in another direction, so he wouldn't see how her hands were shaking.

The story of any long marriage is one that the people involved try not to tell themselves too often. In restaurants, Jacob always studies the menu as if later there's going to be an exam. He is too lean, and too gentle, plus he hides his bald spot by letting his hair grow too long. He makes spreadsheets for their bills, and reads the fine print before he downloads an app. He is a nerd. But that's what she'd *liked*; she had looked up at this boy standing above her in the quad and felt, not desire, but tenderness. And, later, desire born of tenderness, which doesn't burn bright, but maybe burns longer. *Maybe.* Their first date he took her to a bar in Covent Garden, even on his student budget. Walking up Long Acre she had felt so awkward with the lack of conversation that she'd chattered on about how she loved the smell of the city after a good shower of rain, how it was the only time the grimy old cobblestones ever smelled like wet, clean earth. But he had been too shy to answer, and it must have been an off night for the bar, because it turned out there was no one else there but the bartender, so they sat together, silent and self-conscious, the place so dimly lit it felt like they were the only people left alive anywhere, like two survivors working out together how to navigate the aftermath of some apocalyptic event.

What does she want?

They really should *study Baldwin in school*, she thinks, watching Seb over her oat milk latte, his hand in hers beneath the table, waiting for her answer. Because, like Shakespeare, there's a Baldwin quote for everything. *Love him and let him love you. Do you think that anything else under heaven really matters?*

Love him. Let him love you.

That is what she wants.

They agreed to meet the following Monday in a flat he owned in Maida Vale, which he occasionally rented out on Airbnb.

Her tube was delayed a half hour and it was stale and airless in the cab, and after she wound the window down she could smell rain, or the aftermath of rain. The leaves were damp with it. She smelled it again, waiting on the step, while the wind picked up. She breathed in, loving the smell. On either side the street was lined with plane trees. A scrap of crumpled paper blew across the street, from one red-brick building to another.

'It's so perfect,' she said when Seb opened the door. 'And there's the cutest little pub down at the end of the road. I saw it on the way in.'

'You want to go to the *pub*?' He looked her over, and laughed.

'OK. Terrible idea. Maybe later.'

She'd been going mad for the caved-in feeling she got when she was with him. She paced ahead of him down a hallway and found herself in a plain living room that was cleanly, clinically white, save for two green couches and a glass-topped table, picking things up and putting them down without seeing what they were.

'I'm impressed,' he said, at last.

'With what?'

He laughed. He was looking at her in the same focused way he always looked at her, like something he was trying to learn. 'With your restraint. Or maybe mine, since all I want to do is drag you upstairs.'

She laughed too. 'Really,' she told him, looking up, taking in his bulk, his feet (it seemed impossibly intimate, to be seeing his feet), his rolled-up sleeves and that indigo tattoo stalking down his forearm, 'all I want to do is be dragged.' She had never felt closer to anyone. She could ask herself now whether she loved him, but there was no doubt that she loved this feeling, of submitting. She had read somewhere that a person who is drowning can't stop drowning long enough to do anything else. It's why drowning looks no different than going for a swim. The body doles out every flicker of energy, down to the last. It's a kind of shutting down. There is no struggle. No waving your arms, no rasping breaths. In a true drowning, from beginning to end, all you do is drown.

They reached for each other. Within seconds he had lifted her down to one of the couches, pulled her on top, slipped his hands right where she needed them, between her skirt and her skin, and then she felt his breath as his fingers worked away at her, felt herself slipping away above him, felt her body being rewired, she felt, at last, that the nothingness she had been chasing was right within her reach, but then, but then, she stilled. She stopped. She moved his hand away from her, and leaned forward, rested her head on his chest, tried to catch her breath.

'You OK . . . ?' he asked.

She could feel him breathing beneath her, the rise and fall of him. How solid he was, how sexy. It was impossible to stem the tide of feeling flowing through her. She wanted him. She closed her eyes. No woman, in the history of the world, had ever stopped in the middle of sex with this man. She was sure of it.

But she had gotten herself stuck outside, on a word, on the memory of a word.

In that bar, with Jacob. During their first date. He had turned and looked at her, flustered, as if she was an idea that had just occurred to him.

'Petrichor,' he'd said, out of nowhere.

'*What?*'

'That's the name for it – that thing you like. The smell of the earth after it rains.'

A laugh sputtered out of her. What could she do but laugh? She raised her head and looked at Seb.

She had been surprising herself for weeks, but now here was one last surprise, this inkling that within minutes she would go outside, hail another cab and go back home, the place where she had last felt loving, and loved. That she would try never to feel like leaving it again.

Please, she thought, *please don't let it be too late.*

She's going to tell Jacob that she does not agree to a divorce, that they don't yet have good enough reasons. She is going to remind herself that without him she'd never have known there was a word to describe the smell of rain. All she can see now when she looks at him is Sassi's face, and that's what he's running away from, too, because he sees that same face when he looks at her. Their DNA became their mutually assured destruction.

Love him, she thinks. Love him. And let him love you.

Seb looked at her. 'What?'

'No.'

'No?' He shook his head, bemused.

'No, I'm not OK.' He touched her cheek. She pulled away. 'Wait.'

He raised both hands, away from her, above his head. Kept them there. Waiting. Letting her decide.

And, right there, in that moment, she knew she loved him, too. Was it possible? That she could love them both?

'It's only been – what? – four weeks. I can't explain it,' he said. He shook his head. 'Except that I have never felt about anyone else the way I feel about you.'

'Seb,' she said. She began to cry.

Seb. Who had reached into her loneliness, her numbness, and shocked her into wanting to live. Of all the things to love him for, she loved him most for that. She looked at him, hoping she *had* memorised him, because now it would have to be enough. He asked if they could still meet, on the train only, on Mondays. But she knew that if they kept meeting they would never stop. And she knew they had to stop. When she met him, she'd been afraid of leaving her days of madness behind, afraid it would mean she had left her love for Sassi behind also, that it would feel like turning her back on her. But now she knew all these things could stand side by side: love and grief and happiness; they had to, because they always did.

All of these things she told Seb, right before she said goodbye.

Sometimes, she allows herself to go back in memory, to the moment when things that had already been set in motion while she wasn't paying attention started to mean something to her. In other words, she allows herself to daydream about the moment a stranger sat next to her on a train.

On Mondays she and Jacob wake early and walk hand in hand to Kew Gardens, over the bridge, to the café they like that makes the babycinos Sassi used to love, poking her finger at the little rabbit faces in the foam. They let themselves talk about her on the way there. The rule for Mondays now is that they must leave the house and do something together. They go to the café in honour of their daughter, because they are looking for ways to keep her with them, always. Sometimes, on the way home, when they fall quiet, she lets her thoughts wander in secret. She takes herself back to the beginning. To the moment on the train. To the moment before. To the one before that.

The concourse looms overhead as she hurries past the automated ticket machines, the sharp-edged cold driving her straight into

Oliver Bonas in search of a scarf, which means she's going to be late getting her coffee, cutting it close. Her boots are chafing her heels raw. For a moment this morning, before she left Jacob sleeping and stopped to take the bins out because she knew he wouldn't have done it before she got home, she had been hoping to be the woman with new boots, not the woman whose baby had died.

There's a queue at the Caffè Nero kiosk. Already the day is more than she can bear.

She doesn't notice him at first, the man in front of her, eyes on his phone like the rest of them. A small bag rests on the floor beside his feet. They end up at the counter side by side but still she could hardly tell you what he looks like. She's sleeping on her feet. This happens sometimes; she feels like she's slipping outside her skin. Every day for one week after the paramedics came and took her daughter away she still mashed up boiled green bananas with plenty butter (Sassi's favourite) and carried them to the dining table, where she lost track of what was supposed to happen next. Maybe that's what happens to her now – she loses track as she reaches for the cup that's set down in front of them. His hand collides with hers, and she elbows him away from her. 'Excuse me,' she says. She sees only bits and pieces of him. He has dreadlocks, he's well dressed. 'Excuse me.' She sounds so hateful, so angry. 'Get off me.' She sounds like the opposite of herself.

Even three years later it is still very easy for her to lose her grip, emotions still bubble up in the wrong place all the time. There is nowhere in a train station where she can scream or pound her knees or keel over, nowhere to make cow-like noises, why don't they build somewhere like this – like public toilets, but for grief?

All she needs is to get her coffee and go. 'That's mine,' she says. 'That's mine. Would you just fucking well let go of it!'

'I—' he says, then stops. He looks at her. 'Of course,' he says, 'of course. Please. Go ahead.'

The screens above her light up and click and shuffle forwards, changing places, announcing that the platform is ready for her train.

RANI

Amna Saleem

PART I

The story goes that my pregnant mother was visiting her parents when her father had a heart attack, spurring my traumatised human host into an early labour, where I was birthed into existence as my Nanabu slipped out. Rumour has it that his soul now lives aside mine within my chubby brown body. A thought I find both amusing and alarming, as this body of mine has done some very questionable things which I wouldn't want anyone to witness, not least my Nanabu.

Relatives retell the story of my birth as if it were a piece of lore passed down through the generations. Conspicuously linking me to a rich ancestral tapestry where growing up, I half expected to discover that I was a latent vampire slayer waiting to become the brown Buffy Summers of Scotland. Reluctantly destined for a life of fighting demons and protecting my loved ones from the hell-mouth which lived at the foot of the Gorbals.

Unsurprisingly, as I waited for the precocious position of Chosen One to be thrust upon me, I settled into becoming a disappointingly average adult who just happened to be born at the very moment her Nanabu passed away.

Basically, I peaked exiting the womb the way most of my peers peak in high school.

Nani likes to tell me that I saved her life. That a whiff of my baby hair was strong enough to put every grieving heart at ease. My favourite Khala likes to tell me how everyone would demand a turn in feeding me my bottle, which explains why every single one of my childhood portraits features a pudgy round baby who looks like she'd eaten all the other babies. To this day, I hold all twelve aunts and uncles collectively responsible for the stubborn twelve pounds I can't seem to shift. My Ma likes to tell me that I was a Band-Aid taped over her broken heart. Buying her precious time before grief eventually overwhelmed her body, shutting it down as soon as the strenuous task of breastfeeding was complete.

Every birthday, like clockwork, my first gift would be guilt. Not only did the date mark another year of my existence, for others it was also a depressing reminder of exactly how long my grandfather had been gone. As was routine, I'd ask my Nani for a story about my Nanabu, who had become deeply intertwined within the increasingly scratchy fabric of my being. By the time I was a young adult, I knew his history – the PG-13 version – as if it were my own.

It was undoubtedly a privilege to be raised with the surplus of love that was meant for my grandfather, but over time being showered in attention that I hadn't earned became more bitter than sweet. In consequence, I inadvertently internalised the misguided notion that it was my responsibility to heal others.

On my nineteenth birthday, after hearing one of the stories I could now repeat verbatim, it occurred to me that I didn't know anything about my grandmother. We'd spent so much time canonising her husband that we forgot about ourselves. And so, a new birthday tradition began and we gently put memories of my Nanabu to rest. It was time. Not to say we never spoke of him again; we did, plenty. We simply stopped turning my birthday into an unofficial prolonged wake, reserving the stories and tears for the graveyard where he rested undisturbed under the protective shade of an apple tree. My Nani became the new protagonist, with my Nanabu making guest appearances like a famous actor on a popular TV show where the audience claps wildly every time they appear on screen.

'Happy Birthday, darling. Ready for your story?' says Nani in Urdu, before taking a nibble of her cake. Mindful of her diabetes, she removes most of the icing and puts it on my plate, as if her South Asian genes aren't the reason I'm predisposed to it myself.

The contrast between my life and my Nani's life fascinates me. In eighty-seven minutes, I'll officially be thirty-one, an age where, I'm not afraid to admit, I expected to have a husband and kid, yet have neither. I'm not necessarily sad that I don't, but everyone else seems to be on my behalf. I wouldn't be surprised if a 'Save Rani from Spinsterhood' club is in the works, complete with matching T-shirts and a Facebook page.

I resent the implication that everything I've achieved so far pales in comparison to the possibility of one day getting a ring on my finger. Why can't both be worthy of celebration? I have a small but great group of friends, I finally have a disposable income, I'm now a senior graphic designer with my own team and I get to travel a lot due to the head offices being based in London and Toronto. The dream! But, whenever I rave about my job, which I really do love, they read my enthusiasm as overcompensation for everything they feel I'm lacking.

Admittedly, my dating life has been historically less than stellar. In my defence, however, it's only recently that I stopped actively investing my time in terrible men. What I've gained back in mental real estate, I now lose in money to a slightly eccentric therapist with a hardcore plant addiction. The arboretum in Dr Campbell's fifth-floor Merchant City office is home to flora with Latin names that contort my Glaswegian tongue into positions more awkward than my last sexual encounter. Always with a coffee in one hand and a watering can in the other, Dr C feels like my very own Mary Poppins.

An image of Raf with his cute dimples, curly wild hair and tawny skin suddenly flashes through my mind. He didn't need me. He wanted me. And I blew it. *Nope, not thinking about that today.* I shut my eyes and imagine placing my finger on a photograph of his face then flick it upwards as if closing an app on my iPhone.

Nani's fork gently hits my plate as she fails to sneakily take back some of the cake she prematurely gave away. Taking her last bite, she hands her empty dish to a passing cousin and begins to weave my birthday tale.

'Wait, wait. Stop,' I say. 'I need a quick recap. So last year, you left me with a massive cliffhanger! You were in

India, Nanabu was due home from working in the big city but never turned up. Mum didn't exist yet, but my uncles did at that point, right?'

'Yes, and I had just started as a teacher at the local private school so your great-granddad would look after the rascals while I worked, which was considered unusual back then but he didn't care. Dad was my rock,' says Nani, reminding me in Urdu.

'Please, tell me this is the year Nanabu returns. Obviously, I know he eventually found his way back, since it's been well established that I accidentally stole his soul, but I need to know what happened. The last thing I remember is something about a lamp?'

'The gas lamp, that's right. So, he went missing on a humid Tuesday and by Friday a storm threatened to break, as did my heart. That's the day I got the lamp. I needed him to be able to easily find me even in a blackout during a monsoon,' Nani says.

'I mean, that sounds like the perfect way to burn down your house and entire village, but it is very romantic.'

'When he didn't return and others began to disappear, the lamps became a symbol of hope adopted by the village. For all the men injured, missing or gone forever in the wake of the ongoing civil unrest.'

'I can't imagine what it must have been like to live during the Partition. I get mad when people eat crisps too loudly around me, and you were literally torn from your home. Sorry, I—' Shame prickles inside me.

'Don't be sorry. I pray to god every day that you never know what it feels like. I'm very proud of you and your little drawings.'

Only Nani could refer to my illustrations as 'little draw-ings' yet make it sound like the best compliment I've ever received. 'It sounds like you started a movement in the village with your lamp. I hope you're proud of your impact.'

'I am.' Nani's eyes shine at the memory. 'I wish I had a photograph to show you. At night, all the lamps, combined with the marigold fields, made the place look hauntingly beautiful.'

'Hauntingly?' I say. It's not a word I've heard in Urdu before.

'Yes, like what jinn do,' Nani explains.

I'm flummoxed. Then it clicks. Jinn *haunt* people and places. The place looked hauntingly beautiful. Got it. Nani regularly makes profound observations that when trans-lated straight into English probably sound less inspiring, but they always feel special to me even if it initially goes over my head. Early on, Nani and I fell into a habit where she spoke in Urdu while I replied in English, which means that on the odd occasion our conversations would veer wildly off track.

'Ah, right, yes, OK.'

'In fact, do you remember the painting we saw last year? The one with the orange? It was like that.'

I do remember. I'd never seen Nani look so entranced. We were visiting the Gallery of Modern Art and the ladies' bathroom had a ridiculously long line as usual. When I eventually re-emerged, I worried Nani would be upset but she'd barely noticed my brief vacation to the museum's basement. In fact, she was still staring at the same oil painting I'd left her by. It's only now that I recall its burnt-orange hues, estuarial river flanked by a field of flowers on each side, that I understand why she was so captivated. It wasn't her village in India on the canvas, but for that moment it was.

'It was beautiful, Nani.'

'Sometimes when we go to the Highlands it reminds me of India. They are both places of deep beauty.'

'I've only ever been to Pakistan, but I understand what you mean. Well, other than the vastly opposing climates. Does it feel strange that you call India home, but to Mum Pakistan is home, and to me home is Scotland?'

'Not strange, it's more that I simply would never have predicted that future grandchildren would have a Scottish accent and love the rain, but here we are. I wouldn't change a single thing. I learned a long time ago, however, that home can also be found in those with whom you choose to share your whole heart. I see my home in you just like I did your grandfather.'

'I don't think I know how to love someone like you loved Nanabu. I don't know if I'll find a home for my heart like that. I thought I did once but I . . . was wrong.'

'Being wrong is part of the process, beta. My heart once belonged to two men. One being your grandfather and the other, a musician I met when I was a teacher.'

'Two men? Hang on, do you mean while training to be a teacher, or—'

Of course, Nani had two men fighting over her. No one likes to talk about the time Nanabu disappeared, which I can understand due to the unpleasant nature of the situation, but I've never heard even a whisper about this. Instead of blood, my family has gossip running through their veins, so for none of this to have reached me over the last three decades is suspect. It's either nothing of note or I'm about to find out that I absorbed the soul of the wrong old man. Is Nanabu not my Nanabu? Nani is watching me and I don't want her to know I'm internally freaking out, so I paste on the polite face I use when people try to show me endless photographs of their pets.

'. . . Yes, there was an overlap. I'm not proud of it but your Nanabu was still missing over a year later and the pain had barely lessened with time. Jassah was a newly hired music teacher, he had been in a locally famous Indian rock band when I was a teenager. Not only could he sing but he also played over twelve instruments and had perfect pitch. A prodigy.'

The way Nani is bragging about him does kind of feel like she's proud of it, but then again, if I hooked up with a rock star, I probably would be too. She clearly must have been into him because the last time I saw her face light up this brightly was on Eid, when she successfully matched all the loose lids under the sink to the corresponding Tupperware boxes stacked in her pantry.

'Jassah quickly became popular with students and staff alike with his good looks and velvety-smooth voice. Single women would vie for his attention, but he only had eyes for me.'

'Did he now?' I'm well aware that I don't actually share a soul with my deceased grandfather but I still feel the urge to pop on a pair of metaphysical earphones to shield him from what I hope are forthcoming racy details.

'In the beginning I paid him little mind, his confidence bordered on arrogance. And . . . I didn't want him to think he could win me over as easily as the others.' Nani is blushing. It's sweet. 'He taught me how to play the drums and I taught him how to dance.'

'You know how to play the drums? No way. This would have been useful information when I was fourteen and wanted to be Dave Grohl. For Nirvana, not Foo Fighters.'

I know Nani was young once, but this is blowing my mind. The image of her in shalwar kameez rocking out on the drums with a handsome musician during monsoon season is not where I thought this story was going.

'The following semester we orchestrated our classrooms to be opposite one another so we could sneak peeks of each other from across the narrow hallway. After class, he'd serenade me with my own private concert. He wrote me love songs, we stole kisses in the supply closet, it was magical.'

'You didn't worry about getting caught?'

The women in my family tend to speak about romance exclusively as an afterthought or fantasy, so this smashes a lot of my preconceived notions about how I believed my elders lived. Although, now that I think about it, I shouldn't be so shocked, after all, my own mother keeps her Mills & Boon collection hidden under her bed like a teenager.

'Of course, but it felt worth the risk. That doesn't mean that guilt didn't gnaw at me or that I didn't long for my husband. Jassah watched me cry over your Nanabu count-less times. He had no desire to replace him, he was smart enough to know that he couldn't. But it was as if my heart got bigger and there was suddenly space for both to inhabit it at the same time. His love made me a better mother, a better teacher and a better daughter than I had been while swallowed whole in my grief. I'd say I was . . .'

Nani falls silent, and panic rises in my gut. Sometimes revisiting the past becomes too much and sends her into an episode where she has to retire to bed for the day and sleep it off. I've insisted time and time again that we don't need to do this, but she insists right back that we do. Nani is staring off into space and I follow her line of sight to where a nosy relative is making a beeline for us. Relieved that I haven't caused Nani any pain, thoughts of Raf fly by again to remind me of my own. I hope when I'm a grandmother I'm half as interesting as Nani. Though, I can't quite imagine telling my grandkids about the times Raf and I worked late, which coincidentally also involved making out in a supply cupboard. Nani passed down some very horny genes. Suddenly, it's as if I can feel Raf's hand on my thigh again . . .

The noise from the cleaners next door was loud but it by no means drowned us out. It did give me enough of an opportunity to casually lean in closer to whisper in his ear. Unusually confident, I was banking on him reciprocating, so when his hand slowly slid up my bare leg I'd felt vindicated and highly aroused. It was all flashing back now. *Raf pushing me up against the wall, his six-foot stocky frame swiftly lifting me off the floor and carrying me to the nearest meeting room with my legs wrapped around his waist, my hands undoing his jeans, his leg kicking the door shut behind us . . .*

That encounter with Raf was the product of two years of light petting and mounting lust subsequently released in one unforgettable night, leaving us both exhausted but extremely satisfied. The next afternoon featured no sex yet I still managed to screw him. I haven't let myself think of Raf this freely in a long time. I never stop wishing that I could go back in time to the moment where I said no but should have said yes . . . Auntie Seema's bag hits me square in the face, bringing me back to the present as she bids Nani goodbye. It feels like karma. The universe gave me everything I wanted on a silver platter and I still messed it up. No wonder it seeks revenge.

As if she was never interrupted, Nani launches straight back into her story after ensuring my nose is definitely not broken. 'Jassah returned to his home town, a few hundred miles away, due to a death in his family. He wrote every single day for two months. Even distance wasn't enough to keep us apart – only for the letters to come to an abrupt halt. It wasn't until a year had passed that I realised why.'

'Please tell me he didn't also go missing.'

'Jassah, thankfully, avoided that cruel twist of fate. One ordinary morning, I was tidying my classroom when I caught a glimpse of him through the small window on the door where we had once stolen glances at each other.'

'Drummer boy was back?'

'Yes. I couldn't believe it was him at first. I'd spent the last summer looking through that window searching for any sign of him and now there he was like he had never been away. Even to this day, thinking about this makes me want to smash that stupid window into a million tiny little pieces like he did to my heart.'

'You sound totally over him . . . I've seen enough Bollywood movies to know the dumb idiot got married? Am I right?'

'The dumb idiot did indeed get married. Would it have killed him to write that in a letter instead of turning up with his pregnant wife?'

'Oh wow, pregnant. Yeah, that's . . . What a dick. Sorry for saying dick . . .'

'Before he left, he promised to return with a proposal. Not that I needed or wanted one. We were in love, but your grandfather had never left my mind. I still hoped I'd see him again. When I said I loved both of them, I meant it. Maybe I was selfish, I don't know, but I felt what I felt.'

'I believe you. Not to be Team Jassah, but that must have been a confusing limbo for him to live in, too.'

'I know. It's more that he was so adamant about us. Marriage was so far from my mind until he mentioned it. Then it was all I could think about. The complications, the consequences. I tied myself up in knots deciding what I would do when he asked. I considered risking everything for him, but there he was in his classroom standing with another woman in his arms.'

'It was pretty shady of him to not give you a heads-up. Do you think he did it on purpose? To make a point or something?'

'I honestly don't know what he was thinking. Although, the next day I did find a letter on my desk. It was sealed with one of those bright red stamps made from wax and the precise handwriting on the envelope unmistakably belonged to him. I searched the school grounds but he was nowhere to be found.'

'What did the letter say?'

'I don't know.'

'What do you mean, you don't know?'

'I've never read it. It's in my attic. I couldn't bring myself to throw it out or read it.'

'So, you're telling me that this letter languishes in your dusty attic alongside my mediocre report cards even though you thoughtfully and consciously transported it from one continent to another? I don't buy it. You must have at least peeked?'

Nani shrugs as if she is just as confused by her actions as I am. I have to bite my lip to stop myself asking if I can read the letter. It would also be a bit pointless. The last time I could read Urdu was when I was seven years old, before I lost the skill from underuse – which is quite sad now that I think about it.

An hour passes, though it feels like mere minutes. The food has stopped flowing, which means that Aunt Jameela will soon interrupt with a lazy excuse and insist on taking Nani home. Just as I tell Nani my theory, Aunt Jameela pops up behind us, as predicted. As they leave, I have a mild epiphany. If Nani was out there getting laid at thirty-one while living under a civil war with a missing-presumed-dead husband and after bearing a few children, then there was no reason I shouldn't be. This is probably not the life lesson she was hoping to impart to me, but it was the one I was taking.

Seven weeks after my birthday, tragedy struck and Nani suddenly passed away from complications induced by a lurking, undetected cancer. The time between diagnosis and deterioration was barely a few weeks. It felt like a meteor had slammed into my chest leaving a crater so deep that the threat of extinction was almost merciful. She was really gone. Selfishly, I mourned just as much for all the stories Nani never got around to telling me. After the funeral, we began clearing out her large Victorian house, where I found the legendary box in the attic like she had said. It felt unnerving that the letter she never read would now remain unread by her forever.

I can't stop wishing I'd just asked if it was OK to read it, like I'd planned to the last time Nani and I spoke. Jassah and the letter had been on the tip of my tongue, but I chickened out. I never once considered I wouldn't get the opportunity. Now I find myself in the kitchen mindlessly rubbing the box like a lamp, as if waiting for it to magically open and grant me permission. Taking a break from pacing back and forth, I stretch out on the sofa but accidentally sit on the remote, which lights up the TV with Nani's favourite film. I wasn't looking for an arbitrary sign but I got one.

I choose a quiet Saturday where I have exactly zero plans, obligations or major distractions. After settling into my cosy reading chair, it occurs to me that I've created the ambience of a seance with the curtains drawn and lit candles everywhere. I don't have time to be haunted by a malignant ghost right now, so I blow out a few candles to be safe. The key for the box is nowhere to be found, which leaves me with an ingenious Plan B. Hammer time. I give it a few goes, and with only a minor pinky finger injury, it cracks open. Google Translate is on standby and my hands are in a pair of yellow rubber gloves to protect the letter, as if this unveiling is an unaired episode of *CSI*.

The lid flips over with a creak and reveals not one letter but what looks like *fifty* letters. Staring at them, I instantly start to cast doubt on my actions. Nani had only chosen to tell me about one letter. She'd kept these locked and hidden for a reason. My moral compass swings back around and I end my shenanigans. Overwhelmed and uncertain, I tuck the box beneath my bed then slink under the covers.

The box is out of sight and mind, but Nani's confession of having loved two men at the same time is still very much present. I'm determined to be as bold as she had been in life. 'I didn't want to be an obstacle to joy,' I remember Nani saying more than once. Guilt lingered in the background like white noise but she refused to succumb to it. I don't want to be an obstacle to joy either, so I summon courage from Nani's words and plan the best way to slide into Raf's inbox.

'Hi Raf, long time, huh?' I read out loud as I type, only to immediately delete. Ugh, why is this so hard? I just need to ask him to lunch, that's all. I write seven different versions, each worse than the last. Before I talk myself out of it altogether, I hit send on my current draft, then close my eyes so I can't see the envelope symbol grow wings and flutter off to deliver my heart. I mean, email.

Despite knowing better, I click on the email tracker info box every hour to see if he's read it. At 17:21, the email is recorded as having been opened. At this point, I know if I don't walk away from my laptop, I'll have to bring this up with Dr Campbell and I don't want her to be disappointed in me. Quickly, I realise that wanting my therapist to like me is a red flag, but I shelve it for later.

Two days pass and no reply. I take the silence as an answer in itself. Rejection always stings but I am still pleased I put myself out there. Naturally, the minute

I decide to put Raf behind me is, of course, the very moment he replies.

As much as I want to click open the email, I'm afraid to have Raf's disinterest in me confirmed on my screen in black and white. What scares me more, however, is Raf showing interest only for me to discover I have once again built up a guy in my head and granted him permission to use me as his very own personal human rehabilitation centre. The sealed letters under my bed pop into my head. To read or not to read. That is the question.

Downing my coffee, I physically brace myself as if ready for impact and read the email out loud.

Rani! What a lovely surprise to find you in my inbox. Apologies for the delay. I was in Barra with no Wi-Fi or 4G. I've never been off the grid before. It was nice but eerie. I'd love to meet up for lunch, but . . .

This is it. This is where he is, quite rightly, going to tell me where to get off after I left things so weird between us in New York. What was I thinking? This was stupid, I should never have reached out. Nani can put a curse on me for all I care. This is her fault.

'. . . I'm on Stornoway for a week. What about when I'm back? Do you want to come through to Edinburgh or shall I come through to you in Glasgow? Is this the subtle beginning of a turf war? Maybe Danny Boyle will make a movie out of it.'

Oh. Or, maybe I overreacted a wee bit. Sorry, Nani. He does want to see me. Fuck, I was not expecting that. What the hell am I going to wear?

I consider turning my lunch request into dinner, but it feels too audacious and loaded with expectations I'm not sure I can meet. There is something honest about hanging out in the daylight as opposed to clinging to the cover of night where I feel more confident but less at ease. An evening can be ruined but an afternoon can be salvaged.

Raf and I first met at my old job when I was a junior designer tasked with settling him in. The buddy system assigned me as his 'person'. He had a quiet intensity, and struck me as the type of person who took the time to think before he spoke. A notable talent I still don't have. It was in between showing him the printer and the good biscuit cupboard that I knew I was smitten, but back then I believed that connecting with someone romantically meant they needed to be able to make me laugh and cry in equal measure, which my then-boyfriend had expertly covered. Beanstalk, as I came to call him, was a man whose main skill was giving me emotional whiplash. He would insist that I was the only person to ever 'truly get him'. A sentiment I naively clung to whenever he cheated on me. I originally mistook his ability for introspection as progressive but really I just wanted Beanstalk to be better than he was, so I gave him qualities that never existed to justify staying.

Next came Well Actually, who earned his nickname for reasons that can be easily surmised. I convinced myself that Well Actually was one of the rare 'good guys' with his feminist T-shirts and enthusiasm for the Women's March, but his habit of trying to coerce me into sex got old real fast. The incessant badgering was funnily enough not exactly a turn-on.

Embarrassingly, Raf had met both Beanstalk and Well Actually, and although that period of my life was five bad hairstyles, two jobs and an existential crisis ago, I worry that, to Raf, I am his Well Actually or dumb Beanstalk after the poor way I handled things. I guess there is only one way to find out.

PART II

Raf is already seated when I arrive, and for a few seconds I let myself admire him from afar as I internally squeal with joy that he's actually here. I lost the turf war, but I got to choose where in Edinburgh we met. I settled on a hipster café known locally for its laid-back ambience and robust coffee list. It's an intimate space but not overtly romantic.

'Rani, over here,' Raf says as he stands then gives me a small wave to get my attention, as if I hadn't just been staring at him through the lightly frosted glass screen by reception.

When I reach the table, I have to fight the urge to immediately launch into an overly detailed tirade about how much I've changed. Anxiety starts to rear its ugly head, but then I briefly feel the slight pressure of a pair of soft lips on my left cheek as he greets me, and all at once my energy is directed towards the moment his face touches mine as he pecks my other cheek. He's wearing the same aftershave from the last time I saw him and I'm not sure if I have loins or what they are exactly but they are definitely on fire. He is giving me desi George Clooney in *ER* vibes with the hint of salt peppered through his thick black hair. It only makes him look more handsome. Damn it. I knew I should have worn my push-up bra.

The kiss has given me a much-needed shot of confidence. The nervous energy, however, is still present. I fiddle with the cutlery, my hair and the bookshelf next to me. I discreetly position last month's copy of *The New Yorker* and this month's copy of *The List* so they are casually poking out of the top of my tote bag. I may have returned to Glasgow while he continued to live it up abroad, but that didn't mean I wasn't sophisticated. Or at least couldn't give the illusion of sophistication. I should probably tone it down a notch. Oh great, now I've forgotten how to laugh like a normal human being. The noise that is exploding out of my mouth sounds nothing like anything I've ever made before.

'Are you OK?' Raf asks. 'I know this is . . . weird. It must have taken a lot for you to get in touch. And, look, I'm here.' Raf punctuates his words with what I hope are ironic jazz hands. 'So, you can stop eating your hair. Don't you go to therapy now?'

'How do you know that?' I say, taking the hair out of my mouth.

A waitress swings by to take our coffee order before Raf can answer. He orders while I study the cluster of tiny moles on his neck. Nani used to call moles beauty spots, and on this occasion I wouldn't disagree.

'Instagram. Is that really your therapist's office? It looks more like the rainforest.'

'I know, right? Part of the reason I still go see Dr C at this point is just to hang out there.' I'm not sure if I should say the next thing but it is really bothering me. 'Not that I checked, but you don't follow me on Instagram.'

'Not officially. You soft blocked me, remember?'

'Your girlfriend is offensively attractive and I'm not into self-harm,' I say in my defence.

'G? Genevieve?'

'Of course, she has the coolest name in the world.'

'G is great – and happily engaged to someone who is not me.'

'Oh.' I pretend that this is brand-new information but I noticed Genevieve's conspicuous absence from his grid last Christmas. I might be guilty of my own causal snooping too. 'And you're . . . cool with that?'

Raf laughs lightly, as if the idea of him not being cool with it is ridiculous.

'Yeah. We should have just stayed friends, to be honest, but someone broke my heart and I wasn't thinking straight.'

'God, whoever broke your heart must be a real bitch.'

Raf remains neutral at my awkward attempt to confront the elephant in the room.

'So . . . yeah, we haven't really talked since—'

'—We were on that rooftop bar in Brooklyn and I confessed that I was in love with you?' Raf cuts in.

Safe to say he remembers everything.

It all went wrong at the Wythe Hotel in Williamsburg. It was my last day in New York and he had surprised me with a table that gave us an unobstructed view over the East River to the Manhattan skyline. He knew that I loved looking at the city more than I enjoyed being in it. Although I had fallen in love with him a long time ago, I froze.

'Yes, that and . . .' I begin, nervously shifting my long curly hair from one shoulder to the other.

'I asked you to move over there, which admittedly was not pragmatic in hindsight, considering I was the one with the permanent contract. But I did offer to move back to the UK for you.'

For me. *Me.* He was willing to do that for me. It still feels surreal. 'Yup, then—'

'You said . . . no. Actually, you didn't really say anything. It was radio silence from the moment you hit the tarmac at Heathrow.'

I definitely mistook Raf's default charm to suggest that he was perhaps less hurt now, but every word is laced with simmering pain and frustration. I caused that. I didn't mean to but I did. 'I figured it had to be some sort of game. I mean, now . . . I don't think that.' This is painful. 'You were saying all the right things but I was convinced that the minute I said yes, you would change your mind. Tell me it was just a joke. Then *I'd* be the joke.'

Back then, all I remember thinking was that there was no way someone could love me that much when I'd done so little to deserve it.

'A game? I've met your exes. I'm nothing like them. Did I ever give you reason to believe I'd do what they did to you?'

'No. But I didn't see it coming when they did it either. Everything you said. It all felt too good to be true.' Ugh, I sound pathetic. 'I'm sorry, Raf. I really am. I hate that I hurt you.'

I want to go home, but I excuse myself to the bathroom instead. Raf's intense gaze is becoming harder to decrypt and I can't tell if he hates me or wants to fuck me – not that they are mutually exclusive emotions. I'm momentarily reminded of why I'm in therapy.

The bathroom is surprisingly plush. After liberally applying the free luxury hand lotion, it suddenly occurs to me that Raf might think I'm taking so long because of unladylike bowel extractions. My iced coffee is waiting when I return but before I sit down I make Raf smell my wrist, as proof that I'm a neurotic overthinker who should not be allowed outside.

'Lavender, nice,' Raf says as he holds my hand and gives it a polite whiff.

'The lotion from the bathroom. Got carried away,' I say, in hopes that any thoughts of me taking a poop are banished from his mind.

Raf is still holding my hand; he seems to have a much calmer energy than before. I've owed him that apology for a long time. Discombobulated by the unexpected physical contact, the protracted silence that follows arouses me with the need to dilute the tension by any means necessary. 'Did you know that if your ancestors died from eating brains on a semi-regular basis, you could now potentially have built up immunity, due to a genetic mutation, which would allow you to eat brains without becoming sick or dying?'

Raf stares at me for a few seconds. 'I did not know that.'

This was a new record. I've never blown a date by suggesting I had an interest in eating human brains before. Not that this is technically a date. Or is it? Maybe I should just ask for the check now and save us both the effort of engaging any further.

'Did you know that there is a tribe in the Amazon forest who speak a language that has no words for colours and no concept of numbers as we know them?' Raf asks after a brief beat of silence.

I didn't think it was possible to find him more attractive, but I do.

'I did know that! Did you know that an American evangelical missionary guy was sent to live with them with the aim to convert them but ended up being converted himself? Well, not converted so much as lost his faith entirely due to his time with the tribe and became—'

'—An atheist, and his wife straight-up divorced him, right?' Raf finishes my sentence.

'I feel like you really gotta have loved someone to move to the jungle with them though,' I say.

Raf looks mischievous and I realise I've set myself up. 'Yeah, imagine that. Moving somewhere for someone you love. Who would do such a thing?'

'See, that's where you went wrong. You should have offered me the chance to live in an actual jungle, not a concrete one.'

'You have not changed one bit,' says Raf with a chuckle.

'I've changed. I'd go anywhere for the right person now.' I feel like I've said too much. I might as well have cut my heart out and put it on the table for him to devour like a medium-rare steak.

'Rani, that was a lo—' Raf begins, and I don't want to hear the end of that sentence.

'Reminds me of the Sentinelese, except—'

He looks at me. 'Except they tend to kill any outsiders that dare come near them. I feel like a tribe that throws spears at passing helicopters have made it more than clear they want to be left alone. So . . . how much do you know about serial killers?' Raf says, playing along. Pretending that nothing is happening.

If someone was scanning my brain during this conversation they would have been able to pinpoint the very moment my love for him grew exponentially.

'I have to ask – not that I'm not enjoying this – but,' Raf begins, running his hand through his thick black hair, 'what made you get in touch?'

Caught off guard, my mind races through various answers I could give him that don't end in a restraining order being filed against me.

'My Nani . . . She passed recently and, well, she was an incredible woman who died with a rather big "what if" on her mind. Basically, before she died, she told me a story and it reminded me of you.'

'What was the story?' Raf asks, his eyes bright and full of curiosity.

'Well, it was more a culmination of stories she would regale me with on my birthday.'

'Oh, yes. A belated Happy Birthday. Cheers.' Raf lifts up his coffee, I follow suit and we lightly clink cups.

'Cheers. Thank you.'

'So, tell me more about this birthday tradition?'

I'm tempted to tell him that it all technically began when my grandfather died on the day I was born and his spirit apparently took up residence inside me, but I feel like that's more second-date material.

'It just sort of became this thing where whichever age I was turning, she would tell me what had gone on in her life that same year. So I'd be twenty-four and she'd tell me about her life at twenty-four. If that makes sense?'

'My grandparents are no longer with us now, but I would've loved to know what they were like when they were younger.'

'Sometimes it's heartbreaking, though. Sometimes it felt like I was harming her by letting her relive the more painful memories. I'm amazed by all she survived. It doesn't feel possible that one person can live through so much.'

Raf waits for me to continue and for a moment I'm not sure if I should, but then I remember that Nani very strongly believed that you only truly die after you cross a living person's mind for the last time. A beautiful sentiment, I can't help but find a wee bit creepy. If this were true then that means she and my Nanabu are still with us, but so is Hitler.

'You don't have to tell me. It's private, I get it. It just sounds interesting,' Raf says, noting my hesitation.

'How about the highlights, CliffsNotes edition?' I offer.

Raf nods in agreement and rests his chin on his hands, giving me all of his attention. I keep the details brief. If he were to become bored halfway through I'd feel mortified and offended. However, as I watch Raf lean in and listen intently, my fear gets smaller and smaller.

'Some of the stories are little punches to the gut. For instance when Nani was twenty-one, her younger sister was deathly ill. Cholera was suspected, so Nani took some time off to look after her.'

'Extremely grateful for vaccinations right now.'

'Same. The closest we get to cholera these days is by reading Gabriel García Márquez.'

Raf laughs at my terrible joke. Suddenly, all I want is to make him laugh for the rest of my life. It is such a beautiful sound.

'OK, so, get this . . . By twenty-two, Nani had been proposed to five times. Five times!'

'Wow. Did she accept any of them?'

'Nope, declined every single one of them, until she met my Nanabu. Twenty-three, however, is my favourite story.'

Raf leans back, gets comfy and hugs one of the chair pillows to his chest like it's a stress ball. He's so freaking cute.

'My Nanabu was an award-winning landscaper known for his impressive ability to shape animals out of bushes.'

'Your grandfather did what now? That's cool.'

'Yeah, super random. One sunny day, he took her to the park where he was contracted and showed her his latest creation, which he then promptly proposed to her in front of.'

'A . . . flamingo? A rabbit? Lion? A spaceship . . . ?' Raf excitedly dishes out guesses in rapid succession.

'Giraffe, though a spaceship would have been cool.'

'What animal would you have wanted?'

'Elephant. They're smart and empathetic and people are needlessly mean about their weight.'

Raf leans forward and takes my hand. He circles my palm with his thumb. 'You are—' he begins.

'What about you?' I interrupt, sensing a sincere compliment on the tip of his talented tongue.

'A fish. Sea animals never get fair representation.'

'Topiary diversity aside, at twenty-four, Nani and Nanabu had a glamorous wedding where the whole town danced in the twinkly-lit streets all night. Twenty-five was a sad one.'

'Can I take it? Should we skip it?' Raf looks concerned.

'She gave birth to her first child but developed post-partum depression, which wasn't understood back then. It meant that as well as being in pain she faced a lot of judgement for not suffering in silence. Twenty-six wasn't much better, she almost died in labour.'

'She almost died? Women are amazing,' Raf says in awe.

'And don't you forget it. My Nanabu went grey overnight from fear. Even though she went on to have more kids, she stopped including those stories and I didn't push her on it.'

'Fair. Can't imagine it's an easy thing to talk about.'

'I'm glossing over a lot, but Nani left me in the middle of a story where Nanabu was missing on a work trip. At that point, Nani moved back in with her father, who doted on her children. It made the grief just about bearable.'

Raf drops my hand to wildly gesture about the turn of events. I take the opportunity to discreetly wipe my sweating palm with a napkin.

'This is a movie. You know that, right? Like, I would totally watch this in the cinema.'

'Yeah, I did not see that plot twist coming either when she first told me. I mean, cholera, civil war, a missing husband, five proposals . . .'

'Not to play down the tragedy here, but my life feels exceedingly boring right now.'

'Tell me about it,' I agree.

The waitress stops by with our bill, and it's only then that we notice we've been talking for four hours straight. The cafe is closing. I want to suggest we go elsewhere but lose my nerve – only for Raf to ask if I want to come back to his place.

'It doesn't have to be my place. This isn't like a trick to . . .'

'I know. Do you have Netflix or Amazon Prime?'

'Both. And Disney,' Raf says, while pretending to throw money everywhere.

'Well, now I have to come.'

Raf calls us an Uber. My heart is beating so fast I'm sure he can hear it. Fifteen minutes later, Dean Village springs forth, like a scene straight out of a twisted fairy tale where everyone dies in the end. The Water of Leith runs right out front of his building and the realisation that Raf willingly offered to walk away from the New York salary which now affords him this idyllic oasis washes over me.

Although I shaved last night, I can feel stubble already growing on my legs and curse my Pakistani genes. I didn't have any intentions of having sex tonight but I thank past-me for doing the bare minimum maintenance just in case. Neither of us is paying much attention to the TV, but we are inching closer and closer to each other on the velvety green sofa. Soon we're snuggling as if it's something we do on a regular basis.

'Raf, your flat looks like it's been pulled straight from an *Architectural Digest* spread,' I say as the show ends. 'Show me your kitchen again.'

'If this is your fetish, you should tell me now. It's fine, I just need to know.' Raf stands up and extends his hand towards me, then guides me to the kitchen I saw a glimpse of when we first arrived.

I spot the telltale spice tray that many South Asian households have or are eventually gifted. The colourful spices on display add a dash of colour to the minimalist aesthetic. It is perfect. His flat really is a work of art.

He looks at me apologetically as his phone rings. 'Sorry, I have to get this. It's my dad.'

'Of course, I'm going to snoop, so take your time.'

I hear Raf slide in and out of English and Urdu. Being able to understand both languages makes me feel like I'm eavesdropping, so I return to the living room to snoop there.

We eventually head back to the sofa. During our third hour of binge-watching, Raf and I reminisce about the way we met and when we first knew there was something between us. I wait for him to mention my dramatic behaviour but he is more concerned with all the embarrassing things he felt *he'd* done that I'd simply not noticed.

'All this time, I hesitated to reach out because I was worried you had a mental catalogue of all my stupid mistakes,' I say. 'But all these things you just mentioned, I don't even remember. If you fell down the stairs at work, I don't remember it. It sounds really, really, really, really funny but I don't remember.'

'Funny, huh?' Raf says, before launching into a full-blown tickle attack, making me squirm all the way to the ground – and then suddenly he's on top of me. His face is inches away from mine. We're seconds from kissing. I just know it.

'Raf . . . ?'

'Yes, Rani?'

'Not to ruin this moment, but your tickling has made me need to pee.'

'Wow, the dirty talk this soon in our reconciliation? Really?'

'Noooo . . . don't make me laugh. I will pee right here. I'm serious.'

Raf raises his hand, jokingly threatening to tickle me more then shows me mercy, releasing me to the bathroom.

Oh my God, the bathroom. A natural stone walk-in wet room with a separate section for the porcelain tub. It's like he has access to my Pinterest. By the time I return, the kissing moment has passed, but we resume cuddling. I've already seen this episode of *Mindhunter*, so I bathe in the day's events. Burrowed into his side, I tilt my head up, and when his eyes meet mine I decide I need to kiss him now or I may very well die.

'Raf?'

'Do you need to pee again? I'm not even tickling you.'

'No, I'm all peed out. I was wondering . . .'

'Yeah?'

'Can we kiss now?'

Raf grins the widest smile I've ever seen, and the next thing I know we're making out.

'You're so easily spooked, I didn't want to scare you off by moving too fast,' Raf says when we come up for air.

'I should have said yes.'

'What?'

'When you asked me to be in your life. To be with you. I should have said yes. I hate that I wasted all this time by being, as you say, easily spooked.'

'Hey, no, look, my timing was very poor. And we're here now. A lot to talk about but at least we're in the same country this time.'

Raf gently strokes my hair.

'Before Nani died, she said that she found that home isn't necessarily a place. It's wherever the person you love is. I tried to deny it for a long time but it has felt like a piece of me was missing. Now I realise that was just with you all this time.'

'Anything to not have to say the actual words, huh?' Raf boops me on the nose playfully. 'It's fine, I'll take it.' He swoops me into his arms.

Like clockwork, I start feeling spooked. The urge to run returns. I try to fight it. I want to be here. I know I do. 'I should really get home. It's getting late,' I say, overpowered by dread from thinking about all the ways I will inevitably ruin this again.

'Or you could stay a little longer and tell me more stories?'

'You're obsessed.'

'You have to at least tell me if your Nanabu was ever found?' Raf circles my palm with his thumb again and the urge to bolt dies down.

'He was. I don't know the full story behind it, we never got that far before she . . . you know.' Raf caresses my face. His hand is so warm. 'I cleaned out Nani's house, and I found a box in her attic. A box she'd told me about in one of her tales.'

'From the musician?'

'Yeah. The sealed letter was inside the box and had the telltale wax stamp on the back.'

I'd filled him in on my Nani's affair in the Uber, but I couldn't quite remember where we left off.

'Your Nani really didn't read it?' Raf asks.

'Nope, it's wild to me. I'd have to know. I think she felt guilty. This is going to sound so cheesy, but . . .' Raf looks eagerly at me and I feel my cheeks flush just thinking about what I was going to say. 'The sealed letter is what ultimately reminded me of you. I didn't want to go my whole life wondering if what I felt between us was real or imagined.'

'It's very, very real,' Raf says, pausing between each word to place a kiss on my forehead.

'Do you think she told you about the letter and its location on purpose?'

'I did, but then I opened the box and it wasn't just the one letter. There were a ton and it felt wrong to go through them, so now they're just sitting under my bed, potentially to go unread forever.'

'I thought I won the turf war when the coin toss decided you had to come to me, but as usual Glasgow is where all the true hidden treasures are.'

'Well, *this* Glaswegian treasure chest is all yours for the night. Wait . . . I didn't mean it like—'

'Too late,' Raf says while pretending to undo the fake top button of my dress.

'Oh, no, it actually comes undone like this,' I say, standing up, unzipping the back and letting it fall to the floor in the single smoothest moment of my entire life.

Over the next six months, we fell into an easy routine. For the first time, I discovered what it was like to be with someone who only ever wanted to make me laugh, never cry. My birthday soon rolled around again, but the absence of Nani felt too heavy to ignore, so I insisted we take the day to pack up my flat. As much as I loved my place, Raf's was so much nicer. It had more room, more light and most importantly a reading nook built just for me below the window overlooking the river.

'Are you sure you want me to cancel the dinner reservation? You're allowed to have a nice time on your birthday even if some of the people you wish you could celebrate with are no longer here,' Raf says gently.

'I'm sure. Honestly, I just don't feel like it. I really would rather stay home. Wow, this isn't home any more.'

'Wait, I thought home was wherever I was?' Raf teases.

'You know what I mean.'

He pulls me into a big hug. 'Happy Birthday, my favourite weirdo.'

My phone is ringing again – loved ones keep calling on and off all day, wishing me well. I let this one go to voicemail. Part of me still expects to hear Nani's voice at the other end of the line, even though I know that would be impossible unless she figured out how to haunt me after all.

Lost in my own world for a while, I jump when Raf taps me on the shoulder. He's carrying Nani's box of letters. I haven't looked in it since the day I knocked the lock off.

'This is definitely for the "keep" pile, right?' Raf says.

By now I've learned his every facial expression, and the present one is angling for permission to open the box. 'Yes, you can open it. Just be careful. The letters are old.'

Raf returns to pack up what is left of my bedroom, and I resume singing along with Dounia while painting over scratches in the wall on the tiny chance I might get my full deposit back.

'Rani. Rani! Rani, come here, will you?' Raf shouts from the other room. His voice sounds strange – there is a noticeable shake in it.

'If the big prehistoric-looking spider is back then tell me now. I can't deal . . .' I say as I tentatively head towards the room. 'What is all this?' I wasn't prepared to see every single letter from the box laid out on the floor of my bedroom.

'You didn't tell me they were all in Urdu,' Raf says.

'Yeah. I guess I just haven't thought about them in a while. Something wrong?' I ask.

Raf jumps up off the floor. His general vibe is slightly disconcerting. I can't get a read on him like I usually can. 'This one here is from Jassah. The musician, right?' he asks. He places it back in the empty box. 'But the others . . .'

'Yes . . . ?'

'They're for you,' Raf whispers. 'All of them.'

'Sorry?' I'm fatigued from packing and have the beginnings of the emotional hangover that manages to sneak up on me every birthday.

'The letters, they are for you,' Raf says more clearly.

'Look, I can't read Urdu any more but my name is something I would definitely recognise,' I say, a bit more tetchy than I intend. Raf takes a step towards me, reaches for my hands and clasps them in his.

'So, as you know, I still do my dad's taxes.'

'Aye, and?' Raf can't be suggesting what I think he's suggesting.

'And that involves having to translate his notes from Urdu into English every month. My skills aren't the best, I admit.'

His eyebrows are now raised so high I worry they may disappear into his hairline. Exasperated, Raf rests his hands on my shoulders and smiles, making me melt inside.

'Rani. Every single letter says "Happy Birthday, darling. Ready for your story?" Then there is a number. The last story was thirty-one, right?'

I nod to confirm. A meteor strikes my chest again. Surely I haven't sat on a bunch of letters from my Nani for almost a year without knowing that they are for me.

'This one is thirty-two,' Raf says as he holds out the letter in his hand. 'And that one by your foot is forty,' Raf says. He begins to slowly unseal *thirty-two* and when I don't tell him to stop he pulls out the paper inside. I sit down on the bed heavily. Raf flops down beside me, closing the gap between us, and passes me the letter.

'It looks like a piece of art,' I say to him. 'Look at this calligraphy. I feel like we just discovered the Da Vinci Code scrolls or whatever but, like, desi.' I take a few seconds to admire the sheer beauty of the letter then hand it to Raf. He takes a deep breath and starts to read it out loud to me.

'Happy thirty-second birthday, darling. You didn't think I'd forget, did you? Now where were we? Oh yes, your Nanabu's absence. The day you were born wasn't the first time he died. A relative of a relative serving as a nurse for the wounded found him in a hospital three cities away. Within six weeks, my heart was home. We were a family again.

'I saw Jassah once more. I told your Nanabu everything. Do you know what he did? He carved a giraffe into Jassah's lawn out of gratitude for loving me when he couldn't. The two men shook hands, but that was it. We never crossed paths again.

'I know you've read Jassah's letter, or that you soon will . . . Just know that, regardless of what it says, it was written before the giraffe. I'm skipping ahead a little by telling you that, but it is important you know.

'You, my Rani, are made from the fire of stars and the never-dampening embers of curiosity. Never let anyone take that from you.

'Before we get on with your story, I need you to put this down and tell that boy how you feel or I will come back and haunt both of you.'

Raf wipes away my tears, and a few of his own.

'We narrowly escaped a haunting. How about that?' I lean over and kiss an overwhelmed Raf on the forehead. 'You are my favourite person in the whole world.' Raf squeezes my hand and tries to kiss me back. 'Keep reading. I need to know more about this giraffe-shaped olive branch that has to be a Trojan horse. My family are not that chill.'

MOTHERLAND

Sara Jafari

Who are you when your mother dies?

It had been forty days.

She could not believe every day would be like this. Her mother was dead, and this fact would always be true.

It wasn't as though this fear hadn't been a recurring nightmare in Safie's dreams, or a source of anxiety she hadn't lamented to different NHS counsellors, who themselves were overworked, their minds on other things, never quite able to soothe her worries. But in those instances her mother's death was in the future – when she was eighty, or ninety. Even then, the possibility made Safie's stomach churn and her appetite cease. Such thoughts about mortality made her question her faith in God. Because if there was a God, why did the people you love have to be ripped away from you? Either by the decay of old age, or like her mother, who died suddenly in a car accident on the way back from a work conference. The last thing she had said aloud to her mum was a blur; she was already pronounced dead by the time Safie and her sister Maryam made their way to A&E. God didn't even allow her to say goodbye to the person she loved the most.

And that is how Safie found herself here. In Tehran. In a cemetery much grander than those she had seen in England. Her mother's face painted on a plaque quite beautifully; wearing the hijab she sporadically wore, the mole above her lip made bigger than it was, her lips thin, well defined. She was an exaggerated version of herself, not quite the mother Safie knew.

Yasamin Parsi.

The words written on her gravestone were in Farsi. Safie had been taught the alphabet and elementary phrases by her mother later in life, when she had complained about only looking Iranian but knowing nothing of the culture or language.

'You live here now,' her mother had said. 'I didn't think you'd want to learn two languages.' She shrugged, and gave her daughter a crinkled smile. But Safie was young then, so blamed her mother for not caring to divulge her culture, *their* culture.

So, after college her mother began to teach her. But they did not visit Iran, so the teachings were not useful. Until now.

A loving and pious mother, daughter and sister.

Not quite true on the pious part, but she had been good. And Safie felt strongly that if God did exist, surely goodness was what he appreciated the most.

Relatives stood around Safie murmuring prayers under their breath. She held her sister Maryam's hand tighter, despite the sweat that gathered between their hands. Maryam squeezed hers in return, and leaned her head against Safie's shoulder.

This is what it would be like now; she would have to be strong for her, even when she didn't want to be.

Safie never thought she'd be an orphan at twenty-seven years old. They had no extended family in England, so when they returned it would just be herself and Maryam.

'Where's your dad?' Maman Bozorg had asked when they first arrived, as though she had forgotten their mother's – her own daughter's – history.

'What dad?' Maryam snapped.

'Eh?' Maman Bozorg said.

'He's too busy with his other family,' Safie added calmly, yet with a bitter edge to her tone, her comment not much better than her sister's. 'I'm sure he sends his regards though.'

Maman Bozorg muttered an unintelligible phrase that sounded like a mixture of disapproval and a prayer to Allah.

Their backchat was left hanging in the air, because in the eyes of their extended family, the sisters were English, not Iranian. And being rude to one's parents was something Westerners were known for.

Forty days.

Safie was told the mourning period for Muslims typically lasts forty days, and it was now their final day to celebrate the life of their mother. So here they were, mourning their mother's death together, once more. But what happened after forty days? Were they meant to forget about it and move on?

The sun shone on their black hijabs, their long black coats, their black trousers. People walked around the graveyard carrying shrini and refreshments, a good deed intended for mourners and people visiting those long gone. But all these details blurred. A vast future lay ahead, daunting and endlessly dim.

And all Safie could think was: *my mum's really gone.*

*

Her mother had not talked about her family back home often. So little that Safie never thought about them either.

Now, back at Maman Bozorg's house, Safie was confronted again with how large her extended family was. She and Maryam didn't even really know their grandmother either, despite the fact that they were now staying at her house; growing up, they had only spoken to her a handful of times on the phone, their mother next to them, forcing them to speak to her. Looking round now, they noticed how their family were so familiar in the way they talked to each other. Whereas Safie and Maryam sat between them in a bubble of their own.

All these people were here for their mother now, publicly mourning her, but where were they when she'd needed them? When she fell pregnant unmarried and they abandoned her?

Further guests entered, more families they didn't recognise, but were no doubt their relatives. Among the latest to enter was a tall man, in his late twenties, with a dark well-groomed beard and nineties Leonardo DiCaprio-style hair. Safie noticed him speaking to Maman Bozorg. Something about him drew her attention, something beyond his good looks. She wanted to say his aura, but she had never said or thought that in her life before.

Maman Bozorg waved her large hands at Safie and told her to come over. As Safie approached she felt her bitterness dissipate towards her family. Her grandmother's eyes, which were turned downwards, looked so tired. Despite trying to be the best hostess, and hold everything together, it was evident that she too was suffering. Maman Bozorg laid her hand heavy on Safie's back, and said, 'This is your mother's best friend's son, Javad Lajani.'

He waved a hand and said, 'Hey. I'm sorry for your loss.' He spoke in English, in an American accent that startled her.

'Oh,' she muttered. 'Thanks.'

'Talk to each other,' Maman Bozorg said in Farsi, a small smile on her face, giving Safie a prod in the back. Safie hadn't realised her grandmother had noticed how she and Maryam had struggled, watching people talk around them, only understanding certain elementary words. Laughing when others laughed even when they didn't understand the joke, or quite know *why* they were laughing so soon after their mother had died. In those moments Safie would make all the gestures of laughter, shut her eyes slightly, nod her head, say 'ha, ha, ha', but she wasn't laughing at all. It was scary, really, how well she feigned happiness, togetherness even, compared to how she felt inside.

'How are you doing?' he asked, shifting his weight from one leg to the other noticeably. His dark curly hair fell into his eyes and he quickly moved it away, as though annoyed by it. In another world, she might have found the act endearing.

'I'm fine.' She breathed out heavily. She could feel her family looking at them, observing every little detail of this interaction.

He leaned against one of the walls. She noticed his eyes flicker towards them and back at her. 'Do you smoke?'

The question surprised her, gave her pause. 'Not really.'
'That's not a no.'

She shrugged. 'I mean I'd like to smoke now. Or have a drink.' She shut her mouth quickly; needed to remind herself that she was in Tehran, not London. Her heart was beating quickly, a sign that despite her grief she could still feel nervous around good-looking men. She was annoyed at her body for the betrayal at a time like this.

Safie didn't look back at her relatives, didn't want to know for sure if they really were noticing how close they were to each other. It was exactly what they expected of her. She was her mother's daughter after all.

Her extended family were deeply religious – the complete opposite to her mum. Her mother loved her wine; she'd often say, 'a glass of red a day keeps the doctor away'. When Safie was a teenager she had asked to try it, but her mum refused. 'Wait until you're eighteen,' she had said. That didn't stop Safie sneaking a sip when her mother wasn't looking. It tasted awful, nothing like she imagined. Bitter, acidic. She wondered how her mother drunk it so readily, why people got addicted to it.

Her heart hurt even more then. It was the little details that threatened to break her.

Maryam came over, putting herself slightly between Safie and Javad. 'Why'd you leave me alone?' she said, an attitude lodged in her throat. She'd always had an attitude, even before the death of their mother.

'I stole her away,' Javad said. 'Sorry about that.' His voice was so smooth, a bit *too* smooth. Perhaps it was his American accent, which made everything feel movie-like.

It was a stark contrast to Safie and Maryam's very Northern English accents.

'Who are you?' Maryam asked irritably, turning her body slightly to look at him.

Safie pushed her sister with her shoulder. It was normally her mother's job to keep Maryam in line.

'He's Mum's friend's son.'

He nodded, biting his bottom lip slightly. 'I'm only visiting Tehran. I live in Boston.'

This seemed to appease Maryam. 'What's there to do here that's fun, then?'

'You don't find here fun?' he said in mock shock.

'Our mum died, so, no?'

Safie breathed deeply through her nose. Unlike her sister, she couldn't be flippant about their mother's death.

A silence moved between them, heavy and thick. It felt like someone had put their hands around her neck, gripping tighter and tighter, the walls closing in on her. Everything was too much in that moment.

Before anyone could say anything else, a girl approached to offer her condolences. Javad introduced her as his sister, Nina, and she looked a similar age to Maryam. While her presence broke the ice, Safie still felt the hand around her neck. She walked away from them, almost stumbling to the kitchen and then to the back garden. She shut the door firmly behind her, and found herself on the ground, head between her legs.

'I can't do this,' she repeated under her breath.

She heard the back door open and shut, the scraping of furniture, like a chair was being moved, but she couldn't open her eyes or stop speaking to herself. It felt something like insanity; she even wondered if she had gone mad. But when people go mad, do they know that they've gone mad? She imagined not.

'Safie?' she heard Javad say from nearby. Then she heard the striking of a match. She opened her eyes to find him stood holding a lit cigarette out for her.

'People might come—'

'I barricaded the door,' he said. 'With a plastic chair, so not sure how effective it will be, but it's better than nothing.'

'I don't want people to think we're up to no good.'

'They already think that.'

'True,' she said, a shaky laugh escaping her lips. Surprisingly, some of the laugh was real.

He sat on the floor next to her, his arm slightly leaning against hers. She liked the firmness of it, that she had something to lean on. She immediately wiped such thoughts from her mind, embarrassed at herself.

'Jesus,' he said. 'You don't get weather like this back home.'

She took a long drag of the cigarette and felt light in a pleasant, almost grounding way. Exhaled. Didn't say anything.

'Our sisters are one and the same,' he went on.

'What do you mean?' she asked, opening her eyes fully.

Maman Bozorg's garden was modest, overrun in places. They had a small pond in the corner that reflected the sky so it looked a perfect blue. The orange and lemon trees were in bloom. Back home the weather made everything grey. Here everything appeared so full of colour, as though her own personal hell was made even more vivid just to torture her that bit more. She wanted heavy rain, thunderstorms, and winds so intense garden fences broke, not this.

'I left them discussing their favourite make-up YouTubers.' He had a slight smile on his face as he spoke.

She was glad Maryam was making friends, that she still could. A part of her, though, wondered why her sister was so better adjusted to this tragedy. Safie couldn't imagine talking about YouTube and make-up right now. But that didn't stop her from saying, 'Are you looking down on that?' She didn't really mean it, but she wanted – no, needed – to argue with someone.

'No,' he said quickly, but she didn't let him finish.

'Because people always put down things that girls like and it's bullshit,' she continued. 'Anything that's popular and has a predominantly female following is ridiculed as being low-brow, but things like sports – which serve equally no value for society – aren't.'

There was a short silence, in which Safie caught her breath. Javad broke it by clearing his throat. He straightened his back against the wall.

'I'll have you know I'm often a guinea pig for my sisters when they test make-up. I'm partial to Jeffree Star's strong looks, actually.'

The image threatened her composure, almost causing her to break into a smile, but not quite. He noticed this and smirked to himself, before shutting his eyes. The sun shone directly onto their faces and his skin was glistening. His eyelashes impossibly long and dark; her friends back home would kill to have natural lashes like his.

After a few moments he said, 'I know how you're feeling, you know. My dad died four years ago.'

She softened then. He looked at her briefly, caught her eye, and she looked away. She pinched her wrist with her thumb and forefinger. Let the nails really dig into the flesh, giving her a tiny bit of clarity.

Her whole body had been so impossibly tight, and she hadn't realised that fact until now. Her mind, which wanted to accuse him for every wrong thing in the world, relinquished some of its pent-up anger.

'That's shit,' she said. 'I'm sorry.'

He waved his hand. 'I'm not saying it for you to apologise. I just mean you're not alone, even though it probably feels like it right now. What you're feeling, it'll pass. I'm not saying it will stop hurting, but it will somehow be bearable, and you'll feel like you again.'

His words – and how much she didn't believe them – brought fresh tears to her eyes, and she looked away, hoping he hadn't noticed.

'I dyed my hair pink,' she said suddenly, inhaling deeply and turning to look back at him.

He raised an eyebrow, his lips parting. She tried to ignore that. 'Pink?'

'Yep,' she said, moving some of her hijab back so he could see the top of her hair. It was bubble-gum pink. 'I had to bleach it twice in the space of a week to get it light enough. My hair is pretty fucked. Is that a sign of grief? Giving yourself a makeover your twenty-year-old self would have loved?'

He smiled and it touched his eyes.

'I like it, from what I can see, if that's any consolation.'

She looked away and down at her hands, at the grown-out, chipped shellac nail polish there. She had gotten them done before her mum had died. Each nail was a different rainbow colour. When she first got them done they looked Instagram-worthy; now they just looked tacky. Maryam kept telling her to remove them, had even offered to do it for her, because she couldn't stand the sight, but Safie couldn't bring herself to do it.

She could hear increasingly loud chatter coming from the kitchen. Most likely some of the women in her family making another samovar of chai. In the pit of her stomach she felt a sudden rush, a need to run, escape.

'God, I don't want to be here,' she said, attempting to steady her quavering voice. 'I'd literally want to be anywhere but here right now.'

'We could go for a drive?'

'How?'

'I've got a car.'

That surprised her. As someone who was only visiting, she hadn't expected him to have a car, but maybe that was because she still didn't know how to drive. You didn't need to drive in London.

'Would that be allowed?'

He shrugged, and flashed her a small, tentative smile. His teeth were almost straight and almost white; it was rather charming. If she wasn't feeling the way she was, she might have felt butterflies.

When Safie's mother had died, a part of her was taken away. Callum – her now ex-boyfriend, whom she'd been with for two years – didn't understand. He wanted everything to be the same, wanted her to be the same. He didn't understand why she went to such lengths to dye her hair pink; why she didn't want to talk any more, didn't want to go for their regular dinners out and cinema dates. 'I just feel like I don't really have a girlfriend any more,' he said one evening.

'You know what? You don't,' she had said, before getting up and leaving his house. It was the cleanest break-up she'd ever had. She discovered she didn't even care, wondered in fact if she'd ever really loved him.

'Let's go,' she said to Javad now.

They were inside Javad's rented Land Rover, the open windows letting in a little breeze. The sun in Tehran was so sharp, so heavy. Again it seemed odd to her that the world managed to be so bright when her mother was no longer in it.

'I'll put on the air con,' he said, reaching over to close the windows.

She put her hand lightly on his arm. 'No,' she said. 'I like the fresh air.'

'But it'll be way cooler with air con.'

'Leave it, please.' She quickly let go of his arm then, realising herself, put it back on her lap.

He looked straight ahead at the road, giving a small nod of acknowledgement.

Safie adjusted the polyester-silk blend scarf on her head. It was itchy and cheap. Despite only being here two days longer, she still considered buying a better-quality, fashionable one, rather than Maman Bozorg's hand-me-downs.

She looked out the window, at the murals and graffiti painted directly onto the sides of buildings. Many were lifelike portraits of what she presumed were important people in Iran – none of whom she knew. She wondered at this feature of Tehran, the way their leaders were celebrated in such a way.

'Who is that?' she asked, pointing at a large painting on the side of a building of a man with a white beard waving at a mass of people. The sky in the painting was a perfect baby blue, the rest of the image black and white.

Javad followed her gaze, and let out a laugh. 'Ayatollah Khomeini. You know, the leader of the Iranian Revolution? That guy.'

She had never been that interested in politics – or rather political figures – but even she felt she should know what the man who completely changed Iran had looked like. She remembered her mum's stories about Iran, how, before the Iranian Revolution, it was much like many Western countries today. She had seen pictures of her mum in miniskirts, high heels, dramatic eye make-up and lightened voluminous hair. Those images looked so different to the Iran Safie was seeing now. But her mum always warned that people romanticised life pre-revolution.

'Many people weren't happy then, either,' she had said. '*I* wasn't happy then. There was no democracy, the Shah lived well and many others did not. But now,' she sighed. 'It's a different kind of discontentment for some now.'

Safie shook away the memory.

'How come you're here, anyway? A holiday?' she asked, her voice a little too flat.

'Something like that,' he said. 'I come every few years.'

'I wish I had done that before now. I don't really feel any connection to Iran.' She paused, frowning at her own words.

'It's your motherland,' he said. 'You just haven't been to the right places.'

'I mean, I don't really understand why my mum's buried here. She didn't even like Iran.'

'I heard from my mom that she requested it in her will,' Javad said gently.

Safie knew that, but it didn't make it make sense. She thought back to who his mother was, and had a lightbulb moment.

'Wait, is your mum Jeleh?'

He nodded, keeping his eyes on the road ahead. 'The one and only.'

Every month her mum would talk on the phone to her friend who lived in America. She'd even joked, years ago, that Jeleh had a handsome, successful son that one of her daughters should get married off to. Safie had imagined a man quite different to Javad. In that moment, she wanted nothing more than to discuss this with her mum, to laugh about how good-looking he really was, how the proposition wasn't that bad after all.

'Is your mum here?' she asked.

'Yes. We had planned to fly over in summer anyway, and when she heard about your mom we got plane tickets immediately. My mom stayed at the cemetery a little longer, then she decided she needed to find sunflowers to lay for your mom. The flower shop by the roadside didn't have any, and the man tried to sell her pink roses, which pissed her off. "Yasamin Parsi is worth more than some cheap roses".' He impersonated his mother's Iranian accent. 'My uncle took her to find some and she said she'd meet us at your place later. My mom is similar to yours, though – she didn't like your family much either. So, if I'm being honest, she was probably avoiding the gathering.'

She liked the sound of his mother.

'My mum always said her family didn't accept her, that her country didn't accept her. They didn't approve that she had me and Maryam unmarried.' Safie's throat was dry and she stopped to clear it, wondering when she'd last drunk some water. She couldn't remember. 'Did you know that? That we're bastards?' In that moment she felt like an angsty teenager, her words theatrical, and even though she didn't mean it she couldn't stop them from leaving her mouth. She just wanted to complain forever sometimes, and at other times not speak for days. She wasn't sure which part of herself she hated the most.

She looked to Javad briefly, and they locked eyes. Only for a second or so, but it was enough. She bit hard on the inside of her mouth to stop herself speaking further. Javad must have picked up on this because he put the radio on, the volume low, the soft hum of a song in a language she barely knew filling the car.

On the streets she noted the different ways women wore their hijabs. Some had pashminas loosely placed over their heads, the fabric draping over their shoulders, the top of their hair visible. Others wore silk fitted scarves, pinned together at the front, no strand of hair on show. Some, like her aunties, wore chadors; huge pieces of thin, breathable fabric that were wrapped around their heads and bodies, kept in place either by the clutch of their hand or through their gritted teeth. The latter initially looked extreme when Safie first saw someone wearing one in the airport. But she soon learned it was the most comfortable garment of all, especially in the summer months. With the chador you were able to wear whatever you wanted underneath.

She wondered how her mother would style a head-scarf if she were here. She would likely be the type to show her hair and wear a tight monto that skimmed her bottom – toeing the line between what was and was not acceptable.

'Where are we going, anyway?' she asked, after a while.

'I thought we could go to Mellat Park. It's nice there, very peaceful.'

She continued to look out of the window, observing the world pass by. 'Sounds good.'

At Mellat Park, Safie was taken aback by the mountains that she hadn't noticed in the distance, at how expansive the space was, at how extravagant everything was. The flowers were bright, the trees tall, the statues grand. It was quite unlike her imaginings. Since arriving in Iran she had been confined to relatives' homes and her mother's graveyard, had seen nothing of the beauty of her motherland. As they walked she saw two elderly men playing chess, watched as they considered their next move with painstaking concentration. Javad walked ahead of her, unaware, and she had to power-walk now to catch up with him.

'They have coloured water fountains here at night,' he said. 'People really like that.'

'You don't?'

He shrugged. 'It's a bit gimmicky. I like the natural elements more.'

They stopped off at a hut selling refreshments. They got café glace to go. It was her new favourite drink since coming to Tehran. A combination of coffee and ice cream. She had spent many years on diets, but now she found it hard to care about the push and pull of the pleasure of food, and the restricting of it.

The sweetness rushed to her immediately. She drank until she got brain freeze and had to stop.

'What's Boston like, then?' she said, at the same time that he said, 'Where in England do you live?'

He indicated that she go first. 'London, until about a month ago. I moved back home with my sister in Bradford,' she said. Seeing the blank look on his face, she continued, 'It's in Yorkshire. The North of England.'

He nodded. 'I've been to London once,' he said, his lips turned downwards. 'Very busy. Maybe I'd like Yorkshire better.'

'You probably only went to the tourist areas,' she said, a touch too defensively.

There was a small smile on his lips at this, the edges turned upwards ever so slightly. 'Maybe I did. To answer your earlier question, I love Boston. I moved there for college and have lived there ever since. The people are straightforward. They say what they mean. I appreciate that.'

The way his face lit up when he spoke almost made Safie smile. Almost.

'Very much unlike Iranians, then,' she joked.

'Yeah, there's no tarofing in Boston.' He gave her a sidelong smile and her heart quickened in a pleasant way. He really was quite handsome. He looked like a *man*, which sounded odd. All the men she knew back home resembled boys, but the way Javad carried himself was confident, assured.

Iranians were renowned for tarof. She remembered her mum teaching her the custom of never accepting an offer the first time, even if it was something you wanted. But that particular teaching hadn't stuck.

They walked in silence for a while, during which time Safie noted the people in the park, the way they looked like her, and that for the first time ever she felt she visually belonged. Their noses were all like hers, except for those who'd had nose jobs. Their eyes all dark and large, even their mannerisms were a familiar sight.

'Iranians – we're passionate people,' her mum had once told her. 'We're loud, dramatic, make large gestures.' She had laughed as she said it. Safie couldn't quite remember, but she thought her mum was explaining this after she'd thrown a tantrum, and couldn't understand the extent of her emotions. 'Of course, I'm generalising a tiny bit,' her mum had continued, winking. She had had such a natural ability to dissipate Safie's anger.

If she was in a film, this would be the point at which she would realise she was home. The moment in which she finally understood why her mother chose to be buried in Tehran, rather than in the country her children lived in. But Safie didn't feel any more at home here than she did in England. In England she was physically a foreigner; here she was one mentally.

'What do you do again?'

'I'm a researcher at the college. How about you? I heard you worked in fashion?' He stumbled slightly on his last question. His tone made her wonder if he knew more than he was saying.

She looked at him then, and saw the way he was looking at her. Like what she said mattered to him, that he cared and this wasn't just idle chit-chat with a stranger. A thought she desperately tried to repress crept up then: was he curious about her? In the same way she was curious about him? She pushed down such thoughts.

'I *worked* in fashion PR. I quit my job when I moved back home to be with my sister. I doubt they would have let me have time off to come here for so long, anyway.' She shrugged like she didn't care, like everything in her life ending was of no consequence. Like she wasn't terrified about what would happen when her small inheritance ran out and she had to find a job in Bradford, of all places. 'What are you a researcher in?' she asked, swiftly changing the subject.

'Biomedical science.'

Somehow, she hadn't expected that. She looked at people who studied the sciences and maths with awe. She couldn't imagine her brain computing – or wanting to compute – the type of information they had memorised.

'Wow,' she muttered.

'You'll find something great,' he said, as though reading her mind. 'The bumps in the road in life, they all lead you to where you need to be. It's OK to pause sometimes.'

They continued walking in silence.

When her mind was sick of spiralling, of worrying about her future, Safie began to focus on how far apart they were from each other. Probably ten centimetres? She didn't understand what was and wasn't allowed in Iran. Before she came here, she'd scrolled through a plethora of online forums which warned that men and women who were not related were not allowed to be together in public. The internet was full of horror stories about the various punishments inflicted on those who disobeyed the rules.

But the reality was quite different. Ahead of them she saw young men and women walking together, albeit not hand in hand, but from their body language she doubted they were related.

She tried to imagine what she and Javad would look like from an outsider's perspective. Her arms were folded as she walked, which she knew was making her appear closed off, but the fleeting glances they kept exchanging, she knew, communicated something different.

They had circled back the way they'd come and had ended up outside his car.

'Are we going back?' she asked.

'Do you want to?'

She thought for a moment. Imagined her busy extended family, their inquisitive stares as Maman Bozorg asked her where she had been. The answer to Javad's question seemed obvious, at first, but when she imagined Maryam alone, Safie felt a pang of guilt. Then again, she was tired of being a rock; she longed to forget about everything, if only for a few more hours. Maryam would understand.

'Not really,' she leaned against the car. 'But I know you probably have lots to do . . .'

'No,' he said quickly. They both smiled at this, before quickly looking away from each other. 'In fact, I know somewhere we could go to have some fun.'

He flashed her a large, excited grin that made her insides leap. She couldn't tell if he was feeling sorry for her, or whether he genuinely did want to spend more time with her. She hoped it was the latter. In response, she squeezed her hands together, to stop herself from smiling too broadly back at him.

*

They drove for twenty minutes, during which time Safie shut her eyes and let her mind rest. She hadn't been able to do that in ages and it felt so freeing to settle her thoughts.

'We're here,' he said gently.

She opened her eyes, slowly at first, and saw Javad studying her face. His expression was soft, unguarded. She looked back at him for a moment, and then partly because this felt too intimate, and partly because she then saw where they were, she sat up straight, moved her head back. 'Go-karting?'

He let out a bashful laugh. 'Was this not a good idea? A bad idea?' He looked sheepish.

'Not bad, just random.' She couldn't help the small smile on her face; she didn't know what she was expecting, but it wasn't this.

There were eight of them in the race. The men and women were given separate areas to get dressed in. She was about to take her hijab off, given that she would be wearing a helmet, but the other women kept theirs on underneath the helmet, so she did too. It was an interesting look.

As they lined up to get in, Javad leaned into her ear, 'Prepare to get your butt kicked.'

She laughed, despite the chill she felt at being so close to him, his breath warm against her cheek. It was the first time she had genuinely laughed in a very long time; the sound, the sensation in her stomach, felt alien – but freeing, like her body had been desperate for such a release. 'Yeah, yeah, pal.'

It was only when she was inside her car, once she had been fastened in and could only see ahead with the restrictive helmet, that Safie realised that for the first time in forty days – momentarily at least – she had not thought about her mother.

'I can't believe you beat me,' Javad said, a wounded expression on his face, his lips curved gently upwards. 'My car definitely wasn't going as fast as everyone else's – I think it had a fault.' He scratched his head theatrically. 'When I came here with my cousins, I came first.'

'Yep, sure.'

He narrowed his eyes at her.

Safie chuckled quietly. 'I guess I'm going to have to take your word for it.'

He looked like he wanted to say more but thought better of it.

It was getting dark out now. She looked up to the evening sky and wondered what her family would say when she came back, what they were saying to Maryam right now. Her phone didn't work here, and for that reason she had never really left Maman Bozorg's house without a family member with her. She resolved she would deal with her family later, pushing them from her mind.

'You hungry?' Javad asked as they got into the car.

'Yes, actually,' she said, though she wasn't sure if she was. In spite of everything, she just wanted more time. Time away from her reality, her family, and, though she disliked herself for such thoughts: more time with Javad. Knowing what she would be going back to only made her want to stay out more, savour this rare moment of escape with a man she might never see again.

'Are you in the mood for a burger?' Javad asked.

'Always.'

He nodded, and started the engine.

She side-eyed him, noticing the way his hands gripped the steering wheel, the veins on his hands. She forced herself to look away, to push down on the rising feeling of attraction.

Javad was by no means her usual type.

Her ex-boyfriend, Callum, was constantly in the gym – his defining feature in his own words was his six-pack. He was a typical lad: obsessed with sports and beer. He never picked up a book, which irrationally annoyed her on many occasions. Even though they had been dating two years, towards the end he still mixed up aspects of her culture, didn't know – and didn't care to know – much about Iran. For the entirety of their relationship she had always thought it was her fault, because she didn't know much about her mother's country, so how could she guide him? But it was only now that she realised it wasn't her job to teach him, to correct him. He could have cared enough to do the research himself.

Why had she even stayed with him for as long as she did? Safie didn't quite know. Before her mother's death she was a passenger in life. She went along with things, didn't question what she was doing or really consider taking control of her life or what she wanted. She had thought there would always be time to get things right later.

Javad, unlike Callum, had an artistic look about him, akin to the kind of men she had liked on Tumblr as a teenager, but always thought were mythical. He was lean, his jaw strong, his thick hair curly and flopping. But beyond looks, Javad was intelligent, didn't seem to conform to any one stereotype. He constantly surprised her.

'What do you do for fun?' Safie asked him. 'Apart from go-karting?'

He thought about it for a moment, squinting his eyes at the traffic ahead. 'Lots of things, I guess. I'm into gaming. I play basketball in a league with my friends, which I'm really missing right now.' She saw him smiling to himself. 'I fucking love karaoke.'

'Seriously?'

He turned to look at her briefly, their eyes locking for a moment. 'I swear. It's an excellent stress reliever. If I'd known a good place here, I would have taken you.'

Hearing him saying he would take her somewhere, like that was something they now did, initially raised excitement within her, but it was quickly replaced by sadness. After tonight they would likely never see each other again.

He cleared his throat, and ever so briefly his eyebrows furrowed, as though he'd remembered something he'd rather not. 'Anyway, what about you? What do you like to do?' His tone was cooler now, more detached.

'Weekdays were usually pretty busy with work. You're expected to work really long hours in fashion. But on the weekends I used to paint. I'm not a spectacular painter or anything, but I always found it nice to sit in a park and paint and be away from technology for a while.'

'That sounds really nice.'

'Yeah, it was.' She thought about what she would do when she returned to Bradford, and resolved she would try, at least, to paint, to reconnect with an activity she'd once enjoyed, even if the thought of doing so felt wrong, like life shouldn't be allowed to resume again.

They ended up in a quaint restaurant, the interior a fusion of Iran and the West. The menu listed both traditional Iranian dishes, such as kashke bademjan, and more Western ones like hamburgers with fries.

Javad ordered for them, his Farsi so smooth and seamless. He said words she didn't understand, and watching him and the waiter converse and laugh brought her a mixture of admiration and frustration.

'Are you OK?' he asked, once the waiter had left.

She was pulled out of her reverie, attempted to smile, but was sure it came out as a grimace instead.

'That was a stupid question,' he said, moving his fork slightly to the side, perhaps simply to have something to do with his hands. 'The type of question I hated people asking me when my dad died, and here I am asking you.'

She sat a little straighter, and looked at him properly, waiting until his eyes locked with hers. She could see the grief in them then. It was a small glimmer, so slight she probably wouldn't have noticed if her own mother had not died.

'How did he pass away?'

She saw the way his Adam's apple bobbed then, before he bit his bottom lip in what looked like concentration, as if he was trying to control emotions threatening to bubble to the surface.

'Cancer,' he said.

She reached her hand out, almost touched his, but then remembered herself, who they were, where they were.

Her hand hovered above his awkwardly before she smoothly, or so she thought, picked up the off-brand cola the waiter had put on the table.

The waiter returned with the food. Javad had ordered them a variety of Iranian side dishes as well as burgers and fries for them both. It was exactly what she wanted. She dipped the warm nan-e barbari, the traditional oven-cooked flatbread, into what Javad told her was kashke bademjan, a creamy roasted aubergine dip with herbs and walnuts scattered on the top. It was delicious, and eating it made her realise just how hungry she had been. If she were not with Javad she could have finished the bowl in two minutes flat, but she forced herself to slow down and savour the food.

Javad must have picked up on this because when she looked up she saw him smiling. 'You like it, then?'

She could feel her cheeks colouring. 'It's really good. You chose well, I have to say.'

He winked, before taking a piece of flatbread and dipping it into the kashke bademjan.

The waiter returned with their burgers, and for the rest of the evening they talked of their families, mostly his, because Safie was a master of deflection when she wanted to be. Javad had two siblings, one Safie had already met, the other was fifteen years younger than him, only thirteen years old. He spoke of her with such joy.

Throughout dinner Safie felt herself drawing closer to him, feeling almost drunk in the busy atmosphere. But of course she hadn't been drinking, bar her soft drink.

Their knees were touching under the table by the end of the meal, and she let herself lean into him slightly, allowing her legs to be between his. Back home, doing this could indicate closeness but not necessarily romance, but here, right now, it felt like a bold act.

She looked around the restaurant. No one was looking at them; no one cared. The image of Iran being so strict was fading away during her evening with Javad. It was easy to forget the laws here were so different to the laws in England. If anyone did say anything, she thought she could play dumb, not realising their closeness. That didn't mean her heart wasn't beating wildly the entire time, though.

More than anything else, she couldn't help but notice that he didn't move away. She could not tell what his feelings towards her were; could not tell if he was only being friendly this entire evening, if she had misread the signals.

During all their time together, Javad had not made mention of a girlfriend waiting for him at home. But that didn't mean there wasn't one.

'What does your partner do?' she asked, a blank look on her face. It was much less embarrassing to be corrected if she was wrong with this line of questioning, than presume he was single.

He was polishing off the last of his fries. He paused, putting one back down and brushing his hands together.

Oh.

'It's complicated,' he finally said.

She looked around the restaurant, at friends, families and couples eating together, the look of joy on their faces. She had misread the situation and needed to play it cool. She sat back straight on her chair, her legs no longer touching his.

'Oh, really?'

He cleared his throat, gave a short humourless laugh.

'I know I said I'm here for a holiday but there's a little more to it than that.'

She frowned. 'Care to elaborate?'

He looked pained. It was bad.

'I came for an engagement. My engagement.'

'You're engaged?'

The noise around them died away, or perhaps it amplified; either way it was like they were the only ones in the room, like no one else could hear them.

He made a small noise of frustration. 'Technically, yes, but I only met her a week ago.'

Love at first sight? This was even worse than she suspected. She wished he would just stop talking now.

'My dad and her dad had always planned for us to marry,' he continued. 'When my dad died, somehow it felt even more important that I do the only thing he wanted me to do. My mom and dad got married without really knowing each other and had the most perfect marriage, so even though it sounds old-fashioned, I guess it really does work? I don't know . . .'

'So, you met last week and now you're getting married?'

She had to feign interest for her own self-preservation at this point.

'Mona – that's her name – she's a sweet girl, and I thought I could settle for a "friendship" kind of marriage. I think it's obvious we both don't feel that spark. But it's only today that I've realised that's not what I want.'

Her heart stuttered at this.

'Today?'

His face coloured then. He looked visibly uncomfortable, squinted his eyes slightly as he asked, 'What about you? Do you . . . ?'

God this is awkward, she thought. Surely there was an easier way to ask each other if they were single. She realised back home with her friends that they'd just resort to social-media-stalking a man – or they'd find them on a dating app and then the answer would be clear (but admittedly not always). She knew nothing about Javad other than what he told her, and that was oddly both exciting and terrifying.

'I'm single,' she said. It was the first time she had said it with such certainty since her break-up with Callum. She tasted the words in her mouth. She thought she would hate saying it; she had been conditioned to think that being single was shameful, that it made her lesser somehow, but actually she quite liked the way it sounded. She was no longer in a relationship she was too scared to leave. She was free.

Javad smiled. It was a big, toothy smile, which made her smile in return.

'I have an idea,' he said. 'After this, would you be up for going to one more place?'

Javad didn't tell her where he was taking her and she didn't press him. She liked not knowing, liked the weightless excitement that came with no longer having control, of letting someone else lead.

During the drive, she noticed when the cars stopped at the lights that the people inside rolled down their windows and talked to each other.

'What are they doing?' she asked Javad.

He smirked. 'Flirting, probably exchanging numbers.'

Her eyebrows furrowed; she was not sure she had heard correctly. 'Why?'

'Well, they can't meet in clubs or bars, so this is the next best thing.' He glanced at her and smiled. 'It's kind of romantic, if you think about it.'

The look in his eyes as he said this made her cheeks flush.

She diverted her gaze to the scene ahead of her, and watched as the person in the jeep in front – a boy who looked to be in his late teens – stuck his head further out the window, a smile on his face. She could hear shrill laughter coming from the car next to him. The lights switched to green and the jeep beeped three times excitedly before speeding away.

Their methods were different, but really young people here were no different to young people in England. Of course they weren't; it shamed Safie that she expected otherwise. People were all the same, everywhere.

Javad drove up towards the mountains, the roads narrow and bendy, making the car jolt occasionally, always when she least expected it. She knew she should be wary of being in a car with a man she had only known for half a day, but she was totally at ease with him. She trusted him, even though it made no sense.

They ended up parked in a clearing, high up the mountain track. He got out of the car, opened her door for her.

'Very gentlemanly,' she commented as she stepped out, a teasing smile on her lips.

Up this high the view of Tehran's skyline was magnificent. She could see the cars on the network of roads below, their headlights illuminating the city quite beautifully, the patches of greenery, Milad Tower, the high-rise buildings. She had been wrong about Iran, she realised then. It had its own charm. She had initially expected to feel a surge of fondness towards her mother country as soon as they stepped off the plane and into Tehran Imam Khomeini airport, but after weeks of no such feelings she'd thought it would never come. This evening with Javad had shown her another side to the country, and that she would never forget.

More than that, she could finally see her mother here. She could see her eating the food Safie had eaten the last few weeks, could see her as a teenager flirting through car windows, could see her mother in the mannerisms of the people around her. Though she would never fully understand why she chose to be buried here, she finally felt she could accept it.

Javad got a blanket out from his boot and laid it on the hood of his car.

Safie laughed at this. 'God, you really are American, aren't you?'

'What do you mean?' he asked, a goofy smile on his face.

She waved her hand. 'It doesn't matter.'

They sat on the hood of his car, looking at the view. She had loosened her hijab so it was no longer tied under her neck but hung loose around her head. She pulled her knees to her chest, wrapping her arms around her legs. Javad seemed at ease, spreading his whole body as he lay out, his hands behind his head. With her gaze ahead, taking in the view, she could feel him looking at her, and she let him look for a few moments. It was a strange feeling, like she knew what he was thinking.

'Do you have any regrets in life?' she asked suddenly.

She turned to him, and they maintained eye contact for a beat longer than what would be normal. He deliberated before he answered her question; she could almost see him weighing up his answer in his mind, turning it over and over.

'Not really. I don't believe in regrets. You can't change the past, and I'm a firm believer in the cliché that everything happens for a reason,' he said, clearly unaware of how his healthy approach to life was not shared by many – including Safie. 'Why, do you?'

'Lots. I regret staying with my ex for as long as I did. I regret not spending more time with my mum while I still could. I barely went home once I moved to London. I thought I had all the time in the world. I regret being so stupid, most of all.'

Javad's hand lay on top of hers then, seemingly to stop her from fidgeting. It was warm, rough and soft all at the same time. Just his hand on hers was enough to give her chills, make her forget what she was saying, even when what she was saying was so important. Did that make her a bad person?

He wove his fingers through hers like it was the most natural thing in the world. They were truly alone here, and for a moment she thought she was back in England, that he was a man she was on a date with, that what they were doing was not strictly forbidden. His thumb traced circles around her knuckles.

'You're not stupid. None of that is your fault. You can't have known what would happen. You had to still live your life. I'm sure the time you did spend with your mom was special. Sometimes that's what matters more – the quality of time you spend with your loved ones, rather than the quantity. That's what my dad told me when he was ill. I worried I wasn't seeing him enough. That I was a bad son. I didn't even say it, but he must have known what I was thinking. I'm sure your mom would say the same thing,' he said. 'In fact, I have it on good authority that your mom was very proud of you.'

'How would you know that?'

'She always told my mom as much, which was then relayed to me. Even before meeting you, I knew you were pretty cool.'

Her heart began beating even quicker. His hand was still holding hers, and somehow they were sitting much closer now. She could easily lean in, kiss him, like she'd wanted to pretty much all day; perhaps, if she was being honest with herself, from the moment she first saw him.

His eyes locked with hers, hazel on hazel, and his only moved to look down at her lips. She had visions of him pulling her towards him, kissing her, pinning her down on the car bonnet . . . but there was one small problem.

'You're engaged,' she said. She let the words fester in the air.

He moved away at that. 'I'm not going to be for long,' he said, the words quiet; so quiet she wasn't sure she heard correctly. 'I've decided.'

'What?'

'I meant what I said before: today confirmed something that deep down I've known for a while. I don't want that kind of marriage. I want more. I love my dad, but I can't live my life for him. He would understand.'

'What about today confirmed that for you?' she said, clutching at his words, her breath caught, hanging onto his every word, but attempting to look like she was not.

'You,' he said.

Her lips parted at this, and she let out a small, slow sigh.

His hand was on her cheek, cupping it, and she felt like a plant leaning into the light then. His touch felt so right, like they had known each other much longer than a mere five hours.

'Can I kiss you?' he said quietly, his lips already inches from hers.

'Yes,' she said. 'Please.'

His lips were soft and expert, both his hands now on either side of her face, holding her to him. It was all so effortless, so dreamlike, as though they had kissed many times before in some other life.

After a moment, he leaned back, his hand moving under her chin. Somewhere along the way her scarf had come completely undone, and now hung around her neck, her pink hair truly on show in all its glory.

'You're so beautiful,' he said. 'I really don't want this to end.'

The combination of the intensity of the kiss, his eyes that seemed to be boring into her soul and his words sent chills through her.

She realised, with a start, that she really didn't want this to end either. That for Javad to simply go away after this evening, for her to never learn more about this man, was a painful thought.

'It doesn't have to end,' she said, now smiling against his lips.

He lifted her quite easily so that she was on top of him, straddling him. His eyes were so intense, that every time she pulled away after kissing she would feel a tingle inside just looking at them. She never did understand why blue eyes were considered to be so special; darker eyes were the ones that you could really lose yourself in.

The remainder of their evening was a blur of conversation about any and everything, and chaste – and not so chaste – kisses.

As they approached Maman Bozorg's house, the underlying dread at what she was returning to began to encroach on Safie. It was midnight, now, and she sincerely hoped that they had not sent a search party out for her.

'God, do you think they're going to kill me when I get home?'

'Not kill you.' Javad flashed her a joking smile, which was by no means reassuring, given the situation. 'It'll be fine, honestly.'

She wasn't sure she agreed, but wondered if their opinion of her mattered in the grand scheme of things. Her mother had died, and this evening was the only thing that scooped her out of her pit of despair. No matter the consequences, if she could go back in time she knew she'd do it again.

When they were parked outside Maman Bozorg's house, she could see the lights were on inside. Javad switched the engine off and turned to her.

'I want to see you again,' he said. She was surprised by how direct he was, so unlike the boys she was used to.

The fluttering feeling in her stomach returned, and she put her hand over his.

'I do, too.'

Her flight was in two days, though, and he knew this.

'I mean, beyond this trip,' he hesitated then. She squeezed his hand, and he gave her a breathtaking smile. 'Long distance? Is that crazy? It's crazy, right?'

'It is!' she exclaimed. She couldn't stop smiling, though. 'Is it crazy that that's what I want, too?'

He let out a held breath, before cupping her cheek lightly, the car dark, the street lights only illuminating certain parts of the car. She was sure that they would not be seen here, and even if they could be, in this moment she didn't care.

'I guess life itself is crazy,' he said. 'The things you really want aren't easy. And I want you, Safie.'

Looking at this man, she realised that through him she saw beauty in the world again. She now held some excitement for the future, for what lay ahead for her and Javad, and this motherland that she expected she would return to one day.

She leaned in, let her lips brush his.

It had been forty days since her mother had died, and while her life would never be the same again, Safie now felt something like hope.

It was a start.

RAIN . . . DOUBTFUL

Kuchenga

Dear Mum,

The first and last time I wrote to you I was fifteen years old. I was too angry then because I was so devastated and you only gave us a few days to say goodbye. You hadn't told me what was going on until the end was close. You wore wigs most days anyway, so that was easy for you to hide. It was the coldest day in May I can ever remember and I had my head inside a hood for over a month after you left. I can still feel the place in my chest where it felt like I had been stabbed with a steak knife. But I'm in love now and she has healed the young hurt boy in me, and also made me grow up, because that's what she does. She makes everyone love themselves.

We met in Dalston Market on Uncle Harry's stall. Still in the same spot at the top by the station. He finally gave up smoking when Uncle Jim had a heart attack and was practically living in the hospital for weeks at a time afterwards. He never really recovered. His skin was grey and his eyes went yellow. Uncle Harry joked that he looked half elephant when we were walking out of Homerton Hospital, and threw his pack of B&H in the bin when we got to the front entrance car park. He said that just because he was the youngest of the three of you didn't mean he shouldn't do his best to hang about.

'Don't wanna leave you on your own now, do we?'

I think it was that. Him sticking about to look after me. But also, where your going was swift and neat, Uncle Jim's was more harrowing. He couldn't even get up to go to the toilet at the end. Uncle Harry couldn't handle that.

I was meant to be telling you about her, and here I am telling you about him. It's cos you'd wanna know, I guess? Your youngest brother is doing all right, Mum. You and Uncle Jim having a decent time up there, I hope. You asked him to look after me, and Uncle Harry has done that and a whole lot more. When you'd gone and I had to move from ours in Walthamstow to his in Ilford, my bedroom was actually exactly the same. I just watched telly in the living room with my hood up. He even put all my posters up in the same kinda positions because the bedroom was the same size. I get my work ethic from him in a way. No shade to you or nothing, but you did allow me to loaf a bit. You spoiled me. Uncle Harry forced me to be active. It helped. On Saturdays, I'd work with him on the stall selling fruit and veg, and then on Sundays he'd take me to play football on the marshes with my mates.

Outside of that, I just worked a lot. I became a bit of a workaholic from that time onwards now I'm thinking about it. I was grieving for you, but I had no way of talking about it. So instead I just studied well hard. I knew that's what you would have wanted, and when I got three A*s in my GCSEs I decided to go to a different sixth form college. George Monoux in Walthamstow, just off the North Circ. That's when I proper got into cycling, too. Is it funny that I went off to uni, got my degree, came back, got a City job – but still helped Uncle Harry out on the stall on Saturdays when I got back? I wanted to. I love that market. Can't find the banter that you have down there anywhere else. I can't take the piss out of Uncle Harry anywhere near as well as you could, though.

I know you were worried how we'd do without you. We got into a groove quickly. Pam's still quiet most of the time. When you were here, we'd take the piss out of how sour her face looked. One time she slighted you when we were round at theirs, and on the way home you called her a bulldog with a perm. Do you remember? I've never asked why they never had kids. I couldn't ask her and it's really not important. In a way it's like I've become their kid. Emotionally anyway. Funnily enough, people say I look like Uncle Harry sometimes, even though we're not like proper blood-related. Pam said I used to call Uncle Harry 'Dad' but you told me not to. When we go out, people probably think I'm adopted, with me being the dark one. Don't worry though. No one's ever said anything like super nasty, but round our way in summer there was always a neighbour who came back tanned off their holidays and said, 'Well, I'm almost as dark as you now, Daniel!' Every year. The same joke. No variation. Several times a season. Uncle Harry never joked like that though. I wish I had asked you what it was like to be adopted. A Nigerian girl adopted into a white family in the East End in the seventies. It must have been hard. Channel Four would make a film about it these days. You never told me who my dad was and I assume you had a reason. I don't care really. Most of the time anyway. Uncle Harry came to be enough of a dad for me. I know my dad was white because I'm lighter than you. But yeah . . . I dunno. I think about it sometimes. Uncle Harry still loves his reggae. *One Love* tattooed on his arm. Talks about you and him going to shubeens and Notting Hill Carnival and whatever. Even though you were brother and sister, you must have looked like a couple when you went out together. I loved hearing you and Uncle Harry reminisce about the old days. Shubeens and lovers' rock and stuff.

I wish I could have taken her out like that in London. I didn't feel able to. But still, I'm glad I can say I believe in love at first sight now. I belong to a really cool club of people who aren't so bogged down with life that they can't recognise when destiny has come knocking. Her name's Josephine. Her mates call her Jo. I call her Jose.

Mum, I was bowled away. It wasn't lust. Actually, it was that, but that wasn't all it was. She wasn't just golden – she was gold! Her dress was mustardy yellow with little holes in it. Her afro even looked like it had gold in it, almost like . . . wet. Her skin was so smooth I'd have believed her if she said she was on the run from Lindor. I can't really tell you any more about her effect on me, because you're my mum. Actually, I can tell you about her face. If I was thinking lazily, I would say she looked like Cleopatra or Nefertiti, but having read her African history books I have more references to choose from than just Ancient Egypt. She looks like she is a descendant of the Angolan Queen Nzinga . . . or like she was a princess of Old Zimbabwe. Her eyes are a bit far apart, like she's got some alien in her. That sounds weird but when you see the models she works with, you kinda get what I mean. She hasn't got like a button nose. It's a Black nose. It's a cute Black girl's nose. I love giving her an Eskimo kiss. She has a heart-shaped face. You can appreciate the shape of it more when she puts her headscarf on at night. When her face is in neutral, she just looks innocent. Pleasingly round but with these angles that make you think of old films. Lauryn Hill with a lot more meat on her. She'd hate me to say that. I'm probably gonna say it to her. Just so I can get 'the look'.

She gave it to me then.

'Do you want a bag for those oranges?' I asked.

'Yes, obviously?' she said.

I was embarrassed because that was literally my job, that day at least. I was glad to have her full attention though.

''Ere, Jose! Doesn't he look like Thierry Henry?' her mum said, nodding in my direction.

'No, he doesn't, Mum,' she said.

'Yes he does! That one that plays for Arsenal,' she kept on.

'Mum! Please!'

I was flattered, even though I look nothing like him. As a West Ham supporter, I always loved reminding Arsenal fans that Ian Wright started off with us. Anyway, you don't care about all that. The truth is I look like a mixed-race *Love Island* contestant. My head is well square. You'd like *Love Island*, I think. It's ridiculous and no one wears any clothes. Thing is, even though I did have clothes on, I could tell my physique impressed her. I started going gym in sixth form. I preferred how people treated me when I began to get hench.

'Hasn't he got big arms, Jose?'

'Mum, seriously! Can you behave? You're so embarrassing!'

I loved their rapport with each other. The bickering. I could tell this was them all day long. Like Saffy and Eddie in *Absolutely Fabulous*. The mum poking fun and antagonising her long-suffering daughter who pretended to be annoyed, but secretly loved it, and definitely loved her. They walked off into the grubby sunset towards the train station and I longed to follow them and ask for her number. I couldn't stop looking at her. Uncle Harry broke the spell a little bit. 'Careful, son! That one is a bit more Arthur than Martha, if you know what I mean.'

I didn't. But I would soon find out.

'You're always on that bloody phone!' You would say it every night before you told me to lay the table. Well, Mum, if you could see us now! Back then I was only ever playing snake or texting my mates. Now, we live on our phones all day long. We bank through our phones. Watch films on our phones. Everything, Mum! We do everything through our phones. I think – no, I know – you would hate social media. I mean, I do, for sure. The constant scrolling . . . but it was social media that brought us together. That night, after I'd had a shower and was lying on the sofa with a belly full of Pam's shepherd's pie, while she watched *Strictly* – oh, you would bloody love *Strictly Come Dancing*. Such camp dancing and singing celebrities. Lots of glitz. Well, yeah, anyway. I opened up Facebook and there she was in my suggested friends. Josephine Hope. Maybe I should be angry that such things happen these days?

We are obviously being traced constantly. We had no mutual friends. Our phones basically mated without our knowledge. Regardless, I was grateful. No need to become some weird stalker because all I knew was the area in which she shopped with her mum. Now I could research her life and get to know her. She is a fashion stylist. Her Facebook feed was all fashion shows and inspirational quotes. I got bored quickly. Then I found her on Instagram. Here she posted all her work. I didn't have a good understanding of her job back then, but her Instagram was a hell of a lot more interesting. There are more different kinds of models these days. I could see that not only was she high-end and stuff – like, I knew if you were working for *Vogue* you must be doing all right – but more than that, the images were from another world. She helped create that! There were a few photos of her at parties, but not many. She was obviously professional and reserved. It was Twitter that gave me the full whammy. Her memes were hilarious and there was some political stuff. I knew we'd get on. It only took two minutes until I understood what Uncle Harry had meant. There were a lot of posts about Black trans women being murdered in the States. Like – a lot. It started to dawn on me what Uncle Harry had meant, and then I saw a tweet where she said it outright: 'As a Black trans woman . . .' And Mum . . . my heart sank.

Thing is, it did not make me want her any less. It made me want her more, if I'm honest. You're my mum so I can't go into too much detail, but let's just say when I was online as a teenager, and spending some time alone on those sorts of sites, I clicked on that category one day

and surprised myself. I was really turned on by 'em. Don't
know why. I still feel straight, even if no one believes me,
because I don't fancy gay guys or anything, but yeah . . .
There was an experience at university at a rave. And on a
stag do in Amsterdam, I broke off from the crowd and had
another . . . experience. Anyway, the truth is, this woman
who I met in real life mesmerised me. But because Uncle
Harry had 'clocked her T', as she says, I felt exposed. Still,
I had to go after her. Because . . . I just had to. I just
could never tell him, I told myself. So, I liked ten of her
pictures on Instagram, and I messaged her with a terrible
joke and at the end I said, 'I think you're beautiful.' She
responded straight away.

    You're probably wondering why she was so quick to
get back to me when she was not that into me when we
met at Uncle Harry's stall on the market? Well, it's just
the way she is. She'd make a fantastic judge. When you
first meet her or first tell her something, she questions
you to death. She accepts nothing. She believes no one.
She checks everything. Remind you of anyone, Mum? The
same question rephrased and asked in a different tone?
When we started talking on the phone, she refused to
accept that I had no girlfriend and no kids. She interro-
gated me so much I began to wonder if I actually did have
a secret babymother in Ilford I had forgotten about. Her
imagination is wild. She paints scenes, Mum. I learned
that she loves documentaries and this makes her good at
her job. She knows what everyone around the world has
been wearing for the past three thousand years. She reads
a lot. Mostly non-fiction. Her schedule is well random.
Nine days at home planning stuff, then four days in Wales

on a hill somewhere. Then back to London, off to Notting Hill or car boot sales on Sunday mornings, then off to Turkey shooting swimwear at some resort. Then fashion weeks come and she's in turbo mode. She lives on Red Bull and coffee for weeks and then comes home and crashes. She hates Italy. No, that's not fair, she hates the way she is treated in Italy. Because I've never been out with anyone as dark as her, there's things I didn't know. Things you didn't tell me. She is lucky I'm not with her in some of these places because I swear I would knock them out. Still she kept me at a distance emotionally for longer than I would have liked. She didn't trust me. She had every right not to.

She lives on this new development on the Thames. Nine Elms, between Battersea Park and Vauxhall. She has a lot of Russian neighbours. I don't know this part of London that well. That calmed me down. The week after I saw her on the market I was meeting her at Battersea Park train station. Far away from anyone I knew. Like I said, I really didn't know these sides, so I could keep this secret easily. I needed to be . . . discreet. When I was walking down the stairs towards her waiting in the ticket hall I felt like a king. I was only wearing a shirt and jeans, but I felt cleaner that night than I have ever been in my life. Just proper fresh. I scanned her up and down. You really can't tell she's transgender just to look at her. I know it's not politically correct to say this, but it calmed me down no end. She's only a little taller than your average girl. No one would think. This gave us a chance at something. I didn't know how much I could handle with her yet. But it gave us something.

That first night was out of this world. You're my mum so I can't tell you that much, but she was wearing a short floral dress and I definitely fell in love with her form when walking back to hers. The wind was cheeky and the breeze revealed her shape to me. We started in the lift up to hers and then . . . Yeah. I've heard of writers who speak of the body as a landscape. This makes sense to me now. She is a continent to me. Smooth uninterrupted terrains of dunes and jungles and savannas. Her physical being could sustain so many people, but I'm glad to say she's all mine. She said she liked dry rosé, so I had bought her a bottle. Later that night we drank it on her balcony. I knew she was taking me seriously because she had cooked for me.

Stuffed peppers and salad. Roast honey and mustard chicken with lemon potatoes. Roast salmon with bulgur wheat, onion and artichokes. She loves to cook for me, you know. And you know I love to eat. She said she used to have an eating disorder, which I really can't imagine. She looks healthy in all her old pictures. The only quirk she has with food is that she doesn't like eating too late. As a result, most of my memories of us eating together are during sun-filled days. That first summer at hers was just a proper oasis. Uncle Harry didn't care where I was and Pam never asked, so I went round to hers every Saturday evening and returned every Sunday afternoon. On the way to hers I would google shit jokes on the train just so I could enjoy her performance of being disapproving. I like when I tell her a joke and she gets exasperated because it's so shit, but no matter how insufferable I make myself, she still loves me. She is my best friend, Mum. I love her so much. So that's why it got fucked up as autumn drew near. Instead of loafing around on her balcony or drinking in the bar by the barges downstairs, it was time now for cinema visits, museum trips, restaurant dates. She deserved to be shown off and taken out. But I wasn't ready. I should have been proud to be seen with her. Any other girl would have pushed it much earlier. I was glad she didn't because I wouldn't have had the words. It's not manly to say, 'Do you know what? I'm scared.' Looking back, we both were. Neither of us likes confrontation really.

Things came to a head by accident. We were watching that film you like, *The English Patient.* It's a really good film, actually. Anyway, it gets to the end, and I'm cuddling her and she's crying, and I think it's because of the film, but out of nowhere she says, 'I miss my friends.' Well, that knocked me for six. I said, 'Why? What's happened to them?' She goes, 'You. You happened to them.'

'What do you mean?' I said.

'It's been six months.'

'Yeah . . .' I didn't quite know what she was getting at yet. That's the thing with girls, they'll say something that makes it seem like it should be abundantly clear, but it's not.

'You made me sacrifice a whole summer of Saturday nights.'

I just looked at her. I thought she had wanted to.

'I thought you wanted to.'

'What are we doing here? Where are we going?'

Oh for fuck's sake! I said to myself. Pardon my French, Mum, but seriously. Why is it always like this? OK, I've been insensitive and unaware. I genuinely hadn't thought of what she was giving up by seeing me in this way. If she'd been born a girl, this would be the time when I'd say, 'Well, let's meet your friends together then!' Or I'd reassure her with something like, 'Well, you're my girlfriend and I wanna make this official, because I've never loved anyone like you.' But I couldn't do that. My manhood was on the line. If anyone found out about her, that would be it. Those jokes that the lads at football tell each other down the pub. They would be about me. The sniggers and the elbowing and no longer being seen as one of the lads – for life! I couldn't take that.

'I just need more time,' I said.

'Oh, fuck off.'

She had left her e-cigarette thing on the balcony. She went to go and get it and she stubbed her toe on the way there. She soldiered it and swallowed the pain, but hobbled on out. When she finally got it, she toked on it for an eternity and blew out a huge popcorn-smelling cloud stream.

'I genuinely thought you were different,' she said.

'I am different,' I said.

'No, you're not.'

I walked towards her, hoping I could say something that would get her back.

'Oh come on. You're my Victoria and I am your Albert,' I said.

'He wasn't ashamed to be seen with her, and she could actually give him kids.' She turned her back on me and looked out on the Thames. The bright red lights of Dolphin Square felt like they'd been put there to take the piss out of me specifically. I felt ridiculous.

'You should leave,' she said. The finality of that sentence cut through me like a butcher's cleaver. How can it be that only last weekend we had learnt each other's major names and that we both got them from our grandparents? Now look at us. I had been brave enough to dare to dream, saying: 'I, Daniel Albert Baker, take you, Josephine Victoria Hope, to be my lawfully wedded . . .'

I had held her while looking out of the window on a blue sky and imagined having those words. Now look at us. She said it again:

'I think you should leave.'

So I did.

Life without her felt like the way they make Soviet Russia look in movies. Everything had a washed-out sepia tinge. We had lost the Brexit vote. Days after we broke up, Donald Trump won the presidency. Celebrities were dying like flies that year, and I felt like it was all my fault. I missed her interrogation. She's really solutions-based, you see. I loved the fact she always asked me why I did things. 'Why are you still living with your aunt and uncle?' she had asked.

'I'm saving for a house,' I told her, thinking she'd be impressed.

'You're earning hundreds of thousands working as a partner, living at home still and working on your uncle's stall for no reason.'

Forgive me, but because she worked in fashion, I didn't think she'd be able to analyse my life like that. She was right. My life had got mouldy even though money had started to pour in and I was working under loads of pressure. Working on the stall on Saturdays was my only time with Uncle Harry in adulthood. Nothing was unmanageable on the market. It grounded me. I knew where and who I was. Because I had graduated with a first after the recession and done well in my career in spite of it, I kind of felt an unhealthy mix of unstoppable and exhausted. I had got my master's while working. I was at the gym all the time. Girls smiled at me on the tube. Life seemed to be filled with choice and opportunities and decent music was coming out all the time. Then she dumped me and my world was all Wall-Street-Crashing around me. She blocked me EVERYWHERE, Mum. I tried to get hold of her in a number of ways. Her blocking me meant that I ended up sending her postcards. Why postcards? I was hinting that I would be OK with people knowing eventually. We could start with the postman, I thought. Stupid, innit.

She didn't write me back. So, I just walked around feeling ill. Then I actually did get ill. That Christmas I got the flu, didn't I?! Spent the whole day in bed. Came down for the dinner. Ate half a plate. Drank a hot toddy while watching *EastEnders* with Harry and Pam, and then it was back to bed. I was a right state. I actually listened to that George Michael song 'Last Christmas' on Spotify on my headphones loads. Just feeling sorry for myself. Then what does he do? He only went and bloody died, didn't he? I was so angry with him. I was like, 'How could you do that, George? We were good mates. We were in this together. You were the only one who understood.' Anyway, New Year's came, and I don't remember what I did, but I just chugged on through life. January, terrible. February – Valentine's Day. Excruciating. I was still constantly thinking about her. Six months together, then over six months apart, and I was a wreck. Not just a mess, an absolute mess. That winter, taking stock of my life, I realised I'd been whirring on empty fumes for years. GCSEs. A levels. Degree. Training contract. Master's. Only two worthwhile relationships to speak of. Rachel in sixth form. Monica at university. Broke up with both of them neatly. A few girls in the City. Nothing major. They always had their own places, too. I mean, Auntie Pam still ironed all my clothes. The amount I spend on dry cleaning without her is eye-watering. The house in Ilford was big enough that I actually didn't see Uncle Harry and Auntie Pam that much. I mean, I saw them . . . But we didn't hang out. They didn't ask me to leave back then because . . . I think they don't like how quiet it is without me. I played my music loud. Music was what got me through the break-up in the end. Hip-hop and R&B have changed a lot. New stuff. You wouldn't like it. So, spring came about and I was just about feeling better again and then life said, 'Hold on a minute, let's take the piss out of Daniel a bit more!'

I'd been in Hertfordshire with my department for an away day thing. Such a waste of money. 'Let's get away from the City and go sit in a country house to encourage blue-sky thinking.' We would've been better off Skyping in from home on a day off and giving that money to the homeless or something. But whatever. Anyway my boss said he would drive me back to London. I told him to just drive me back to his in Primrose Hill and I'd walk to the station from there. So I'm striding over Primrose Hill with this hefty rucksack and I thought, I'd love to have a sit-down and look at this view. No bloody chance. Barely 11.30 a.m. on a Saturday and the tourists were out in force. So I'm standing at the top, looking away from them all with my headphones in, taking a few deep breaths – and I suddenly thought, 'Do you know what, Daniel, you're all right. It's taken longer than you thought, but you're getting over her. Life is good. You'll fall in love with someone else. You're all right.'

After a while I bid farewell to a view of the City I wouldn't have to battle my way into until Monday morning and go striding down the hill. I get to the bottom and notice a blue plaque for Friedrich Engels on a building. Ironic that one of communism's founding fathers lived at the top of a street that is so comically pretentious: book-shops, pet shops and brunch spots. Honestly, it's the worst that North London has to offer. Hampstead's lowlands, basically. Up ahead there's this green café where it's twenty quid for avocado toast and an almond smoothie. There's a queue outside. A bloody queue. There's surely a decent enough café in Camden just across the bridge. Who's made this place the fashionable place to eat eggs Benedict? Then obviously – OBVIOUSLY – who should be sitting at one of the pavement tables? Her! OBVIOUSLY! Sitting in the shade with her date. Some muscly Viking-looking guy. black-rimmed glasses and an unnecessarily tight grey T-shirt. She looks out on the street and sees me. It actually is like a film. Time slows down. She looks hurt at the sight of me in my washed-out blue hoodie and ruck-sack. I feel like a nothing. She is so obnoxiously pretty that day. She's gone blonde, too. Her eyelashes are like really long. She is looking a bit like she's from the sixties or seventies. I dunno. Hot-pink dress, blonde hair and those full lips with some shiny lip gloss. She really does look like a model. If I didn't know her, she would make me wanna eat at this place, because who would not want to be around girls like her? And what do I do? Like an idiot, I nod. Some stupid bloody nod. She gives me this pitying smile and I scuttle off. I can't run – but I want to. So I just walk extra fast. I'm getting hotter because of my pace but inside I just feel sad. Just so lost and cold and sad. How could I not have taken her out? I mean, look at her. She was born to be on someone's arm and now she was. Some random Scandinavian bloke had swooped in and done what I should have done.

I get to Chalk Farm tube and I go into the corner shop. I buy a bottle of proper Coke and when I'm outside I chug it. Not drink it, chug it! I wanna feel it on my teeth. It's not enough, so what do I do? I go in and I get another one! And I get some chewing gum because . . . I dunno. I just think, if I don't chew, then I'm going to grind my teeth to splinters. I go in the station and I forget that there are lifts at this one. Belching out swarms of tourists because they can't get out at Camden Town, I suppose. I can't deal with the crowds so I go down the stairs instead. I think if I was drunk then I could just slip down the spiral staircase and do myself some damage on the iron. Another man would just cry or something, but I've not cried like that since you've been gone. No, I just visualise me doing myself harm. Don't worry, I wasn't that far gone, but for some reason I just wanted to talk with people who jumped in front of or off of things. I couldn't have her, so why not oblivion? I get to the bottom and the wind coming up from the tube is like a full body punch. I walk past the lifts, head first against the wind, grit making my eyes water, and I get to the top of the stairs, down to the platforms. Walking up the stairs . . . it's her! She came to find me.

Looking at her, for some reason I remembered some idiot on Twitter who had recently said Black girls shouldn't go blonde. Looking at her now made me angry that I had even read it. It wasn't just that she looked phenomenal. More than that, she looked bold! And what's that word . . . ethereal. There was something angelic and futuristic about her. Kind of seventies *Star Trek*. Lieutenant Uhura's niece or something. It was like she had come from the future to deliver a message she didn't have quite enough breath in her lungs for.

'I thought you'd gone . . .' she said.

'I went to the corner shop,' I said.

'Oh OK.'

'Do you want a chewing gum?' I asked, because I'm an idiot.

'No thanks.'

Silence.

'You been OK?'

'No,' she said, looking at the ground. I was ecstatic. If we had both been as miserable as each other . . . Of course, then I remembered.

'You clearly moved on quickly, though,' I said with petulance.

She looked confused and then she must have seen the jealousy in my stare.

'He's a hairstylist I met on a shoot. We just started working for the same agency. He's lovely, but I am very far from his type, Daniel, I assure you.'

Assumptions can be deadly and always seem to make an arse out of only me. I had genuinely thought . . . Thing is, you really can't tell these days. Half the gay blokes at the office have beards and go to the gym way more than me. Rappers are painting their nails. I dunno. Anyway, good news. She was single.

'Do you wanna sit down?'

'Yeah,' she said.

We sat in silence as another northbound train pulled in. I took my rucksack off. She took a wet wipe out of her handbag and cleaned her hands with it. She put it back in her handbag and got hand cream out. She tried to hand it to me. I shook my head. She gestured more emphatically for me to take it. I looked down at my hands and realised how ashy they were. She laughed. I took it. Squeezed too much out, didn't I. She laughed harder. She put the hand cream back in her bag and massaged my hands as I held my arms out to her helplessly. She aroused me so much I could have had her condemned as a witch. She stopped and just held my hands on her knees. She was crying.

'I needed more than the minimum, Daniel.'

'I know. I'm sorry.'

'I didn't need you to shout about me from the rooftops.'

'Yeah. But now I kind of want to.'

'I don't want everyone knowing my tea, though.'

I didn't even know that a trans girl came up with that word before I met her. Now, everyone is spilling tea. Giving all the tea. The young girls at the office saying it every two seconds. 'What's the tea, bitch?' 'Oh give me all the tea, bitch!'

Well, she did not need to worry. I don't share my life and my business like that anyway. No one over the past few months even knew that I was going through anything. How could they? I'd kept everything a secret. Life without her had been actual torture, though. Having her back without the hassle of battling the world outside of us, was all I dreamed about.

'I don't care about other people, I just know that I proper love you, Jose.'

There were a few heartbeats and then she said with a smile, 'I proper love you too, Daniel.' She cupped my jaw with her hand and I clumsily lent in with gusto for a kiss. I had tucked my chewing gum in behind my molars. I'm glad I'd got the chewing gum. Because the kiss was perfect. We needed it. A confirmation that our bodies were as in tune as our minds always are.

'I've got you something,' I said afterwards.

I took my wallet out of my rucksack. I handed her the two tickets and saw her face light up when she saw them.

'I thought it was all sold out. How did you know?'

'I was reading that free magazine they give out on the tube on Fridays. I know you love Alexander McQueen because he's on your coffee table. So I thought, if I see her again, then I'll take her to the museum, which is basically ours, because you're my Victoria and I'm your Albert.'

'You soppy bastard,' she said, even though she was the one smiling and crying. Her hand was on my inner thigh. 'Are you going to come back to mine?' And just like that I was back in.

That wasn't actually our first date. That night we spent in at hers. We went to the Waitrose downstairs and got the fancy ready meals because I didn't want her cooking in the kitchen forever. Our first date was the next day. I did some googling and we went to the BFI and watched this crazy hypnotic Black film called *Daughters of the Dust*. After that we walked along the Thames and went to Nando's. But some weeks later, we did go see Savage Beauty at the V&A. It was stupidly busy, but she was as happy as a kid at Christmas. She likes me most when I am romantic. So that's what I do. I just show her I love her in different ways by listening out for what excites her. So much excites her, it's kind of easy.

I brought her round to meet Uncle Harry and Auntie Pam on a sunny Sunday. We had a roast and ate it in the garden. I know Uncle Harry recognised her from the market but he didn't make a big deal about it. Not at first, anyway. A few weeks later we were watching football down the pub and he goes, 'So, don't you want your own kids?'

'Yeah, but there's lots of ways around that.'

'What, like adoption?'

'No, like surrogacy.'

I could tell he did not want an explanation. He just wanted . . . I don't know. I mean, you were adopted into his family. I knew it was the end of the conversation when he turned to me and said, 'Well, anyway, she's a beautiful girl.' That she is. She gets on well with Auntie Pam, which came as a surprise to me. She insists on calling her Auntie. Some sort of Caribbean respect thing. Anyways, there's always giggling in the kitchen when she's round. I don't ask her to stay over because that would be weird. So I always go to hers. I lived half there, half here. I told Pam I might get my own place, but she wouldn't have it. 'Save your money for your family, Danny,' she said. So that's what I've done.

It's been a couple of years and we live in Frankfurt now. After Brexit, a lot changed. I was sent to Frankfurt to head up my department. She's still got the flat in Vauxhall, but she works more in Europe these days, so Frankfurt is all right as a base. It's a bit boring for her, but it's all right for me. No matter where she is, we send each other memes all day. Not a day has gone by where she hasn't made me laugh out loud. We had a chat about the future the other day. I was fishing for information.

I'm going to marry her. I had to commit a couple of crimes in the past couple of weeks just to make sure I can properly pull this off in the way I want. I know it's bad, but I read her diary just to make sure she's not expecting it. Also, I'm a thief. I stole one of her costume jewellery ring things. It's disgustingly tacky, but as it is so cheap she won't notice it's missing. Or if she does, she won't freak out. The man at Hancock's told me to do it. I came back to London for work and called in at the shop because I'd seen the ring I'm getting for her on Instagram. It was my secretary that showed me their page, actually. That sounds posh, doesn't it? Well, I share her with my colleagues, so it's not like *Mad Men* or anything. Although, even though I'm not like that, HR could really tell you something scandalous about a lot of the blokes I work with. Anyways, I was researching how to get the best ring, and I thought,

why not get a ring that is like the one Albert gave Victoria?
Well, I googled it, and it's hideous. It's an actual snake.
It looks cursed! No wonder they had so much tragedy! So
instead I saw this emerald one. All emeralds round the
outside with a big diamond in the middle and emeralds
around the ring band as well. I like it because it suits us
as Slytherins. Yes, Mum, she is a Slytherin! Judge us as
evil if you want, but we are good for each other. When
you used to read me the books I did not tell you I felt
like a Slytherin for ages. I felt you should be embarrassed
to be a Hufflepuff, but there you go. I can imagine us
all arguing about Harry Potter together. She is just as
obsessed as we are. You would love her, Mum. She says
it was when she was being bullied for being transgender
at school, she could read those books and know that she
would always be accepted at Hogwarts. She thinks Tonks
is trans. I can see that. I don't care about the wedding
much. It's going to be in London, obviously. If I could,
I would propose a Harry Potter wedding. Just 'cos . . .
you know . . . That was our thing, as mother and son. It
would be a way of having you there in spirit. Anyway,
she wouldn't want that, and I'll think of some other way
to involve you. I'm doing something else that feels weird,
but I know I want to.

I am going to take her name. Weird, innit?! OK, hear
me out. So that night we got back together in Vauxhall
we were in bed and I asked her, 'Would you take my
name if we got married?'

'No,' she said.

I was surprised, if I'm honest. A bit hurt even. So I
asked her why.

'I have thought this through already. With your surname being Baker, if I took your name I would become Josephine Baker. While I do love her . . . Well, the first time I went to Paris I had these cornrows in a bun on the side of my head. I kind of looked like her, I suppose. So I was walking through the Marais where all the gay bars are. All the boys started yelling "Josephine! Josephine!" in French accents. It was just so affirming. I mean, they didn't reeeeeeally know my name, but I felt seen. They saw my Black womanhood and they celebrated me in the way she had been.'

'So why wouldn't you want her name forever then?' I asked. I didn't know much about Josephine Baker then. I still don't, if I'm honest.

'Because I already had that moment. I don't want people to see my name written down and think of someone else. She had her wonderful life. I want mine . . . Besides, my brand is Jo Hope.'

I didn't know what she meant by 'brand' until she made me watch this reality TV show with her: *The Rachel Zoe Project*. I kinda got into it in the end. Made me understand her job a whole lot more. She is not at that level yet, but she could be. Hollywood stylist to the stars, sort of thing. I know it's the kind of life she wants. I can give her that. As long as work keep paying me well and stuff. We can go to California, find a surrogate. All of that. So why do I need to take her name, are you asking? Well, if the kids are going to be genetically mine, by giving them her surname, it's like a symbol that they are hers too. Do you know what I mean? The actress that I used to fancy, Zoe Saldana. Her husband took her name. Modern times.

It's just something I want to do. I won't tell Uncle Harry
for a while though. He will be offended.

Anyway, Mum, listen. I've written you this letter over
like a few days. My therapist told me to because I finally
broke down. I can finally admit after sixteen years how
much I still bloody miss you. You're my mum. Girls
think about weddings their whole lives, but until I met
Jose, I just didn't think about it. Now, here I am about to
propose, I'm having all these visions for my future family
life, and you're not going to be a part of it. My kids won't
have the other grandma they deserve. I am gonna have
to read them Harry Potter myself. I will love and raise
them with all the values that you taught me. I will even
love them if they are Hufflepuffs like you! You not being
here and the changing my surname thing, made me ask
my therapist if I was like betraying you. So he said, why
don't I ask you? This is me asking you, Mum. Are you
all right with all this? I'm giving you a chance to tell me
if you're not. I just went and got some strong sandwich
bags from the supermarket. I am going to come to your
grave with this letter triple-sealed and put it inside a jar
and then I'll put it in the gravel on top of your grave.
Next week, I'm taking her on holiday to Switzerland. My
secretary found out Jose has her nails done on Friday after-
noons. I am going to propose to her on Lake Maggiore
on the Monday. She won't expect it. Who proposes on
a Monday? Me! There is this place called the Brissago
Islands Botanical Park. She's gonna love it. So this is your
chance, Mum. If you're not happy with my plans – send
heavy rain. You hated the rain. If you really are not OK
with all this – destroy the moment.

I'm kind of confident you won't. You weren't that kind of person. Also, I know I've done right by you. I am a good boy, Mum. I promise. I still donate to the breast cancer charity every month. I give money to tramps, and I never let Auntie Pam take the rubbish out. I'm a good boy, Mum. I promise. I will always do right by you. I love you.

Yours forever,

Daniel xxx

Ps: You know that thing you said would never happen? It happened. We had a Black president. It was great! In fact when me and Jose go out, that is who drunken strangers say we look like – the Obamas. You would have loved Michelle. I'm not as cool as Barack. Jose is as nice as Michelle is. That's who I say we are these days. 'I'm your Barack. You're my Michelle.' They're definitely not cursed. They're blessed. Anyway, it makes people feel good to see us together. We give people hope. That's who we are going to be. The Hope family.

NO ONE IS LONELY

Rowan Hisayo Buchanan

'Explain again. You're becoming an oven?' her mother asks. Her muddle, projected from the speaker, fills Fiona's flat. It has been a week since Fiona moved to the city. For so long the place seemed part of a distant mist-covered adulthood. Now she is here in a small, clean, barely furnished room.

Fiona is multitasking. She balls her socks, rolling them together, until only the toes poke out. They look like severed rabbit heads. If her mother were here, they'd be doing the task side by side, her mother wondering aloud if maybe her daughter is walking wrong. How does she wear through them so quickly?

Fiona says, 'No, an oven writer. I'll write the things the ovens say. You know, like the one Ms Davies across the road has.'

The job is at a big kitchen goods manufacturer. Their ovens can detect a chicken's juiciness and know when precisely to crisp the skin. It's all AI. But it still needs humans to script the jokes.

'Is it just me or is it getting toasty in here?' The AI regurgitates these phrases. If you are roasting carrots it says, "Happy hoppin', honeybun!" But if you rewarm pizza for the third time it enquires, "How're you feeling, buddy? Can I interest you in seven easy home recipes?"'

Fiona continues, 'I'll come up with stuff that feels timely. So, um, if there's a dish on a popular show, then I find out how it's made. Or, I don't know, festive stuff for the holidays. Apparently the blender writer suggested an avocado milkshake when Mexico won the World Cup.'

'Why do people want to be talked to all the time? I spent almost twenty years waiting for your father to shut up, and now I'm supposed to listen to my appliances?'

'My boss says personality is a big-ticket item.' Fiona tries to repeat the phrasing the man had used as he leaned forward in his chair. His eyes were shadowed, but he'd seemed so certain of his truth. She'd envied the faith.

'Studies show that it fosters brand loyalty,' Fiona adds. Her mother doesn't say anything, so Fiona asks, 'You're happy for me?'

'Of course. If you're happy, I'm happy. But you can come home any time.'

Fiona is alone in this vast city, but she does not want to go home. Here there is the feeling that something special might happen, although Fiona does not know yet what that could be.

One day as she exits the office lobby, her boss is leaving too. They step outside together and she notices that their steps are falling into rhythm, the way Fiona's school friends' steps always synced up. This feels too intimate. She tries to unmatch her pace, which results in a speeding up that seems rude, so she slows down again.

'Do you take the Overground?' he asks.

'Yeah.'

'It's a nicer walk if you go along the canal, rather than up the high street,' he says.

'Oh, I didn't know that.'

Here the canal is the width of a two-way road. Boats are parked up and down it. You can buy artisan coffee from the barges, or bean burgers, or shirts, or speciality magazines with only pictures of dogs or chickens or women eating. Scattered here and there are a few remaining houseboats. The paint on these ripples and warps. Knots of wood show through like barely open eyes.

Usually she avoids the canal, because she doesn't want to buy useless things. She prefers to walk down the colder streets, passing the crystalline office buildings. But she follows her boss. He tells her that he grew up here. Right over there, under where that building is now. He points across the canal. You could afford to live here back then. His parents weren't fancy people, not at all, don't get him wrong.

'Cool,' she says. Although what she is thinking is that it seems absurd to have grown up here. There would be nowhere to travel to. You'd already have arrived.

'What did you do?' she asks.

'What do you mean?'

'What did you do as a child here? Like, did you stay in your room? Go over to your friends' houses? What was it like?'

'We played video games. We played five-a-side in the park. Nothing special.'

Her boss seems to be built at a slightly larger scale than the people they walk past, over-tall, over-broad. It is hard to imagine him skinning his knees in the mud. At that time, Fiona would not have been born yet. Her mother would not have met her father. Her mother would be riding the bus in another town, and doing her lipstick so that it was precisely one shade brighter than her mouth. Her mother would be looking at her own reflection in the bus window, her face half shadow, and thinking her own secret pre-baby thoughts.

'Are you settling in?' he asks.

'Of course,' Fiona says. 'Just fine.' This is a lie. But it is the kind you are expected to tell.

She notices his hands are very large. They seem designed for something more than typing messages. These hands should be holding an axe or stacking bricks or chopping wood.

'Do you like where you live now?' she asks.

'No,' he says.

'Does your,' she pauses, unsure of the right assumption, 'does your partner like it?'

'My ex-wife liked it just fine.'

'Oh, I'm sorry.'

'Don't be sorry.'

'OK.'

'You're too young to be sorry,' he says.

The train is quite full and there is only one seat, which he gestures for her to have, presumably because she is a woman. She gestures for him to have it, because he is her boss and he is old. In the pause, a young guy with lightning tattoos takes the seat. She and her boss make the sort of eye contact that is also laughter.

As the train sways, he asks her about the town she grew up in, the country her grandparents came from, what sort of music she listens to, how does she like the office snack selection? She tells him. The answers she gives him are true, but simple, one or two words, a sentence at most. There is something about the way he looks at her that makes her feel he would've been fine with complicated. The expression is kind, like her favourite teacher from the Saturday Cantonese class her mother insisted she went to, despite the fact that they never saw the relatives from that side of the family.

When she gets home, she is greeted by Leonard. Only the well-off have every appliance individually bespoke. Fiona doesn't have a talking teapot or shower nozzle. What she has is Leonard, a general-use home assistant. She pays for him by subscription. He runs on the system in the flat. For the rest of her life, or as long as she keeps up with the fees, wherever she goes, she can take him with her. She named him after the stuffed lion she slept with as a child. Back in the day, home assistants arrived pre-named. Then marketing departments realised that we're more attached to things we name ourselves. Leonard controls the heat. He is linked to the fire alarms and to the projector. Whenever she comes home, he says, 'Hello, Fiona.'

The first assistants were all women. Of course, many of the personality writers were male. But the machines sounded like women. It was less threatening. Now you can choose. You can even pick the accent – sexy Irish brogue, sweet Southern belle waitress, or husky Darth Vader. Leonard sounds middle-aged, like he wears glasses. It makes Fiona feel good to boss someone around who sounds like her Communications professor.

'Leonard,' she says.

'Yes, Fiona.'

'Show me pictures of London twenty-five years ago.'

It looks the same and different. Like how when she sees old photos of her mother, the person in them looks like a stranger, but is also in some way inevitable.

A few days later, her boss calls her into his office. All the writers work in one open-plan room, but he has an office. It has a glass door. At all times they can see him and he can see them. She is not sure what purpose the glass serves other than to remind them that he is their boss. Not the big boss. That man is a few floors up in the finance department. Her boss is only the boss of the writers. Sometimes they see the engineers or finance guys in the lift. Although there is no uniform, you can tell who works where. The writers wear brighter colours and have less expensive-looking shoes.

'Were the soy chicken recipes OK?' she asks.

If they want the oven to suggest a recipe, they must buy a licence of use. She has clearance to do this for up to five recipes a season. There is a database of pre-bought recipes. She has scrolled through her predecessor's choices, trying to figure out what that person was like. All she knows is that they really loved kale. How anyone could enjoy kale that much is a mystery to her, but there it is.

'They were just fine,' he says. 'Your tone is a little stilted. Try using more humour.'

'I'll work on it. Humour. Yes.'

'Don't look so stressed. It's your first month, everyone takes a while to get into the rhythm of things.'

She waits for him to say more. Right now she can see all her co-workers. Most of them are scrolling, research probably. Though the woman who works on blenders is leaning back in her chair and staring at the ceiling.

'You're settling in OK?' He asked her that only a few days ago and for a moment there is a feeling of snowflakes falling down her throat as she thinks that she has done something wrong. Something unsettling.

'Yeah, great!' she says.

'I find it useful to get away from the screen sometimes,' he says. He lifts up a yellow pad of lined paper. 'Don't look at me like that. I'm not that old. I'm not saying I dislike them. But writing things out longhand helps. Sometimes you have a better feel for the sound.'

He pulls open his drawer and she flinches. She is not sure why. He is not going to cudgel her. He removes a small green notebook. He leans across his desk to hand it to her.

The edges are gold. This was not pulled out of the stationery cupboard. Had he chosen this for her? Or did he just have it to hand? This is her first professional job, paid by the month and not by the hour. To understand what is happening, her mind jumps to childhood and aunts and the general interest of adults. The attentions which, however generous, always made her feel watched. Silly of course, because she is now an adult.

'Thanks,' she says. She feels she should do something more, so she opens it. The paper is soft and fine and slightly translucent, like skin.

Fiona's desk is next to the blender woman's. As she sits back down, her neighbour mouths, 'Are you OK?'

Fiona wonders if something shows on her face and, if so, what it is. She looks down at her fingers and the tips are flushed, as if touching the book has burned them. Fiona nods. Fiona has read reviews of the blender online. It is their star product. Someone started the hashtag #bbf, best blender forever. It can be seen in so many celebrity kitchens. Some reviewers call it overpriced, but everyone says the personality is endearing.

'Let's eat lunch together later,' the girl says, and Fiona remembers that the girl's name is Iris Kazmi.

'OK,' she says. Shamefully, for someone who writes for ovens, she has brought with her only a sandwich that she bought at the station. Fiona does not like to cook. It seems like a lot of effort for one person. And when she goes and looks at the bags of ingredients, they all seem like too much of a commitment. How can she possibly consume twenty carrots? Two litres of milk?

Iris is beautiful the way the city is beautiful. It is the sort of beauty that says nothing you do will ever really touch me. Nothing you do will change me or break me. She always wears red lipstick so dark that from a distance it looks like two slivers of meat. Then again Fiona is not a reliable witness of beauty. Since she moved here, everyone seems beautiful in their own odd way. Everyone she sees on the train she wants to know. She likes to imagine what is in their handbags, in their lunches, in their ovens.

'What are your weekend plans?' Iris asks. Iris is drinking a smoothie. She has smoothies for lunch every day. She says it is kind of like method acting. She is embodying the sort of woman who has a daily smoothie.

'I'll call my mum,' Fiona says, and then because that sounds too tragic, she adds, 'I might check out a street fair that I read about.'

'Do you want to come to an Invisible?'

Fiona has heard about Invisibles on the news. Nobody knows whose idea the parties were, although many try to take credit. The authorities frown on them, though they aren't illegal – just dangerous. The idea of the parties is simple – nothing is recorded. Phones, cameras, laptops are banned. They are free of any device that could be listening or watching. Locations are carefully chosen. Newer buildings are disqualified. Too many have voice-activated air conditioning, motion-sensitive lights, or TVs that know when you wake up.

When Fiona first read about them, she was excited. You could trial an outfit and know that you'd never be confronted with next-day photographic proof of how the sequins clung to your stomach. You could make up a whole new personality just for the night. But they weren't a big thing back home, and here, well, who would invite her?

'You go to a lot?' Fiona asks.

'Some.'

'Is – is the thing about the rapes true?'

'I don't know. Probably. I mean, people get raped everywhere all the time. You can't let that stop you.'

'Wasn't there a murder?'

'Rumour. But you don't have to come.'

'No, I want to. I mean, I'd love to.'

The building is Victorian, maybe older, in a part of town she has to change trains three times to reach. She follows

Iris upstairs, watching the other woman's legs contract and expand. They look like the sort of legs that could carry a person through the Apocalypse – lean and strong. The flat is on the third floor.

As Iris walks in, she enters not only the room but the open arms of another woman. Fiona is not hugged and the other woman looks at her with speculative eyes. Fiona feels as if later this woman will take her apart stitch by vein by stitch until Iris will not want to be Fiona's friend anymore, not even a work friend. The other woman says, 'Welcome to the party. Drinks are in the kitchen.' And then she hooks Iris away by the arm to someone she just *has* to meet.

Fiona pours herself a drink in a paper cup and then doesn't know what to do next. Everyone seems to be standing in groups and she wishes that she had some device to check, some article to scan, something with which she might occupy her eyes. She wanders to the record player which stands on the kitchen table and stares into the black disc. It seems miraculous that these guitars and the fluting voices are trapped on one vinyl plate. Somehow this is stranger than any microprocessor.

Outside the window, Fiona can see across the street into another block of flats and another party, bodies swaying like fronds of coral. She thinks of her younger self who believed that to be in this city all you had to do was get here. Every night her parents fought, until they tired themselves out. Babies scream themselves to sleep the same way. Fiona was left awake. Sometimes, she'd slip into her parents' bedroom to watch them sleep, their facial muscles gone slack, their eyes looking at something she couldn't see. The room was so silent after the shouting and it was this that she found most frightening – the way that in their sleep their thoughts were suddenly cut off from her. It was almost like they had died. She had to stop herself from running over and shaking them. She'd pace the house alone, and think of the day that she would go to the city and escape this silence.

The next Monday at work Iris says, 'What a great party!' and Fiona agrees. During her coffee break, she asks Iris for help editing a particular line. Iris shows Fiona how to optimise her alerts, so that she'll know immediately how reviews are affected by changes in dialogue. This, Iris says, is her secret. It is less about good writing than good listening.

Fiona looks up and sees that their boss is watching them from behind his glass partition. Her brain is still slow from the weekend and she finds herself staring back into his eyes. She wonders what colour they are. From here it is impossible to tell; they are shaded by his unusually long lashes. He smiles and holds up a hand. Fiona constructs her face into a smile. For a tall man, he is delicate-looking. If Iris notices being looked at, she doesn't react.

Fiona receives a memo from her boss saying that it is time to research Halloween recipes. Another memo says improved technology means the AI can hear both the number of times 'Pumpkin' is said in a household, and also the tone of voice in which it is said. Many families, it turns out, do not actually like pumpkin or pumpkin spice. Alternative recipes should be found. It is summer still, but she supposes that to be the voice of the robot kingdom is always to have to be one step ahead.

The office air conditioner is a breath too cold and she tucks her scarf tighter around her neck. There are windows, but they keep the blinds pulled down *for confidentiality reasons*. The day only registers as a fading glow against the white plastic.

Iris leaves early on Mondays for her dance class. No matter how tired she is, Fiona is careful to be the last one to leave the writers' room. She wants to appear serious. Finally, as most of the others are packing up or shuffling on jackets, Fiona gets up, ready to go. But as she walks past the glass partition, her boss calls her in.

'Is the notebook helping?'

'I think so,' she says, not wanting to sound too sure, in case he is still unhappy with her work.

'Let me see,' he says. She goes to her desk to retrieve it and is ashamed of the drunken way her letters wobble across the page. He holds it close to his face, a lick of pale hair falling across his forehead.

He says he is working late and is planning on ordering in. Does she want anything? She is too awkward to say she was about to go home. The food arrives, hot and greasy, but also a little sweet. She will remember this taste for a long time. They eat it sitting together on the floor of his office. After he puts down his fork, he leans down and kisses her. She stays very still, not moving forward or away. His face is slightly scratchy, like the way it feels when a cat licks her hand with its rough tongue. Her brain begins to do fast recalibrations.

'I'm sorry,' he says. 'I couldn't help it. You're just so—'

He pauses like he doesn't know what to say next.

She wants to ask, 'So what? What am I? Please tell me.

Hot? Sexy? Beautiful? Young? Available? Here?' How does he see her? She feels oddly as if she is the one who has made the faux pas. Has something been happening this whole time that she was too dense to see?

Instead, she closes the noodles' cardboard box and tucks the dirty napkin inside, her hands moving on autopilot.

'I'm sorry,' he repeats. 'You can report me. I'll admit it. There won't be any negative . . .' He waves a hand as if he's lost for words again. 'Anything negative for you.'

Her mouth feels greasy. She looks into his eyes and realises they are hazel with a hoop of blue. He doesn't look that much older than her. He still has his hair, even if it is thin and downy at the temples. There are lines around his eyes and mouth, and she thinks they look like smile lines. She wonders what expressions are slowly rising up under her skin. Are there such things as loneliness lines?

And then she says it. 'I'm so what?'

'Lovely.' He says the word slowly, lingeringly, like a child giving one last pat to a toy his mother won't buy him.

'You can kiss me again,' she says.

This time his bottom lip is tense and certain. Tentatively, she touches the back of his head. The hair is short, but not too short. The bristles bend easily under her fingers. She wonders if she is spending too much time with his skull. She feels his big hands wrapped around her and that, despite his size, he is a bony man. She thinks about how the marrow is birthing tiny blood cells which carry oxygen and energy all through his body and about how, if that stopped, his life would too. She thinks of how so much of a body is essential and so little superfluous. Then she thinks that she should be thinking about how he is her boss and this will mean something. Then she realises that she hasn't been thinking about what her mouth is doing. She refocuses on the kiss, trying to remember how her mouth should behave.

In work hours, they act like nothing has changed. He hasn't forbidden her to tell anyone. But she can see from the way that sometimes he looks at and then away from her face that he doesn't want her to. She is in some peculiar way embarrassed. Quickly they find a routine. On Wednesdays, she stays late to talk about 'how she's getting on'.

And sometimes they do. He says, 'It's not about the oven so much as the sort of person who owns the oven. They're probably pretty established, have a family, my age . . .' Here he smiles awkwardly. 'So you don't want to make the jokes too risqué, or the recipes too hard. But you can use quality ingredients. You want them to feel like you're showing them something new and special.'

She writes it down in her green notebook.

He continues, 'But you've got to think of this as more than recipe suggestions. Personality writing isn't about tacos, it's about love. Even if you're in a family you can feel so stranded, so alone, so unhelped.' He speaks with tenderness about these distant customers. She is almost jealous. 'It's our job to give them a friend, someone who cares, to make sure no one is lonely. Well, none of our customers, anyway.'

This seems like too huge a responsibility, so she says, 'I was thinking about updating our factoids, maybe adding little biographies of great female chefs.'

Later, he holds her in his lap and kisses her. The kissing is nice. He kisses her eyelashes and the base of her neck.

It goes on longer than she thought possible. Nobody has ever kissed her this way, as if by their kisses they are trying to preserve her and keep her in one place. She wonders if one day they'll make ovens that do that too.

'Your face is a little scratchy,' she says. And he touches his chin anxiously.

'I guess I'll have to start keeping a razor in the office.'

She thinks he is joking but the next day he calls her into his room and quietly opens a drawer. There it is – lying lengthways – a thin T. The razor is the old-fashioned kind, not the smart kind, not one with sensors, just three strips of steel.

At the Invisibles, sometimes Iris dances with Fiona and they swing back and forth, their arms in the air, their noses almost touching. Then Fiona thinks she understands what her boss meant by lovely. She understands how sometimes you want to lean forward and bite into something. But she doesn't. Other times, Fiona finds herself alone at the edges of rooms, while Iris is busy elsewhere. In those times, she tries to keep looking busy by moving from kitchen to living room to record player. She collects details to tell her boss about later.

One night, a fight breaks out. Two young guys, one tall, the other short. Neither looks frightening. Neither is the type she would hide from. They wear similar screwed-up faces and they both have tattoos, though they are moving too much for Fiona to get a clear look – a tiger, some flowers, a curlicued letter. They push and shove. She feels it should be like dancing, the two of them facing each other and moving back and forth. But it isn't.

When she first saw a porn movie, she was terrified by how sudden and random much of it seemed. This is like that. Shouting, shouting, shove, more shouting, shouting, punch – a glancing thing, a gesticulating of hands, and then all at once blood opening up across the taller man's face. Then more blood. Then he is on the floor, and the shorter man is calling his friends over. They strip the tall man, pulling shirt, and trousers, and sneakers and socks and throwing them across the room, until he is naked as a worm.

Fiona looks around for Iris, but she is on the other side of the room, and wrapped around another body. The only reason Fiona even recognises her is the gold skirt that catches the light of a low table lamp. The body's hands move at 1.5 x speed over Iris's slim shape, as if fast-forwarding towards the end.

So instead, Fiona turns to the girl standing next to her. A girl whose bleached hair is the burned colour of dead grass. 'What's happening?' Fiona asks.

'He had a recording device on him.'

'OK?'

'So they're going to strip him, and throw him outside.'

'But he's naked.'

'Yes, that is rather the point.'

She learns that her boss smells of baguettes, except when they fuck, and then he smells like bacon. She learns that his favourite thing to do at night is to walk through the city. He tells her that Grape Street was once Grope Street and that it was where the prostitutes shared their wares. He points out the street that used to be where all the

Korean restaurants were when he was a boy. He tells her that he used to busk illegally on this train, and middle-aged women would give him enough coins to keep him in beer for a week. He sings softly to Fiona as the train moves and the song seems to change the temperature of the lights.

'That's beautiful,' she says.

'It's sentimental,' he says.

'I liked it,' she counters.

They never go to his place. He says, 'It depresses me, OK? It's this hole that I've gone to ground in. When I have somewhere that actually feels like mine, then we'll go there all the time. Anyway, your place is good.'

It is, she has to agree. The previous tenant had killed themselves. And the landlord had wanted to fill the empty room fast. So instead of having room-mates in a dive above a pub, she has this whole place to herself. It is only forty minutes from the office, and everything still feels shiny. She thinks that of all the places to die in the city, these rooms don't seem so bad. She has not told her boss this; there is something about him that despite his age and status seems small and vulnerable. She doesn't want to alarm him.

After they have sex, he holds her very tightly. Their sweat glues them together, like two pages of a book that has been dropped in the bath.

He brings her coffee that he says is the best in the city. A week later it is a sponge that won't scratch her pans. He takes to doing domestic tasks for her. When Leonard breaks, she calls her boss and he comes over. They read through the manual together. With each option they try,

Leonard's voice comes out crackled and strange. Her boss emails the manufacturer. The bot on the other end asks if they've tried restarting the device – which of course they have. Her boss frowns and says, 'Maybe this will have to wait until the weekend.'

Fiona begins to sniffle and her boss looks at her in confusion. 'Sorry,' she says, 'this is stupid. But he's my only family in this place.' And she thinks that the tears will stop, but they don't.

Gently, her boss bops her on the nose and says, 'Restart device.' When she opens her mouth to smile, she swallows her tears. The taste is a little like crisps. Mysteriously, Leonard fixes himself three days later.

Her boss descales the kettle and love boils in her diaphragm.

The next time Iris invites her out, Fiona says she can't go. Iris shrugs and asks what her plans are and she invents a visit home to her mother. Iris smiles and says that she herself is a bad daughter. Iris knows her mother misses her. But mothers are always there, whereas life must be snatched. Fiona offers Iris a segment of clementine. She bought them that weekend with her boss and they swung from his arms in their loose net bag and she thought yes, yes, this is what your big hands were meant to hold. Iris takes a segment and bites it in half so that little bits of citrus dew cling to her lip. This is the happiest Fiona has been since moving to the city, or perhaps since she can remember.

That Friday, just as her mind is slipping through the meniscus of the night into dreams, her boss says, 'I love you.' She thinks that her heart will split like the skin of an overripe peach, all the sweetness gushing out. She lies very still trying to think of what to say. Of course, she could simply repeat his words, but she feels overwhelmed. She opens her mouth to begin. He coughs. She feels it on the back of her neck.

He says, 'We shouldn't be doing this. I'm your boss. I'm too old for you.'

She pretends to be asleep. She tells herself that perhaps she is, perhaps this is a dream.

In the morning, she wakes up first. She whispers to Leonard to turn on recording. It isn't video, only sound. She can't explain why she does it, other than that she wants to hold onto this moment before it changes again. Leonard catches the sigh of the shower and the thrum of the kettle. Leonard captures the thuck, thuck of two mugs being placed on the counter, as her boss gets them down. They have been together only a month and already he knows where everything is.

Leonard hears the pop of her fridge opening and her boss saying, 'You should eat more vegetables,' and taking out the almond milk, because Fiona likes almond milk in her coffee and also in her porridge. It is Saturday. So Leonard also hears her boss humming as he slowly spins the porridge around in the pot. Her oven is not a smart oven and so it says nothing at all.

That Wednesday, he messages her to say that he has too much work to do and can they postpone? She goes home. Her flat is so quiet. The windows block all sound from the street. Even when she asks Leonard to play her a song, she can hear the quiet behind the music, and behind that she can hear her echo of her boss's voice telling her that he loves her and that she is too young.

Fiona messages to ask Iris if anything is on. She wants to party. She wants to feel young and bright and electric. Iris says she thinks she's coming down with a cold, but there's a place that's started running regular Invisibles and charging only a small cover. If Fiona doesn't mind going alone, Iris can send her the details.

New house, the same skippy records. A guy with beer-heavy breath comes up to her and asks where her boyfriend is.

'In the kitchen,' she replies. Actually, she doesn't know where boss-boyfriend is. She wonders when he will move out of his 'hole'. As it is she has trouble picturing where he might be. The guy steps closer and she sees that there is something not right about his pupils. They seem too small for the low light, small as bee stings. 'I better go find him,' she says. She feels proud of how smoothly she has managed this escape. Even if her boss talks to her again, she thinks she will keep this from him; it will only make him afraid for her in retrospect.

There is a guy in the kitchen, standing awkwardly by the fridge. He is cute like a dog tied up outside a grocery store. He is wearing high-top sneakers, the kind that had been cool when she was a teenager stealing small change from her mum's handbag.

He says his name is Scott. His accent is slightly American, the vowels stretched. She asks him what he does. He replies, 'Why does everyone always want to know that? Next you'll be asking what part of town I live in or my bank balance.'

'Hey, I'm sorry. No offence meant,' she replies and reaches over him to grab a cup to pour some vodka in.

'Sorry, I'm being an ass,' he says. 'What do you do?'

At the end of her explanation, Scott asks, 'People really want their ovens to make small talk? Is it a master of the house thing?' he asks. 'Like wanting a wife from the old days, someone you can come and shout at?'

'I suppose,' she says. 'God, my boss would hate this conversation.' It feels good to describe him like this to this stranger – just a foolish, controlling superior. Not the reason she doesn't sleep on one side of her bed, having decided it is his. Not the person who sat on the same bed and plaited her hair into a French braid to demonstrate what his sisters made him do.

'Isn't the whole point of these things that you can do or say anything here?' Scott says.

'He really believes in them. He says if we do our jobs right, we're reducing the overall loneliness in the world.'

'How?'

Fiona shrugs. 'I suppose an oven is like a friend who can never leave you.'

'What would she say?' Scott asks and points at the oven they are standing next to.

Fiona considers. It is old. Dried food gums the knobs. Scott's shirtsleeves are pushed to the elbows revealing his pale forearms.

Fiona grabs the oven door, flapping it like a mouth. 'If you don't eat your greens, young man, how do you ever expect to grow big and strong?'

He laughs and says, 'You're really not funny. You know that?'

'The doors don't actually flap,' Fiona replies.

'I suspected,' he says.

Outside, a fire alarm moans. She mixes herself vodka and supermarket-brand lemonade.

'Want one?' she asks.

He shakes his head.

Fiona turns to go. 'OK, I guess I'll see you around.'

'Wait,' he says, 'I have a question.'

'Yeah?'

'What's the worst heartbreak you've ever had?'

'What sort of question is that?'

'You look sad. I figured, if you thought about something worse, you'd feel better.' Before she can stop herself, her hand goes to her face to catch whatever sadness has been escaping. Anger spurts up her throat. 'You can't just ask people that.'

'Why not?'

'It's personal.'

'Isn't that the point of talking to a person – to be personal?'

'Fine, my worst heartbreak—' Then she stops. She thinks about her boss and feels the pulse of anxiety. It beats like a second heart. It is as if with each beat it grows more and more engorged. She imagines her heart exploding and bits of ventricle and vein flecking her teeth. 'Actually, you go first.' She gulps her drink.

'When I was young, I believed in ghosts,' Scott says.

'That's not heartbreak.' Fiona leans against the counter-top feeling it press her hip bone.

'Hear me out,' he says. On the kitchen table, the translucent cups cast watery shadows. 'I used to think there was this girl who died in our house. The girl visited me at night. She had the palest skin and this long braid of hair that swayed as she walked. I kept asking her to let me touch it. But she always said no. She said I'd die before I turned thirteen if I did. The end of the braid flared like the brush my mom used to put her face on in the morning. You know the kind I mean.'

He mimes the flick-flick of a blusher brush sweeping over his cheeks.

Fiona says, 'I know what you mean.'

'God, I was so obsessed with that braid,' he says.

'Go on,' she says.

'The ghost girl was homesick. She said the town was different when she was alive. Black squirrels lived in the trees. You'd catch their shadows out of the corner of your eye. Foxes stole chickens and babies. She thought they preferred the babies because feathers are tricky to swallow. She kept trying to describe how the trees grated the sunlight so it came out like little bits of cheese.'

Fiona thinks that her boss would love the ghost. Together they could reminisce about long-gone places. Maybe this is what he means about Fiona being too young. But what is so very wrong with the now? The urge to message her boss comes upon her like a full-body itch. She can't. She has no device that would allow it. But she can feel the messages composing themselves in her head. *Hey, I'm at this stupid party. Hey, do you believe in ghosts? Hey, I met this weird guy.*

Scott continues, 'I wanted to recreate her world. When my mom was buying cigarettes, I'd wander over to where the grocery store kept buckets of plastic animals and slip handfuls into my pockets. The plastic squirrels were too large, out of proportion. But the girl liked the rabbits. She said there were hundreds of rabbits in the spring.'

Fiona closes her eyes. It is hard for her to imagine the ghost. She wonders if he'd asked her the question about heartbreak so he could tell her this story.

'It was tricky to steal the rabbits. I had to be careful. They came in white and brown, but she only wanted brown. You see, in the past, there were no white rabbits. The ghost girl sneered the one time I brought— HEY watch out!'

He grabs her elbow, pulling her forward. Her body connects with his. Her nose finds itself in the crook of his neck.

'Sorry,' says an un-sorry-sounding voice behind them. Fiona turns to see a grumpy-looking Asian guy, beside what is now an open cupboard just above where Fiona has been standing.

'You almost knocked her out,' Scott says.

'We needed the cocktail shaker,' the guy says. 'Anyway, this is my place.' On the shelf glass and metal are stacked and shoved together.

Fiona looks at them both, squaring off their skinny bodies, and takes Scott's hand. 'Let's talk somewhere else,' she says.

The leather sofa is as cracked as old lady feet. As she sits on it, she thinks that she does not want to be in this place.

'Are you sure this story is about heartbreak?' Fiona asks.

'So, the girl told me she'd have to stop visiting soon because only dogs and babies can see ghosts and my body was growing too fast.' He sighs and leans back on the sofa, which sighs also.

'She wouldn't tell me when she was going, only that it would be soon. I couldn't help it, I kept thinking about how I needed to touch her at least once, even if it was only the very tip of that braid. So, one night, I grabbed it. It slipped through my fingers. It didn't feel like hair. It was like when you put your hand over the kettle and the steam burns your skin. She didn't come back after that.'

Fiona has forgotten to bring her drink to the sofa. She doesn't know what to do with her hands. She picks at the seat and succeeds in pulling up a black cornflake of leather. 'So that's the heartbreak?' she asks.

'I could forgive her going away, but . . . I made it to thirteen. I made it through thirteen. I'm still here. I didn't die.'

'You think you made her up?'

'It hurt when I touched her. I always thought that meant she had to be real.'

'So what then? That she went away?'

'Or she lied to me? Maybe. There were no rabbits?'

The sun starts to rise, turning the edge of the sky Bunsen-burner-flame blue. It is late summer, and the sun still has insomnia, unable to rest for more than a few hours. Fiona has not thought about her boss for at least five minutes. She wonders how long he goes without thinking of her? Perhaps because of the drink, Fiona finds herself sliding, leaning against Scott so that her ear meets his shoulder. It is an unsteady position. The thin cotton of his shirt brushes her cheek. He's too slim to be stable and she rights herself again.

'It's your turn to tell me about your heartbreak,' he says.

'I can't.'

'Why not?'

'Do you wish you'd done anything differently?' she asks. 'Do you wish you hadn't reached out?'

'I don't know,' Scott replies. 'What would you have done?'

Things are fine until a Tuesday a few weeks later. Her boss never comes over on Tuesdays. But she has learned to like the slow walks through the city and often takes herself out. She puts in her headphones to listen to songs Leonard thinks she'll like.

This Tuesday she takes the train to a part of town that she has read was once the site of major protests, although now it is the place where all the best restaurants are. It is only by chance that she sees him. If he'd chosen another street or another borough, she would have missed him. If she'd been distracted by a feral cat, she might have walked obliviously by. But she isn't, so she sees him at a window table. A woman is sitting opposite. The woman is older than Fiona, but not old. She is leaning back in her chair, her arms crossed. Her hair falls in loose curls over her cheeks.

Fiona feels her feet stop. And without knowing why, she lifts her hand in a wave – not an energetic one, just a flicker like she'd seen performed by members of the royal family. Her boss's eyes hit her and then pinball away. She waits for a long time, but he never looks back.

At home she cannot sleep. Silence fills her flat.

'Boo,' she says to the empty air. 'Boo!'

No one replies.

*

Fiona and her boss are by the canal again, not the strip near work, but closer to where she lives. Here the towpath is not cluttered with brunchers, picnickers, lovers and friends. It is empty. This is where the bad floods were a few years ago, and many of the buildings are only now being repaired. Wilting bunches of flowers are tied to the posts where the drowned were lost. Small birds hop on the verges where grass grows through the pavements and across the sky flit delicate clouds, with faces that seem to say, *Who, me? Floods?*

'I'm too young for you?' she asks. 'You knew my age when I started. They sent you my documents.'

'I know,' he says, and he slumps. 'But I'm serious. Think about it. When I'm drooling and shitting myself, you'll still be in your early middle age. And then when I die you'll be by yourself for years and years.'

She imagines herself getting her hair done in the afternoon with the other ageing trophy wives, and getting her nails buffed with those powders imported from Japan. Though this doesn't make sense, because her boss is only a normal guy. And you have to go out with someone very fancy to be a trophy wife.

'You don't know that. I might find a hot young widow or widower.'

'You might,' he concedes.

She has the ridiculous feeling that she has won. It hops in her chest like one of those little birds. It should not be possible to argue someone into still loving you.

To secure her triumph, she changes the subject. 'Did you know this canal was almost never used commercially?

Almost as soon as it was built the railroads took over.' She always loved this city for its newness, but perhaps it is also possible to love it for its age.

'I did, actually,' he says. 'Don't look at me like that. I wasn't there. But we learned about it in school.'

'Oh,' she says.

'Fiona,' he says, 'I'm sorry but we really do have to end it.'

'Why?'

'My wife, my ex-wife, and I. I think we might . . .' He trails off, looking into the water. 'You saw her.'

'I know.' It had not been hard to find a photograph of the woman he had been married to, once she knew to look.

'Can we draw a line under this? I think that would be the adult thing to do,' he says. After she stops crying, she reaches her hand up to his nose and whispers, 'Reboot device.' But he does not reboot.

At work, she pretends nothing has happened. She avoids looking at the glass door, until one night after he has left, she sneaks into his office. The razor is still there. But he isn't shaving. In team meetings, she thinks she can see the filaments of hair. She wonders if anyone else notices how they catch the light.

At night she dreams of him. They are doing ordinary daily things. Nothing special. The problem comes in the waking up alone. It is hard to concentrate at work. If her jokes were stilted before, now it seems as if it might have been written by an algorithm. She waits to get fired. Then she decides that he can't fire her. She thinks of his recorded voice and wonders if she'll have to use it against him. The idea depresses her.

It is ridiculous, but she wishes she'd told that boy at the party, Scott, about her boss. There is no one here she can confide in now, not Iris, certainly not her mother. But she barely knew him. He did not give her his full name. When Leonard looks up Scotts, she sees hundreds of faces in every colour and cut, but none of them are her Scott.

She queues up Halloween recipes. She searches for ghost jokes, and the puns hurt her eyeballs. She is thinking of Scott's tilted face when she types in the last auto-response. At her desk, Iris slurps a smoothie and it sounds like someone trying to suck an eyeball up a straw. The juice is the dark green of canal sludge.

On Halloween, all her ovens ask, 'Do you believe in ghosts?'

She wonders if someone will tell Scott, if he will find her. The news alert for her oven chimes and chimes. Across the internet people are writing about the weird question their oven asked them. They trade their own ghost stories, strange broken things. Stories that end badly or mysteriously and end in death and disappearance. She looks for Scott's story. She does not find it. But as the airwaves fill with ghosts, she listens to the stories and stops thinking about Scott or her boss. That night she dreams of a ghost with loose hair that flows around her like spaghetti.

At the end of November, consumers message in to say that their ovens are still asking the ghost question. Someone in tech fixes the issue. Her boss sends a message that she must have tagged it improperly and that she should be more careful in future to distinguish between seasonal and eternal questions.

She goes to another Invisible. She thinks she sees Scott's red shoes, but it is someone else. She tells Iris about him. And Iris makes a long 'Ooooooooooo . . .' of suggestion.

'It's not like that.'

'I knew you had something up your sleeve.'

On New Year's Eve, they go again to an Invisible and Iris kisses her. Their faces seem to warp into one another. She thinks how strange it is that everyone kisses differently. Afterwards, Iris fist-pumps, like she has won at Bingo.

'Glad you enjoyed it,' Fiona says.

'I'm moving to Singapore,' Iris replies, 'and I would have kicked myself if I didn't do that at least once.'

Fiona wonders what it is about her that makes people think she can be kissed without consequence.

On New Year's Day her ovens ask, 'What would you do if you could do anything?' One reviewer calls the question corny. Another says it is too motivational-poster. A meditation app writes a letter saying it will sue them for copyright infringement.

But vloggers and bloggers and other online personalities leap to answers. *Fly*, says one. *Leave my wife*, says another. *Build a city*, says another. *Kill Peter*, says another. Some write essays. Some only epigrams. She asks Leonard to read the answers to her and he does while she eats eggs straight from the pan.

Before Valentine's Day the machines ask, 'What was your greatest heartbreak?' She wonders if Scott got the same thrill, the same tingle and zing, as he asked. She prepares herself for the spattered hearts. Video, audio, written confessions, they all come in. It is a summoning.

She listens to them as she goes to sleep and again as she gets dressed, pulling herself into the loose-fitting dresses and oversized cardigans that have become how she wraps herself for work.

The ratings, which have been sinking, plummet. Online people wonder if the company is losing touch. Others recommend a Korean brand as being superior. Fiona knows she should stop. She knows the ovens are only supposed to ask questions with easy answers.

She receives a message calling her into her boss's office. He sits behind his desk. His big hands are folded together as if he is holding hands with himself. It strikes her that he looks afraid.

'What do you think you're doing?' he asks.

She shrugs.

'Is this some bid for my attention?' he asks. 'I know you're lonely, but . . .'

She thinks of the voices that fill her flat and shakes her head slowly.

'No,' she says. 'I'm not lonely.'

'Well, then,' he sighs. 'Just stop whatever this thing is you're doing.'

She imagines stopping. She imagines the silence. She imagines all those cooks waiting to be asked the right question.

'No,' she says, 'I don't think I will.' She walks back to her desk and begins to type.

THE ROW

Daniellé DASH

Edith stepped off the train in South London. Late-afternoon sun pooled around her. She walked out of the station onto the high road. She tipped her head up momentarily and it felt as if the sun's warm, kind hands were holding her face. Yellow and orange melting into blue sky, the sun pressed its lips against Edith's ear, urging her to complete her journey, to find somewhere to live.

The window in an off-licence displayed room-for-rent adverts handwritten on small cards. Edith stopped and scanned each one. She knew that the right one would call out to her.

There it was:

One double bedroom to rent in family home.
Six hundred pounds a month, reference desired but not
*   required.*

It was signed with the name Gardenia Franklin and a phone number, the penmanship elegant and clear.

'Gardenia Franklin.' It felt right in her mouth. She had nothing on which to pin her confidence, but she walked into the off-licence.

When Edith emerged, she held Gardenia Franklin's card and a small box containing her new, simple mobile phone.

Gardenia closed the door behind them as Edith bent to take her shoes off. 'As long as you no wear outside shoes in my house, we will get on.' Every word, wrapped in a Caribbean lilt, was ushered from her lips by a laughter that was also a warning. Gardenia's feet were snug in a pair of house slippers, the ones only old ladies owned. 'How you no fall over with them small feet you have?' Gardenia's laughter was kind and fulsome.

Edith looked up from her feet and followed Gardenia into her kitchen. Her home was lived-in but clean. Every wall was covered with pictures Edith assumed were of the old woman's family. Edith couldn't tell if the house was big or if she felt small.

The bedroom was spacious.

'My daughter move in with her fiancé.' Gardenia sipped on her tea as Edith ran her hand along the wood of the chest of drawers. 'I no really like people, but you seem sensible. You want to live here, Edith?' When Gardenia said her name, the 'h' at the end went missing so it came out *Eedit*. Edith liked it. She liked Gardenia. Even though her eyes felt like suspicion. She nodded.

The early-evening air was thick and warm, coated with the heady mixture of weed and barbecue. The ice-cream van's 'Greensleeves' called out like a pied piper summoning children, and adults too, for sweet, cold treats. Edith wanted to take her time getting acquainted with the South London area that was now home. But she was on a mission. She needed a job. Once she left Gardenia's – no, *her* house – she soon came to a hair salon wrapped around the end of the road that opened into a tightly packed row of shops. Despite the late hour, the salon was alive. The low rumble of music carried laughter and loud voices, letting them fall out onto the pavement. Edith walked more slowly so she could see into the salon, but not so slowly that she'd be confused for a potential customer.

A woman with eyes so big and bright Edith could swim in them pinned her with a stare.

Edith stopped moving.

The woman's face broke into a devastating smile.

Edith felt her heart churn to a stop.

The edges of Edith's lips tilted upwards.

Reciprocating.

The woman's eyes broke away from Edith's. Her hands were in the scalp of another. Her wrists flicked with experience as she cane-rowed hair thick and high on her client's head. Edith wished she was the woman's client. She made her feet move.

Edith passed an off-licence. Boys in tracksuits tumbled out, giddy with excitement about their haul, carried in black plastic bags. They narrowly missed knocking into Edith. 'Careful, beautiful,' one of the boys called out to her. His friends all followed his lead and stopped so she could pass by unimpeded.

'Thank you,' Edith said in her most confident voice.

'Ey, fam! Come on.' And in a flurry of laughter they left, almost skipping away into their youth.

*

Edith walked past a West Indian takeaway. A man wearing a plastic tabard stood on the pavement jerking chicken in a steel drum balanced on wobbly legs. He gestured towards her, asking wordlessly if she'd like some. Edith shook her head but smiled. His teeth, big and white, preened for her as he nodded and turned his focus to the chicken that sent smoky succulence up into the air.

Edith pushed the door open to the bookies, tucked onto the end of the row of shops. A burst of light and sound jumped at her. Men sat on stools watching television screens that lined the walls. They shone with every sport Edith could imagine and numbers she couldn't easily understand. This wasn't a high street betting chain. To Edith it was like it'd been designed specifically for the area.

At the shop's far end, a woman sat behind glass. Edith hoped this was Carmel.

'Wanting to put a bet on?' The woman's voice reached out to Edith and pulled her the rest of the way to the counter.

'No, miss.' Edith held her hands behind her back and squeezed them, encouraging herself on. 'Gardenia sent me. Said I should ask for Carmel?'

'Oh yeah?' A raised eyebrow. The woman hopped off her seat and got close to the glass. 'That's me. How can I help?'

'I'm looking for a job. I'm really trustworthy and I'll work hard, miss.' The words chased each other out of her mouth. Now empty, Edith sighed. Relieved.

'It's Carmel, love.' Her eyes flicked up to the clock on the wall. 'You're gonna have to step aside for a sec.'

Edith did as she was told and a bell went off. Two men sat scribbling in front of the screens rushed towards the counter. Edith watched as they pushed their betting slips and money under the glass at the same time. Carmel's hands moved in a flash; taking their slips and cash, her fingers flew across a computer keyboard then returned each slip along with any change to their owners. The men rushed back to the screens as a second bell sounded out.

'So, you're taking over Malika's room?' Carmel stepped back from the glass and out of sight.

A door to Edith's back opened and Carmel appeared. Her locs, so startlingly grey they were almost white, were braided elaborately into a ponytail that swept at her shoulders. Carmel looked at Edith. Really looked at her.

'Yes, I only moved in today.' Edith squeezed her hands again.

'You good at numbers?' Carmel put her hand on her hip, leaned against the door, and Edith knew then that this woman was younger than Gardenia, despite what her hair suggested. It was hard for Edith to guess her age. Or maybe it felt wrong to try.

'I am.' Edith made sure to look Carmel in the eyes, those knowing eyes, even though everything in her wanted to look at her feet.

'What's your timekeeping like?' Edith wondered if this was the job interview. She hoped she was impressing Carmel.

'I'm punctual.'

The door to the bookies clattered open. The woman from the hair salon ran in from the street towards the counter holding her own betting slip.

Carmel held her palm up. 'No. Nope. It's not happening.'

The woman's run slowed into heavy steps like she was wading through water. Edith could see now that it wasn't just her eyes; all of her was beautiful.

'Come on, Car. Please.' Edith wanted the woman to say more so she could identify every note that lent itself to her harmony.

'The second bell's gone. I don't make exceptions for anyone. Not even you, Mariah.' Carmel folded her arms and leaned back against the counter.

Edith felt awkward but excitement traced its way up her back. Now she knew her name. Mariah.

'But that's the last race.' Mariah pouted.

'You're free to play on the machines.' Carmel used her chin to point towards the colourful slot machines.

'Car, I only wanna put on a fiver. All this talking when you could've just put the bet on for me. The race ain't even gone off yet.' Edith didn't know where to look. This felt like an exchange she shouldn't be present for but hoped she could stay and listen to.

'Mariah, I'm not playing this game with you. You know what time the races go off. If you don't make it before that second bell goes, I don't know what to tell you.' Carmel's tone was firm but loving. Like a mother's might be.

'Next time you come in, I'm gonna do your hair so tight.' Mariah pointed her betting slip at Carmel. A smile in her eyes.

'Do what you're doing, Mariah.' Carmel's face spread out into a smile as she moved to pick up slips abandoned on the counter.

Mariah balled hers up and threw it towards a bin next to Edith. Her aim was perfect. The paper sailed through the air and landed neatly inside. Mariah winked at Edith. 'See you on Saturday?' Mariah asked, heading back towards the door.

'You know it,' Carmel called out.

'It's month's end. So, come early if you're coming. Unless you wanna be in there all day.'

Carmel kissed her teeth long and loud. The door clattered shut behind her and Mariah was gone.

Carmel shook her head as she came back to Edith, hands full of discarded slips, and deposited them in the bin. 'She's right, though. I'll get there early.' She laughed then and fixed Edith with a stare. 'So, you. What's your name again?'

'Edith.' She squeezed her hands. 'Edith Harris.'

'OK, Edith Harris. Come back tomorrow morning at eleven. I'll give you a trial.'

'Really?' Edith's eyes gleamed.

'Why not? And take Miss Mariah as your first lesson.' Her head nodded towards the door through which Mariah had walked. 'No let no pretty woman, no pretty man come make you break my rules. You hear?'

'Yes, Carmel.'

'Go on. See you in the morning.'

'Thank you.' Edith started towards the door.

'Tell Gardenia I'll see her at church.'

Edith pushed open the front door and was met by an aroma so tantalising she could taste it. She toed off her shoes and moved through the house.

'Wash your hands and come sit down.' Gardenia was dishing up at the stove and when she turned around she had two plates in her hands piled high with stew chicken, rice and peas and macaroni and cheese.

The table was set for two.

Edith wanted to cry.

Edith was looking down at a jewellery box on a kitchen counter. Inside, a ring, simple and unremarkable. Its stone as unappealing as the proposition it posed. The jewellery box snapped shut, gobbling her hand in one bite. She tried to cry out, but the ring's stone covered her mouth. The box continued eating her arm, then her shoulder, her torso then her legs. The jewellery box took bites of her neck then swallowed her head whole.

Edith snapped upright in her bed. Her eyes tried to pierce the darkness. Looking for light. Her breath leapt out of her, sharp and ragged. Her shoulders sagged and she lay back down.

She didn't want to go back.

Eleven the next morning, Edith was standing outside Carmel's. She was punctual. She'd been there ten minutes already, examining the drawn shutters. On them, Carmel had let some graffiti artists spray-paint a mural. 'Carmel's' swirled in bold, bright colours.

'My sons' work, that.' Edith heard Carmel's voice before she saw her. She was approaching with a coffee in hand, her keys out. 'He's a big, serious man now. With a big, serious job.' Carmel pushed her keys into a lock and the shutters ascended. 'Coulda been a artist. But he just do the art 'ting on the side. So smart, is my Lucas.'

Edith didn't know what to say, so she said nothing and smiled.

Edith's morning passed in a blur. Carmel's induction was rigorous, and Edith had to keep up. Carmel wasn't going to make it easy for her; she needed to know her business was safe in Edith's hands. Edith respected her. Edith learned how to put on bets and watched as Carmel paid out complicated winnings. Carmel's clientele were mostly men of different ages, all of whom she was on a first-name basis with. Edith liked the familiarity and wanted to be rooted in it. Maybe she could be like Carmel one day. A woman who, on the surface at least, was calm, didn't wring her hands when she was nervous. Edith let her hands go and made a conscious effort to keep them on her lap.

Time warped when the door clattered open and Mariah stormed in. The lightness she moved with the night before was gone. She marched up to the counter with her betting slip and cash. Edith was sweeping and tidying up the shop. She paused and hoped against hope to catch Mariah's eye; maybe she'd secure herself one of Mariah's smiles.

Mariah, though, was thunder and lightning.

'I made it before your bell, Carmel. Please, put on my bet for the one fifteen.'

'Good afternoon to you too.' Carmel made the transaction look effortless.

'Thanks,' Mariah said, snatching the betting slip from under the glass. She headed back towards the door, focused only on her escape. It was almost as if she didn't notice Edith. Disappointment sprouted in her belly.

'No mind her,' Carmel called out. 'A so she stay.' It wasn't comforting.

*

The rest of Edith's day felt like she was swimming through batter. She thought so much about how Mariah looked when she had come in. Mariah took up space, more space than Edith would dare. The air around her earlier had been heavy with clouds threatening to burst into angry rain. The hours trudged forwards and sometimes, Edith swore, backwards too. The end of the day wouldn't come fast enough. Edith thought about how she could unknit Mariah's brow, make whatever it was better. Every so often, she'd shake her head. Trying to dislodge this absurd thought. Then, at five thirty, there she was. Sailing through the door, free from whatever had made her thunder and lightning.

Mariah floated up towards the counter.

'Hello, Carmel. Hello . . . ?'

'Edith. My name's Edith.' She surprised herself with how quickly she gave that up to her. She wanted to hear her name in the other woman's mouth.

'Hello, Edith.' Mariah smiled.

The hair on Edith's forearms stood up to meet the syllables rolling across Mariah's lips.

'Sorry about before.' Mariah dipped her head, abashed.

'Mmm-hmm.' Carmel smoothly stood up and took the betting slip Mariah had pushed through the glass. Putting it in the machine, she began counting money. Sixty pounds and a receipt were pushed back through the glass into Mariah's waiting hands.

'Thank you, Car.' Mariah slid another betting slip through the glass with a five-pound note.

'I'm gonna let you do this one, Edith.' Edith's heart pounded in her chest so hard, so immediately terrified, she worried Mariah would hear it.

Edith was flustered but quickly inspected Mariah's handwriting.

Five thirty-five, Haybridge, looped and cursive.

Six to one circled twice.

Queen Seaton to win.

Five pounds underlined twice.

Mariah fanned out her winnings, turned her back to the glass and held her phone aloft ready to pose for a selfie. Edith, focused on the task at hand, felt Carmel shift beside her.

Only then did she look up and see what Mariah was doing.

The first bell sounded out.

Edith smashed enter on the keyboard.

She ducked out of the way of the camera's flash.

'You OK, love?' Carmel asked.

'Yes. Sorry.' She tried to regain her composure. 'I don't like taking pictures.'

Mariah quickly put her money and betting slip away. 'I'm sorry. I should have asked.'

'No, it's OK,' Edith lied.

'I have to get back.' Mariah laughed nervously. 'I'm sure that perm's ready to come out now.' Mariah tapped the glass. 'Thank you, and see you later.' Edith hoped she was talking specifically to her.

'Later,' Carmel called out to the woman leaving her shop.

Edith's heart dropped to her knees.

'You can go home now,' Carmel said as the second bell sounded out.

Worry must have been stretched across Edith's face because Carmel put a reassuring hand on her shoulder. 'You did well today. Come back tomorrow with your ID and NI number and we'll get your paperwork sorted out.'

'I got the job?' Edith's eyebrows arched up on her face.

'Yes. Now go before I change my mind.'

Edith was running along a station platform that moved. It was alive. She was desperately trying to find a door that would open and let her onto the waiting train. Something grabbing at her ankles. The platform was made of hands. One reached out and pulled her shoe from her foot. Another snatched at her ankle. She fell over and the hands were everywhere, pulling her back down the platform. She fought with everything in her and made it to her feet. She was off again, sprinting. She stopped at the next set of doors and beat on the button, then banged on the glass, hoping that someone on the train would help her. A rope of pure, blinding gold snapped towards her, sweeping her off her feet. Her face smashed into the hands. She was pulled back across the platform by the gold lasso around her waist. Screaming, she tried and failed to find purchase. She was sucked into darkness, her hollering swallowed up by its infinity.

Edith snapped up in her bed. Her hand whipped up to cover her mouth. She hoped that Gardenia had not heard her. Her chest heaved as she tried to get her breathing under control. Her heart squeezed. A tear landed on her naked thigh. Her head hit her pillow and the last thing she remembered when sleep claimed her was the wetness under her face.

She didn't want to go back.

In the morning, Edith met Gardenia in the kitchen where she'd pushed open the doors out into the garden.

'Good morning, child,' Gardenia greeted Edith as she came to stand next to her.

'Good morning.' The outdoor space was so beautiful. The flowers planted along the edge of the garden were unashamed and opened themselves up to the sun.

'I want you to come with me to my church dance on Saturday.' Gardenia heaved herself from her seat and moved towards the kettle. 'Ask Carmel 'bout it. The music and food real nice. You meet lots of nice people.'

Edith's hands squeezed one another. 'I'd like that,' she said, unsure if she really would or if she didn't want to hurt the old woman's feelings.

'Why you don't go see that Mariah?' Gardenia was picking mint leaves from her windowsill and putting them in two mugs that waited patiently. 'She could do your hair nice. Maybe you could buy a dress? Or you bring one?'

Edith's mind raced. She didn't know which question to answer first. She wanted to live in the idea of Mariah doing her hair.

Gardenia sliced the last of a spiced bun and laid the pieces on two plates. Butter and cheese. She handed Edith her plate and her tea. 'Sit down and go on, go eat this so you belly no empty for work.'

Edith did as she was told.

'Oh!' Gardenia clapped her hands together. Delighted. 'A night on the town.'

Edith smiled widely then blew on the boiling hot tea she wasn't sure she wanted. Her mind bursting with possibilities.

*

Edith and Carmel worked alongside each other and the morning turned to afternoon. Edith tried not to look at the clock that taunted her on the wall. She thought not looking would make time go faster. She'd become attuned to the rhythm of the days and when she didn't see Mariah as the first then second bells went off for the one fifteen race, she didn't panic. Edith was certain she'd get to see her soon.

Standing at the door of the salon, Edith found Mariah alone. Busying herself. Swaying to the low rumble of music Edith could feel through the soles of her shoes. Mariah looked up.

'Edith. You OK?' Mariah's voice called out to her.

'Hi, yes. I'm— I'm OK. Thank you. You?' Her voice a whisper, lost in among the bass of the music.

'Come in, babes. I can't hardly hear you.' Mariah beckoned for Edith to come closer.

Edith willed herself forward.

'That's better. What's up? I upset Carmel again?'

'N-no. No. Not that.' A host of butterflies took flight at once in Edith's belly. 'I wanted to get my hair done.' She begged herself to calm down. 'For the dance this Saturday?'

'Of course! I'd love to.' Mariah patted the salon chair in front of her. 'Come, lemme give you a consultation.'

'Oh. Oh. I have to get back.' Edith's hands could have wrung one another off their wrists.

Mariah dipped her head, flicked her eyes, those big eyes, up at Edith and pouted. *Please.*

Edith acquiesced.

Mariah swept a hairdressing gown over Edith.

'Can I take out your hairband?' Edith nodded. Mariah released her hair from the simple black tie. Edith's hair popped out, preening for Mariah. Mariah pulled both her hands through Edith's hair. Her fingers drawing across her scalp. Edith wanted to close her eyes so she could record the feeling. She never did anything to it herself, other than washing it once a week. When it dried, she pulled it into a band, where it stayed until she washed it again. 'Your hair's dry, babes,' Mariah said.

Edith looked down at her lap. Under the gown she squeezed her hands together.

'No, no. There's nothing to be embarrassed about.' Mariah pushed the dry flakes of dead skin off Edith's shoulders. Her hands stayed there and she searched the mirror for Edith's eyes. 'When you come in on Saturday, I'll give you a treatment. Show you how to moisturise it.' Mariah's kindness squashed the bad feeling inside and the butterflies took flight once more. Mariah's eyes lingered a moment too long. She swept her hands down Edith's shoulders to her arms.

A simple gesture.

Edith hoped it meant something.

Mariah leaned forward over Edith's shoulder. 'Hold these for me.' Mariah dropped hairbands into Edith's lap. Mariah sprayed her hands and then sprayed Edith's hair. She parted her hair into sections and made sure the oil got down into the roots. Edith had never smelled anything so sweet.

Mariah hitched the spray bottle to her apron, then her hands were massaging the oil into Edith's hair. Edith was scared she'd moan out loud. She closed her eyes to help fight the temptation.

'How . . . how long have you been doing hair?' Her own voice surprised her. Edith couldn't believe how much she needed to know about Mariah. That need, primal and unfamiliar, pushed past her fear.

Mariah laughed. A sound like wind chimes and rain. 'Since I knew hair could be done.'

Edith laughed.

They both went to speak at the same time.

A pause.

They did it again.

They both laughed.

Edith stopped, so her laugh wouldn't crowd Mariah's. She had to hear more of it. She needed to know if Mariah was really enjoying this as much as she was.

She opened her eyes. Mariah was looking straight back at her. Studying her.

Edith's heart stopped.

She had to will it to beat again.

Mariah's full cheeks pushed up high under her eyes. Her mouth cut into a smile that asked Edith to smile too. Looking at Mariah when she smiled was like looking into the sun. Edith wanted to look away. But she didn't. Couldn't. She smiled instead, their smiles crashing into one another.

'Go on, babe, what you gonna say?' Wind chimes and rain.

'No, no. You go.'

'When's the last time you let anyone do your hair?' Mariah's eyes moved away from Edith's to focus on her hair. The broken connection, though temporary, felt to Edith like a little loss.

'I . . .' Edith searched her memory. 'You know? I can't remember.'

Mariah's laugh poured out all around Edith. 'Don't forget me like that.'

Mariah had pulled Edith's hair into a bun high on her head. Simple yet transformative.

'I won't.' A promise.

Mariah leaned forward over Edith's shoulder again. Edith caught her perfume, separating it from the scent of the hair oil. Mariah's oil-slick hands undid the lid of a jar, her index finger dipping in and bringing a glob of clear jelly to Edith's hairline. Expertly, she used a small brush to curl and shape Edith's baby hairs. Mariah worked silently, concentrating.

Too soon it was over. Mariah was gently patting Edith's head.

'There you go, babe.' Mariah rested her hands on Edith's shoulders. 'Come back on Saturday at six and I'll get you ready for the dance.'

'Thank you, Mariah,' Edith said as Mariah swept the gown off her and packed her tools away. She was methodical. 'How much do I owe you?'

'For this bun and some hair oil? Don't irritate me, Edith.' Mariah was smiling.

Edith was up, desperate not to overstay her welcome. 'Thank you.' She searched for something else to say. 'You coming in for the five thirty-five? I haven't seen you in Carmel's for a while.'

Mariah was washing her hands at a sink. Drying them with a towel that she flipped onto her shoulder when she was done. 'Am I that predictable?'

'No, no. No— I just . . .' Edith was panicking.

'I'm joking, babes.' Wind chimes and rain. 'You're funny, Edith.' Was she? Edith had never heard this before. Mariah looked at Edith then and her lip corners tipped upwards.

Edith's hands, clasped at her back, gripped so hard.

Mariah moved towards her.

They were a breath away from each other.

Mariah was whispering.

'I'm trying to be better,' Mariah confessed.

'Than who?'

'My dad. Myself. I don't want you to think I'm some gambling lout. You know?'

'Oh. I don't think that.'

Mariah raised an eyebrow. 'What do you think of me, Edith?'

Before she could stop them, the words came running out of her mouth. 'I think that you're smart and pretty and really good at your job.'

'I'm an addict.' Her admission landed heavily in the space between them.

'I'm sorry.'

'Don't be sorry, Edith. It is what it is.' She was casual about her pain.

Edith didn't know what to say.

'Do you want to know what I think of you?' A lion playing with her prey.

'What?' Edith asked.

'You have secrets too.'

'Hey. Hey. Hey!' A man's voice and presence broke the moment. Shattered it. Mariah peeled her eyes away from

Edith's. 'I have clothes to sell. You want dresses? I have jeans too. Good ones.'

Mariah stepped back away from Edith. Edith felt altogether empty and angry at this man.

'Marvin, where you steal these clothes from?'

'Don't mind that.' Marvin opened his duffle bag and started laying out the clothes on the chairs.

Edith moved towards the door. 'Thank you again.'

'Saturday. Six,' Mariah said, her hands on her hips and her focus on the merchandise.

Edith was jealous of the clothes.

'Oh, and Edith?' Mariah called out to her.

Edith, hopeful, stopped and looked at her. Quiet.

'I think you're pretty too.'

Edith wanted to fight the clock on the wall. Late Saturday afternoon seemed to stand still for all eternity. She found herself asking Carmel about the Bible just to check her hearing was working. She hadn't heard a bell go off in years.

'Gwan go get your hair done,' Carmel said at five o'clock. Edith could cry. 'It's quiet. Go.'

Edith kissed Carmel's cheek.

'Don't forget. I want you to meet Lucas. I told you 'bout him?'

How could Edith forget the apple of Carmel's eye? Edith had a front-row seat to every coming and going in Lucas's life. His new job in town that Carmel couldn't quite remember the title of. His car and flat in Canary Wharf that overlooked not some but all of London. Edith had seen every picture of him, knew his height and at a push might be able to guess his blood type.

'I can't wait to meet him,' Edith lied, and she was sure Carmel enjoyed it.

Edith finally settled into Mariah's salon chair. Her hair wet and limp about her shoulders, a towel around her neck like a boxer.

Mariah's fingers curled over Edith's shoulder and she brought her face right up close to Edith's so they were looking into each other's eyes in the mirror. 'Edith, babes. I know you only came in to get your hair done, but I'm giving you the works.'

'The works?' Edith had never been so excited before.

'I don't want to call it a makeover, because that would mean there was something wrong with what was there before and that's simply not the case, darling.' Mariah spun Edith around in the salon chair. A disobedient squeal fell out of Edith, her heart charging like wild horses. 'Soon, my girl Pam will be here to do your make-up. I have a dress and some heels for you. I guessed your shoe size. Six, innit?'

Edith nodded.

'I want you to feel as beautiful as you are.'

Edith's eyes were filled with tears that threatened to spill. 'Why?'

'Everyone should get to feel special.' Mariah caught Edith's tear, swiped it away. 'Plus, I like you.' She said it so casually. So easily. Edith wanted to say it back, but she wasn't so brave. Mariah took out a pair of scissors, fine and sharp, and flexed them in her right hand, a tail comb in her left. She posed. A lone Charlie's Angel.

Edith's laugh dislodged the tears.

'Do you trust me?'

Edith freed her hands from under her gown and covered her face. When she emerged, Mariah was still waiting for an answer.

Edith would do anything for her.

She nodded.

Laughed.

Sniffed up her tears.

Exhaled.

The music swallowed them up as Mariah went to work. Edith watched hair fall to the salon floor as Mariah fell silent, an artist at her easel. Edith didn't want to breathe too deep lest she break Mariah's concentration. She sat still and patient. Eventually the scissors and comb were abandoned for oils and pastes and creams. A blow-dryer that she expected to scream silently chased the dampness in her hair away, her tight curls too. Edith would miss the latter but knew in a week they'd be back, so she wouldn't dwell. A pair of straighteners came out next.

When Mariah was done, Edith's hair framed her face with a bounce and boastfulness Edith never imagined for herself. She didn't have time to gawp at herself because Mariah's friend Pam was in her face with so many brushes, she couldn't believe she possibly needed every one.

Unlike Mariah, Pam spoke as she worked. Mariah swept the salon while they caught up. Edith only spoke when she was spoken to, content rather to listen to the two of them. They had a shorthand; a secret language Edith couldn't fully grasp. But she liked it and hoped she and Mariah would have their own one day.

Edith wobbled when she took her first steps though the heels weren't very high. The dress felt painted on but was surprisingly demure.

Pam and Mariah gasped when Edith walked back into the salon. 'You look incredible.'

In the church hall, music was all around her. Small children held hands in a circle and danced the uncoordinated jig universal to small humans the world over. Balloons were kicked up into the air. Serious-looking older people sat with paper plates in their hands, sucking at curry goat bones. Men stood by sky-high speakers slapping their thighs, doubled over in fits of laughter. Teenagers waited patiently in line at the buffet, passing flirtatious looks between each other.

Edith heard Gardenia and Carmel before she saw them.

'Edith?!' Carmel took Edith's hands.

Gardenia's hands shot up to cover her mouth.

Carmel grabbed her up into a hug. Over Carmel's shoulder, Edith spotted Lucas dutifully sitting at a table looking right back at her. A sympathetic smile on his face.

'It can't be my Edith this!' Gardenia looked her over with admiration.

Edith's heart swelled at the idea she was Gardenia's.

The two of them cooed over her and praised Mariah's work before Carmel all but dragged Edith to formally introduce her to Lucas.

Gardenia scooted Carmel away. The two of them sitting at a table far away but close enough that they could see their meddling take root.

'My mum's mad.' A rumble deep in Lucas's chest. 'But she was right, you are very beautiful.'

'Thank you.' Edith told her hands to take the night off.

'I have to be honest, when she said there was someone called Edith she wanted me to meet, I was suspicious.' They laughed together. 'I was convinced the old lady had finally gone arms wide open into one of her fantasies. She hates Adjua, my girlfriend.' His smile when it opened up into its fullness was heartbreaking. Edith could feel it in her chest. He made her want to smile.

'I was suspicious when Carmel kept on saying how it was a shame that you were single.' Lucas nearly choked on his drink.

'Where are my manners?' He stood up. Tall and steady like an oak tree. 'What would you like to drink?'

'Please may I have some water?' Edith looked up into his eyes.

'Absolutely.' He strode towards the makeshift bar. She watched him go and wondered what kind of person his girlfriend was that Carmel hated her out of existence.

Edith felt eyes from outside the church on her as she and Lucas danced. Their hands clasped, his hand at her lower back. Edith's hand at his shoulder. She looked around, hoping to find the source of the feeling of being watched. Lucas, however, said something to pull her back into his orbit and that's where she stayed as he led her through the music.

Edith listened more than she spoke. Lucas offloaded about the one-sided war between Carmel and Adjua as they swayed to the music.

Gardenia and Carmel, alcohol making them unsteady on their feet, encouraged the young couple to stay. More old-woman meddling. They'd get a lift with some of their church friends. Lucas and Edith waved them off.

'You hungry? The oxtail's pretty good,' Lucas asked as they sat back at their table. Edith was grateful for the reprieve; her feet throbbed as loudly as the music.

Edith's hands threatened to hold onto one another. She dipped her head. 'Can I tell you the truth?'

'Please.'

'I would like to go home,' she confessed.

Lucas grabbed his heart dramatically. 'You've wounded me, Edith. I'm a broken man.'

Edith's laughter leapt out of her mouth. He dropped to his knees. 'However will I recover?' A little girl in a too-big dress took cautious steps towards Lucas and put her hand on his shoulder, worried. He swept her up into his arms. 'This pretty lady doesn't want to hang out with me any more, little one.' The girl squealed with delight. He put her down and she spun away in circles and skipped, dizzy.

'Let me drive you home.'

'I want to walk.' Edith surprised herself with her candour.

'Edith . . .' He crouched in front of her. His hands on her hands. 'You can't walk in these heels.'

Edith rested her head on his hands, her shoulders going up and down, laughing. When she caught her breath, she unfolded herself and smiled into his eyes. 'I have my other shoes in my bag.'

Lucas wasn't happy but he slipped his phone into her hand, made her put her number in and told her he'd call her to make sure she'd got home safe. She wasn't to upset his mum by being kidnapped. She was grateful he didn't push it.

'I want you to meet Adjua. You'd love each other,' he said into her ear as her face met his chest in a hug. His kiss on her cheek was chaste and chivalrous. 'Be safe, Edith.'

Edith changed into her other shoes and stepped out of the church into the night. The air was cool, a welcome change to the thickness in the hall. Time shattered like shards of broken glass around her at once when Edith felt hands grab at her shoulders, swinging her around so her back was against the church wall.

Mariah's face came into focus.

Edith's heart, which she hadn't realised had stopped, started beating again.

'I'm sorry. I'm sorry. That was harder than I meant.' Mariah searched Edith's face in the darkness of the bushes.

Edith's chest heaved. She stared at Mariah. Eyes wild, a mixture of fear and relief.

'I'm sorry.'

'Why did you do that?' Her voice hoarse. Her breaths ragged.

'I saw you dancing. With Lucas.'

Edith looked at Mariah, confused.

'Yeah, and I . . . I didn't want you to go with him.'

'I wasn't.' Edith put her hand on her chest. Hurrying on the calm. 'You can't do that.'

'Can I kiss you?' Mariah's eyes pinned Edith.

'Why?'

'To say I'm sorry.' She inched forward.

Edith turned her face away. She was hurt.

Mariah inched forward some more.

'Don't do that again.' Edith crossed her arms.

'I'm sorry.'

'Ask before assuming things.'

Mariah took a step backwards.

Edith had never told anyone off before.

Mariah went to speak but went quiet. Waited.

'I like you too, but I have to be in control of what happens to me.' Edith searched Mariah's eyes. 'I want to make decisions about what I do. This is important to me, Mariah.'

Mariah nodded then looked down at her feet and kicked at something.

Edith imagined this was what Mariah felt like when she took up as much space as she did, never apologising for it. It felt good filling up everything under your skin. 'You can kiss me now.'

Mariah looked up.

Edith fell into her eyes.

Edith's back pressed against the wall.

Mariah's lips on her shoulder.

Her neck.

Her lips.

They parted.

Her moan fell into Mariah's mouth.

It felt like Mariah searched Edith's lips for acceptance of her apology. Her tongue licked desperately against Edith's own. Mariah's hand gently rested on Edith's hip. Her other hand on Edith's neck. Edith grabbed at Mariah's back. Eager.

'Can I take you to mine?'

'Yes.'

Edith slept peacefully. Morning light framed her face.

Edith heard a camera shutter go off.

Her eyes fluttered open.

She turned to see Mariah smiling into her phone. *She wouldn't have—?* A loud banging on her front door startled her, ripping Edith from her thoughts.

'Oh my god!' Edith flew out of bed. 'Who's that?' She held the sheets to herself. She was scared.

Mariah slinked out of bed and into a dressing gown. Her face was stern. 'I'm gonna find out.' She walked over to Edith and cupped her face. She kissed her.

Edith's heart stilled. The night before came rushing back. Cool sand over a raging fire.

'Don't worry,' Mariah assured her. Edith watched Mariah head out of the room.

Another banging on the door before Mariah reached it made Edith jump again.

'Why the fuck are you knocking on my door like that?' Mariah's voice had an edge so razor-sharp, it could cut Edith where she stood.

She looked for her clothes.

It sounded like Mariah had pulled the door closed behind her. The voices were muffled but Edith heard every hard, cold word. Angry words only people who'd once loved one another could say. They slashed and ripped at each other.

'You wouldn't even have that blasted shop if it wasn't for how I make my money!' The man's voice was gruff and bellowing. Edith felt shame for Mariah.

She dressed quickly. Pulling the scarf from her head, making quick work of pulling out the hairpins Mariah had carefully secured her hair with the night before. She shook her hair free. A memory between her legs stopped her. She remembered in her knees a feeling from their lovemaking. *Lovemaking.* A concept she'd reserved strictly for people in books or on the telly. She moved again, hoping it would repeat its murmur. She wanted it again. She wanted Mariah again. She felt guilty for wanting something so carnal while a battle raged on so close by.

'Don't fucking come back here!' The front door slammed. Edith listened as Mariah stomped back through her small flat. She heard a tap running.

Mariah was at the bedroom door with two glasses of water.

'Are you OK?' Edith's voice was small.

Mariah walked towards her and handed her a glass. 'My dad . . .'

Her pain was palpable. A raw, animal thing Edith could almost reach out and touch. If Mariah blinked, tears would betray her strength. Edith put her hand on Mariah's shoulder. 'How can I help?'

Mariah's eyes were pleading. 'Can you stay with me?'

'I . . . I have to go open up Carmel's.'

Under Edith's hand, Mariah's shoulder turned to stone. Edith pulled her hand away.

Mariah went to speak but shook her head, laughed, no wind chimes. Only rain. She drank some more.

Edith had no compass to navigate all the emotions crashing into each other.

'Fine. Just go if you're going.'

'Can we talk later?' Edith moved towards the door, holding her bag. Edith needed Mariah to say something to fill up the silence lying open between them.

'Bye.' Mariah folded her arms. The weight of Mariah's rejection pushed Edith out of the flat.

Edith walked home. Their lovemaking repeating between her legs. Their row repeating all around her.

*

Edith's shift was lonely. This was her first shift without Carmel, but every part of her body cried out for Mariah. Every time the door clattered open and with every bell that went off, Edith knew it was wrong to hope Mariah would come but she did anyway. She just wanted to see her so she knew it wasn't over.

The second bell for the last race of the night sounded out. With her shoulders slumped, Edith let herself out into the front of the shop and started cleaning up. The door clattered and Mariah stormed in. Thunder and lightning, a betting slip and a fiver in her hand.

'Can you put this on for me?'

Edith looked at Mariah. Incredulous. She wished she could kiss her teeth long and loud like Carmel. Words failed her.

'The race ain't even gone off yet.'

Edith held onto her broom to keep her upright. Mariah's brazenness threatened to push her over.

'Are you gonna do it or not?'

'No.'

'I'm not gonna beg you.'

'I don't want you to.'

'Why are you doing this?' Mariah's voice was a mix of desperation and venom. 'Did you want to be my girlfriend or something?'

Edith was at a disadvantage. She'd never argued like this. 'What?'

'You heard what I said. Were you looking for a relationship?'

'That's not fair.' Tears sprang to her eyes.

'So what is it then? Why won't you put my bet on?'

'You're an addict, Mariah!' Edith roared.

Mariah jumped, shocked.

'This is my job! There are rules, and I feel like I can do anything for you but I can't lose my job. It's too important to me. You don't understand.'

Tears poured down Edith's face. She had scared herself. Her poise slipped its leash.

Mariah took steps backwards like the impact of what Edith had said threatened to push her over.

'Your dad upset you this morning. I had to come to work and you're hurting me for it!' Edith threw her crutch, the broom, to the floor. 'You've been hurting me all day! It hurts!' Edith clawed at her chest, trying to get her heart out so it would stop the pain. 'I'm not putting on your stupid bet!'

'You're sitting on your high horse judging me!' Mariah fought back.

'You said it yourself!'

Their voices, lovers' voices, landed blow after blow. So loud, so focused on pushing this aching back and forth between one another they didn't notice when he walked in.

It was after his third attempt at calling her name that she heard him. 'Edith!' He yelled. Louder than them both.

Edith's eyes peeled open. Her reckoning made human. Her fears in flesh. The space she'd learned to occupy only the night before shrinking. All that could be heard were Edith and Mariah's breaths leaping out of their open mouths. Their chests rising and falling.

'Edith, get your things. You're coming home.' He spoke to her like a child he was picking up from a sleepover.

'How did you find me, Tony?' Edith's voice was small again. She could feel the hands at her ankles, pulling her backwards along the platform.

She'd thought they were Tony's.

They weren't.

'Ask your friend.' Tony nodded towards Mariah.

Edith turned to Mariah.

A tear slid down Edith's cheek.

She *knew*.

Mariah looked back at her with apologetic pleading.

'You just looked so beautiful sleeping. I didn't think . . .'

Edith's face, twisted with hurt. Realisation slowly crystallising. 'I told you . . . I told you. I don't like taking pictures.'

'Lucky for me, Mariah don't listen.' The air in the room vanished. 'Still got that nasty little gambling habit?' Tony spat out into the betrayal in front of him.

Edith looked between them. Her chest rose and fell, she was finding it hard to catch her breath. 'You know each other?'

'Me and Mariah go way back. Don't we?'

'Edith, look at me.' Mariah waited for Edith's eyes to meet hers before she spoke again. 'I got into some trouble back in the day. Tony was my bookie. That's all he was. I haven't seen him in years. I didn't even know he was following me on Insta. I'm sorry. I'm sorry, babe.'

'Bless. I make sure to keep an eye out for all my old punters. It's good business.'

Edith stared at Mariah. Disbelief and profound sadness fighting inside her. The silence stretched out endlessly between them. Tony clapped his hands loudly once and Edith jumped.

'Right. Get your things. Let's go home.'

Edith did as she was told.

'Nah, wait. No. Hold on.' Mariah looked back and forth between them. 'What is this?'

Edith, deflated, defeated, picked up the broom and moved through the shop turning off machines and screens. Tony's voice shaming her.

'Edith and I were together. Years. Lived together and everything. I come home one day and proposed. We been together long enough, might as well get married, make an honest woman out of her. And she walks out. Leaves my ring and the cooking on the fire. Just walks out.'

Mariah looked at Edith standing with her head down and her bag over her shoulder.

'She took my bank cards and cleared out what she could get her hands on and disappeared.'

'Why?' Mariah's voice now small and confused. 'What did he do to you?'

Edith shook her head. 'Nothing . . .' Tired, she squeezed her hands together, wringing what little strength she had left to explain. 'Yeah, he's a bit controlling and a bit rough, but he didn't *do* anything to me. It was the idea . . .' She searched her mind for the words to explain what drove her to leave. 'The idea of being with him forever, it was choking me.' She locked eyes with Mariah then. Tears chasing each other over her cheeks and off her chin. 'I was . . . I was bored and lonely. It scared me how alone I was with him.' Head bowed, embarrassed by how very petty it all sounded but buoyed that she was finally giving voice to what stalked her in her sleep. 'I couldn't breathe for the nothingness of him.'

'What you on about?' Tony held his arms out.

Edith took a hiccupping breath and steadied herself. 'I'd never felt special, really special until you.' She looked at Mariah, who was looking at her. 'I never made love before you, Mariah.'

'Come off it! We had sex. Plenty of sex.' Tony's voice was pitched higher, incredulous and wounded.

Edith looked up at Tony. '*You* had sex.' She exhaled, releasing a truth she'd never admitted to herself until now. 'I was just . . . there.'

'Well, now you've had your fun. Your little adventure.' He nodded at Mariah. 'Time to go home.' Tony turned slightly towards the door as if to help her out of it.

Edith did not move.

'I don't want to.' Edith's confession was for Mariah. 'I don't want to go back.'

'Either you come home with me or I tell the police where my bank cards and money went.' A threat.

Mariah, taking back control of the room, took steps towards Edith. Her hands cupped Edith's face, kissed her shame away. She tasted like she was asking for forgiveness in return.

'You don't have to go back.' She kissed her again. Deeply. 'Stay with me?'

Edith nodded.

Mariah slipped her hand into Edith's. Edith squeezed. A thank you. Mariah's face crept into a smile, inviting Edith to smile with her. Together.

*

A barbecue's smoke bellowed in the garden. Derek and Malika, who both had their mother's face, tended to the meat on the grill. Gardenia sat staring out at her people. Content. Edith poured two glasses of rum punch for Carmel. Carmel's teenage sons, who must have had their father's face, sketched caricatures for some of the guests. Mariah sprang up from a basin full of ice and drinks when she heard the doorbell go. Inside she passed the TV on her way to the front door. The TV quietly played the news. *Authorities baffled by missing Bradford man* captioned a picture of Tony. Mariah walked back towards the garden with Lucas and Adjua. Carmel rolled her eyes when she saw the woman the apple of her eye called his. She held onto him tightly when he bent for a hug. Mariah introduced Adjua to Edith and they hugged. Edith thought Adjua was even prettier than her name suggested. She knew Mariah must have read her mind because she felt Mariah's fingers thread themselves through her own.

Edith liked it.

She liked this beginning.

Was thankful for it.

MY HEART BEATS

Dorothy Koomson

AUGUST 2020

The knocking and ringing at my door had been driving me crazy. I'd ignored it for as long as I could, but now I had to drag myself out of bed and move my body along the corridor, holding onto the walls as I went.

I use the anger at having been woken up and forced out of bed to swing the door open.

'Remember me?' he says, following the question with a grin. Anyone who doesn't know him would think that grin was arrogance, that he'd turned up here expecting a hero's welcome. I knew him. And I knew he was nervous, worried, fearful that I would slam the door in his face.

And, come on, why wouldn't I slam the door in his face, nervousness or not? I mean, how dare he stand there in his beautifulness asking me if I remember him, as though I could ever forget him. Or that grin. Or exactly what he did.

FEBRUARY 2010

Dane sat beside me at Hove train station, staring at his bag that he had nestled on his feet so it wasn't touching the ground. He was down in Brighton for work and had asked if he could stay over at mine instead of schlepping back to London or staying in a hotel. Of course, had been the answer. I always leapt at any chance to spend time with Dane. We had first met when we both got a job in a warehouse up near Leeds. We were studying up there, and instead of going home for the holidays, we got jobs. And then we'd discovered we were actually at the same college. We'd built a circle of friends around us, but college friendship had quickly moved into adult friendship, even though he now lived in London and me in Brighton.

Last night had been our usual night of takeaway, big bags of popcorn, watching our shared favourite movie. Of course, I'd fallen asleep, probably snoring like a chainsaw. He'd gently woken me up, tried to encourage me to go to bed. Outraged at the very idea that I'd fallen asleep, I'd refused, we'd carried on with the movie and then *he'd* fallen asleep. I'd leaned over to wake him up, to laugh at him as he'd laughed at me, but I'd had to stop.

The feelings I had for him, had *always* had for him, hit me full force at that moment. I'd stared at the smooth dark skin of his face and the perfection that was every line, every curve, every feature, every blemish, made the breath catch in my chest. His tall, slender frame was so wonderfully free and relaxed that all I wanted was to snuggle myself against him and feel the beat of his heart against mine.

I'd felt like this about him for years but had never had the courage to do anything beyond fantasise. Beyond imagining him sweeping me into his arms in a grand gesture and kissing me, before his lips confessed his undying love . . . Last night, I stopped trying to wake him up and sat back. I inhaled and inhaled until I was light-headed, woozy. It didn't change anything – it didn't stop me finally admitting that my crush was more. My crush was . . . *more*. It was more, and I had to tell him.

And there I was, at Hove train station, the words I needed to say stuck in my head and not going anywhere near my mouth; my courage – which I needed to be big and mighty – was a tiny ball that did nothing except make me pick at my nails and bite my lower lip.

'You're quiet,' Dane said suddenly.

'Am I?' I replied.

'Yes. You've been quiet all morning. Is something on your mind?'

'Yes,' I unintentionally admitted.

'Anything I can help with?' he asked.

'No, I don't think so.'

'Are you sure?'

'No, I'm not sure. But there's something I need to work out and I'm not sure you're the best person to help me make sense of it.'

'Are you sure about that now?' Dane teased. 'I am really rather excellent at listening, offering hugs, deciphering the most tricky of problems.'

Yes, I know, I thought. *That's why you're so perfect for me.* I glanced up at the info board, and it taunted me, telling with its bright orange lettering that the train was on time; reminding me that if I didn't get on with it, his train would arrive and this opportunity would be lost.

'No . . . I mean, yes, I am sure that I'm not sure if you can help me with this thing.'

Dane laughed. 'Don't change, all right, Zari? Stay exactly as you are. Stay as incredible as you are.'

That made me spin to look at him. 'Pardon me?'

He grinned at me. 'You always make me laugh with the things you say. I like having that constancy in my life.'

'Constancy. That's a big fancy word and I'm not sure it's that much of a compliment – basically, you're saying you like me because I'm boring.'

'How did you get that from one word? I'm saying I like you because you've always been like this. I adore that about you.'

I blinked at him. Was he trying to tell me he felt something for me? I stared at his sensationally shaped lips, wondering what their bowed perfection would be like to kiss. . .

Suddenly the air was filled with the metallic tingle of the tracks, indicating the train was on its way. It was decision time: tell him now or shut up forever.

He picked up his bag, stood up and pulled it onto his shoulder. I stood, too. 'Excellent to see you, as always,' he said.

He moved to draw me into a goodbye hug, and . . . 'I think I'm in love with you,' came hurtling out of my mouth before I could stop it.

I was not meant to say that! 'Fancy,' 'crushing on,' 'feelings for,' 'got the horn for' – all acceptable; all non-scary, gateway expressions to start a conversation. Love? *Love*?

Dane's body froze, stopping him from completing the hug. His face froze too, the expression etched into his features as though he'd been suddenly turned to stone. Over his shoulder, the train drew closer like a green and white snake, coming to take him away.

'I'm sorry,' I added quickly. 'I shouldn't have blurted it out like that. I was aiming for a better word, a better way of telling you. But it came out like that. And, well, I think it's love . . . you know what, I really wish my mouth would stop saying that word. I just . . . I have all these feelings for you and I thought I should tell you. I wanted you to know, in case, you know, you kind of . . .'

The more I spoke, the more his face changed, each feature drawing in until his eyes were wide and his lips were pressed together in a grim line, and he looked utterly terrified.

The train pulled into the station and the doors opened, letting a few people off. Dane said nothing, he just continued to stare at me, before he blinked, pulled himself together and moved away. He didn't hug me, didn't do anything, except get on the train.

After he was at a safe distance, he turned to face me. He stood in the gap of the doorway, staring at me with the same horrified expression creasing his features. The doors started to bleep, causing him to step back. He was still staring as the doors closed and the train hitched itself up and carried him away from me.

AUGUST 2020

'Go away, Dane,' I say. 'I don't have the time or energy for you and your . . . *you*-ness.'

'Zari—'

'Go away,' I manage, before I have to press my hand over my chest, to ease the burning. 'I don't need you, I don't want you around. Just go away.' I step back and, with the last of my strength, I swing my front door shut in his face.

FEBRUARY 2010

The ticket woman from the barriers stood watching me from the platform by the exit on the other side of the tracks. She'd let me through without making me buy a station ticket and she was keeping her eye on me in case I decided to cheat the train company.

My legs were wobbling too much for me to begin the walk down the steps, through the tunnel that ran under the tracks and back up to the other side. Instead, I stepped back a couple of paces and lowered myself onto the bench. *How am I going to fix this?* I asked myself. *How am I going to make this right?*

My mobile began vibrating in my pocket, and I pulled it out to find Dane's name flashing on the screen.

'I'm sorry, I'm sorry. I'm sorry I froze,' he said quietly but firmly before I could even manage a cautious hello. 'I wasn't expecting you to say that. So, I'm sorry I didn't speak.'

'It's—' I began, but he ploughed right over me: 'As I said, you're incredible and thank you for loving me. But I've been seeing someone for a while now. It's serious. I haven't told you about her before because . . . because it's Leigh.' He stopped then, obviously expecting a reaction to the name.

Who the hell is Leigh? I asked in my head. 'Who's Leigh?' I asked with my mouth.

'*Leigh*,' he stated. 'Your friend.'

Leigh? Leigh? Do I know a Leigh? It's not like it's a common name. 'Who's Leigh?' I repeated because my scrambled brain would not make any connections.

'She was there on your birthday, six months ago. That's when I met her.'

Lei— What? Her? Seriously? SERIOUSLY?

'We've been together ever since,' Dane was saying into my ear. 'We've just moved in together. We weren't sure how you would take it so it became easier to say nothing. I meant to tell you last night, but— Look, I'm sorry. Can we put this all behind us? Maybe speak in a few days? I'm sure Leigh will want to call you to explain, too. I'm sorry. I'll talk to you soon. Bye.'

And then he was gone. He'd hung up without giving me a chance to really say anything.

The woman from the ticket barriers continued to watch me and I had to close my eyes. To brace my body as the full force of what he told me hit me. He didn't love me, I could just about deal with that. But he was dating her. Of all the women he could have picked, he chose *her*? And at my birthday gathering that I'd held in London so he could definitely come? When I'd squeezed my curves into a hot-pink dress he'd once told me he liked, when I'd squandered valuable fizz-drinking time waiting in the hairdressers to get my hair done, when I'd chickened out at the last minute of telling him how I felt, he had found someone else.

It's fine, I told myself as I stood up and began to leave the station. *We're much better off as friends,* I repeated to myself, as the ticket barrier woman let me out.

Yes, we're better off as friends. Anything else will ruin it. This is all for the best.

I told myself all those things as I walked home from the station, humiliation burning up my body, hurt tears rolling down my face, pain cracking up my heart.

AUGUST 2020

My letterbox creaks almost painfully as its heavy hinge is forced open. 'I'm not going away,' Dane calls through the metal rectangle in my red door. 'I'm not going away until you talk to me.'

I place the flats of my hands against the corridor wall to lever myself away from the front door. I really don't have the energy or headspace for this. I need more than anything to lie down. Dane can be Mr Drama without me as an audience because I am not— I have the sensation of falling. I'm not falling, my body doesn't feel like it's falling but I have the sensation of it, the idea of it floating around my head. And then, up is way, way up there out of reach. Down is right here, next to me. And the pain is like the falling – an idea of a feeling.

'Zari!' Dane calls through the letterbox. 'Zari! Can you hear me? Is it your heart?' He sounds worried, he sounds desperate. I don't know why – it's not like I'm anything to him. Like I've ever been anything to him. 'I'll get help,' he calls through the letterbox. 'I'll get help.'

JUNE 2015

'You do think I'm doing the right thing, don't you?' Elise asked. She was an absolute vision of perfection in her ivory dress, and her shiny dark curls pinned up to emphasise every beautiful thing about her face, topped with a diamond and platinum tiara. 'You do think I should be marrying Randal, don't you?' She had been saying this all morning Since she walked into her spare room where I was staying as head bridesmaid, she had been seeking reassurance that she should be doing this. Of course she should. I had never seen a couple more suited to each other.

'Yes, yes, I do,' I replied. 'You are perfect for each other. Come on, you know that.'

'I know, but you and Moses are perfect for each other and you're nowhere near marriage. Maybe I should wait, like you guys.'

'Yes, maybe you should,' I said.

Elise froze, her eyes wide and terrified. 'You think? *Really?*'

'No, I don't think! I promised myself when you hit a hundred times of asking that, I would say you should wait to make you see that you shouldn't wait. You hit a hundred a while back, but I gave you extra credit. Now I'm calling in the marker.'

'I don't understand what you're saying to me,' Elise replied, her eyes wild with worry.'Do you think I should wait or not? My nerves are shot to pieces and my mind is like jelly. Tell me yes or no if you think I should wait like you and Moses.'

I reached out and took my best friend's hands. 'I don't think you should wait. Moses and I aren't waiting, we're comfortable as we are. If I thought for one moment that you should wait, I would tell you. I would have told you well before the moment when you're wearing this gorgeous dress and we're about to go out there and you're about to say vows in front of everyone. I wouldn't be any kind of best friend if I didn't, would I?'

'No, no you wouldn't.' Elise visibly calmed down, her bare shoulders falling and the terror on her face draining away. I was about to take my hands away when she clung onto them, tight. 'And I wouldn't be any kind of best friend if I didn't ask you why you don't think you or Moses deserve more than "comfortable"?' she added. 'You are both such wonderful people and you are so fantastic together. Why are you "comfortable"?'

My mind, my heart, my entire being went straight back to Hove train station, to standing on a platform and finding out loving someone with all your heart wasn't what it was cracked up to be. Since then, I've held back. Never going into anything without knowing what I could stand to lose, how much hurt I could take if that person left or rejected me. I had learnt my lesson. I could pretend I was fine with love as long as I didn't have to have anything to do with feeling it. Experiencing it. I could be comfortable. I could be with Moses because it was easy, simple and always at the edge of the boundary of feeling.

'Can you not start therapising me, please? Not when you're about to get married.'

Elise stood stock-still – petrified all over again.

'And it'll be the best thing you ever do,' I added quickly. 'Come on, let's go get your dad so we can get this wedding on the road.'

And *then* she relaxed, then the grin returned to her face, then she remembered why she was doing this. And I looked at my best friend, knowing that was why I would never be doing this – I didn't think I could ever allow myself to feel like that when there was the risk of getting it so monumentally wrong.

AUGUST 2020

'Zari, your neighbour is getting her spare key. You're going to be all right. You're going to be all right,' Dane continues to shout through my letterbox.

Sure I'll be all right, I reply in my head because my mouth doesn't work. My heart is speeding too much and I feel the numbness edging down from my jaw and along my arm. *As long as you go away, I'm sure I'll be perfectly fine.*

JUNE 2015

The big old church in the heart of Brighton seemed full. Not just with people, but with joy and happiness, and everyone wishing Elise and Randal the very best. I'd been to lots of weddings, but this one seemed especially jubilant

– maybe because there was a double dose of Ghanaian parent relief at children they thought would never marry finally tying the knot. (My parents had given up all hope of me doing this, I was sure.) Moses, standing beside the groom, cocked his eyebrow at me. From how he looked at me, he clearly appreciated the way this strapless, dark sapphire dress emphasised every single one of my curves. And I was definitely appreciating everything his navy morning suit with its cream waistcoat and kente tie did for his body. Moses smiled at me and I grinned at him, then we both remembered we were in the house of God, we were meant to be standing by our two best people, so we focused again.

Despite how it might have sounded to Elise, Moses and I were happy. We adored each other, we enjoyed each other, we clicked on every level. What I felt for him was reflected 100 per cent by him in what he felt for me, but I always knew to be careful. To not let my heart ever forget to beat within the boundaries of what it was allowed: never too much, never enough to properly feel.

'To love and to cherish,' Elise was saying while Randal was weeping; openly crying with happiness. I saw Moses's eyes well up, seeing his friend so emotional, and even the priest seemed a bit dewy-eyed.

I looked over the congregation of people gathered here to celebrate, and my heart was lifted by the many different faces; the glorious, beautiful, traditional outfits; the tears shining in their eyes or glistening on their cheeks. This was love. This was what was so wonderful about love: it brought people together, it broke down their inner barriers, it made them *feel*. I was about to tear my eyes away from the people in the pews when they became locked with another person's pale blue eyes. *Her*. Leigh. My gaze shifted right. Beside her, of course, was Dane.

AUGUST 2020

I'm fine. Truly, I'm fine. I am getting up, getting to my feet and I am walking head high to my bedroom where I'm going to sleep this off. I do not need to wait here, listening to the key turning in the lock, the door being pushed open and Dane rushing in.

'Do I need to call an ambulance?' I hear my neighbour say anxiously.

'I don't know,' Dane calls back. He stops beside me, then gets down to his knees and brushes a hand over my cheek. 'I'm here, Zari, I'm here,' he coos.

They're the last words I hear before everything disappears.

JUNE 2015

'I'd ask if you're bride or groom, but seeing as you're a bridesmaid, I'm guessing bride?' Dane has come to stand beside me at the bar. I'd been careful, so careful, not to be anywhere near him or to be alone for too long so he'd feel brave enough to speak to me.

But while we were buying drinks, Moses had spotted one of Randal's aunties sitting alone and had gone to speak to her. She was fine, but Moses couldn't help flashing his good-guy halo when it came to the aunties. I loved that about him. The moment he'd gone, though, Dane had arrived.

I didn't turn to Dane, but I wished the sound of his voice didn't hit a certain part of me, that the warmth of his body wasn't so deliciously welcome. 'Yes, bride. Elise and I went to school together and we drifted apart for a while. But now she's moved to Brighton, we've become best friends again. Having said that, my partner is "groom" and they met through us, so I'm "groom", too, I suppose.'

'I'm guessing your partner was the man who couldn't take his eyes off you,' he said.

'How's your wife?'

'We're not married.'

'Yet. I'm guessing you actually mean we're not married "yet".'

'I guess.'

The barman placed my prosecco and Moses's whisky in front of me. Before I could give him my card, Dane handed over his in payment. 'Thank you,' I said, still not looking at him.

He edged closer to me, so close I felt my body moving to bring us closer still. 'Was cutting me off the only way?' he asked, the hurt in his voice evident despite the volume of the music, and sounds of people dancing. 'Did I really not get to be your friend any longer?'

He'd spent weeks – months – trying to contact me, trying to speak to me and I couldn't. Wouldn't. The humiliation was too great. It was one thing not to have feelings for me, but to lie about a relationship with someone I knew . . . it was all too much. It showed me the lack of basic respect he had for me as a friend.

'I didn't ask, are you bride or groom?' I replied, ignoring his question.

He sighed. 'The groom is my second cousin. I'm sure there's a removed or two in there.'

'I see.'

'I didn't mean to hurt you, Zari,' he tried again. 'I had no idea you felt like that about me . . . if I had—'

'You would have told me who you were screwing before I humiliated myself?'

'She was your friend. We thought—'

'Let's get this straight: she was never my friend, Dane.'

Leigh had never been my friend, and I resented the fact she had twisted the truth so much he believed it. She was someone I had worked with a few years earlier who had basically bullied everyone. Being slightly new to the media department, I was the only person who wouldn't put up with it. I decided, even though everyone else was too scared, because of her position and her ability to cry at the drop of a hat, to put in a formal complaint. After she was called in to HR for a 'chat', she had a Road-to-Damascus-type epiphany and changed her ways. She brought me flowers and publicly apologised so I had to give her another chance because otherwise I would have looked bad. I didn't believe she'd changed. No way. And when I left, she spent a lot of time trying to keep in touch. I avoided her as much as possible, even when I saw her on nights out with other people. She was careful to hide the general contempt and disdain she had for most people, but in unguarded moments I saw it sitting behind her eyes whenever she thought no one was watching her. Leigh thought she was better than most people, but obviously didn't have a big enough pool of friends to avoid the ones she particularly didn't like.

If there was one thing that was certain, it was that Leigh had never been my friend.

Dane frowned at me, clearly confused. I couldn't explain to him what our relationship was really like because, well, as he was still with her five years later, he obviously loved her. But I couldn't let him go on thinking she was some great ally of mine, either.

'We worked together,' I stated, keeping the anger out of my voice. 'I often saw her when she was at other people's nights out because she basically invited herself to them. Like my birthday night out – one of my friends mentioned we were going out, Leigh turns up unannounced and uninvited. She'd brought me a present and she started buying people drinks, so how could I tell her to leave without *me* looking terrible? On my birthday. So, no, she wasn't my friend. There was no need for you and her to lie about your relationship. To allow me to humiliate myself like that.'

'I didn't like keeping it from you, but Leigh kept saying you'd told her how much you disliked people in your circle going out together because it always led to awkwardness when it went wrong.'

'You've known me longer than her – when have I ever said something like that?'

Dane said nothing; he had no answer because what he was saying was nonsense.

'Were you not going to tell me until you got married, or something?' I asked next.

'No, of course not. That was why I came to stay. I wanted to tell you, to explain, and then she sent me a message when I was on the train down saying she'd done a test and she was pregnant. My mind was blown and I couldn't tell you without saying she was pregnant, so I kept quiet.'

Pregnant? *Pregnant*? 'So you've got a child?' I asked.

He shook his head. 'No, it was a false positive. It said she was pregnant when she wasn't.'

Pregnant my left foot! I didn't bother telling him how rare false positives are – you're more likely to be told you're not pregnant when you are than the other way round. She had obviously said it to throw him off telling me, but why? Was she scared I'd tell him we weren't friends? That I'd declare my undying love and he'd dump her?

'Right,' I said.

'And you didn't humiliate yourself. You basically said what I'd been waiting half my life to hear.'

My gaze snapped up to look at him, then. He was staring intently at me. Seconds passed, each one of them like several lifetimes where everything around us faded, until we were the only ones left in the room, the whole world for all I knew. 'What did you say?'

'I've been in love with you since we first met. I've tried to ask you out dozens of times over the years. And every time you'd make a joke of it, or you'd invite other people. You kept pushing me away, or acting like you could never see me as anything other than a friend.'

Was this true? All the hugs, the late-night talks on the phone, the nights out initiated by him, was that him trying to get things going?

'Why didn't you just tell me, if this is all true?'

'I tried, many times. I tried to talk to you that night at your party. You looked incredible, and I was determined to tell you. I didn't even care how you reacted, I wanted you to know. But you kept running away. *Every* time I came near you, you ran. After a while, I figured that you'd worked out what I was going to say and didn't want to hear it.'

I kept running away because I kept chickening out of telling him how I felt.

'Why didn't you just kiss me or something?'

He pulled a face. 'I've never felt right about kissing a woman unless I know she's at least partially interested. And anyway, why didn't *you* tell me? You don't go from nothing to love overnight. Why didn't you say something?'

'Honey,' from nowhere, Leigh appeared. 'You said you were getting us drinks, and here you are, no drinks and talking to . . . oh, hello.'

She was good, I had to give her that. Pretending she didn't notice who he was talking to and hadn't come over to put herself in the middle of us.

'Hello,' I replied, matching the coolness from her tone.

'I thought it was you up there,' she said. 'You were an *excellent* bridesmaid.'

'And you were an *excellent* guest,' I replied. 'You both were.'

'Thank you,' she said with a gracious smile before she wrapped her hand around Dane's. An arrow of agony shot through me: she could do that and I couldn't. Because I hadn't been brave enough; because I'd given in to the fears of humiliation instead of the longing in my heart.

'I hope you enjoy the rest of the wedding,' I said after a beat of awkward silence passed between us. I picked up my drink and Moses's drink. 'Oh, and congratulations,' I said, nodding to the solitaire diamond engagement ring on Leigh's finger. 'I wish you all good things.'

'Zari,' Dane called as I walked away. I stopped and turned back. 'I'll A-B-C you?' He came up with that when we worked in the warehouse and those were my assigned aisles.

'Not if I-D-E-F you first,' I replied, instantly recalling his aisles.

He grinned, and I couldn't help grinning too. He dipped his head in the smallest of nods, I dipped mine in return. We needed to go back to how it was before – him out of my head, me focused on Moses and our life together; him continuing his life with Leigh. It was honestly that simple.

AUGUST 2020

Another sensation. Everything was blurry, confused and confusing, but I had another sensation of being lifted. Someone had their arms around me and was lifting me up. *That'd better not be you, Dane,* I said with my non-working mouth. *That had better not be you picking me up and carrying me to my bedroom.*

NOVEMBER 2019

The things I do for my friends. Speed dating. I didn't even do dating at a normal speed, let alone rapidly. But Francesca had no other single female friends.

The downstairs of the bar, not far from the seafront, had perfectly modulated lighting, low music and well-priced drinks – everything was conducive to having a good time. I would have been having a great time if I hadn't, so far, had three four-minute 'dates' with Mr Too Loud, Mr Too Quiet, and Mr Too Arrogant. Who was going to be next, Mr Too Self-Effacing? Mr Too Boring To Speak? Mr—

The next 'Mr' pulled out the chair opposite me and I automatically clicked on the timer without looking up.

'Ah,' he said as he lowered himself opposite me. 'Ah.'

I looked up as a lightning bolt of shock ricocheted through me. 'Ah, indeed,' I replied.

'Would it make any difference if I told you I was here with a friend?' Dane said.

'Why would it make any difference to me? It's your wife you need to worry about.' They finally got married two years ago – Elise and Randal went to their wedding that I (unsurprisingly) wasn't invited to. Although Moses and I had split up by then, we were still the best of friends. I felt nothing when Elise told me about the wedding. And *everything*. It felt like a crater opened up in the middle of my chest, and then it felt like oil had been poured on the troubled waters of my mind about this. Not long after, they had a baby boy, which further cemented their relationship. It was truly over and out for me and him.

'I don't have a wife,' he said, looking me right in the eye. 'We split up eight months ago. I really am here to offer moral support to my friend.'

My chest was suddenly aflutter, my heart beating in quadruple time. Opportunity. OPPORTUNITY. 'Me too,' I replied.

Silence. Silence from both of us as we let the revelation settle between us.

'Hello, my name is Dane,' he said to break the silence. 'I'm from London but I've been staying in Brighton for work these last few months. I go back to London every weekend to visit my son. My interests are music, movies and reading. I wasn't looking for anything tonight, but I think I've found her.'

I swallowed the excitement and fear that was clogging up my throat and trembling my fingers.

'Hello, Dane, my name is Zari. I'm also from London but I live here in Brighton. I don't have any children. My interests are music, movies and reading. I'm not looking for anything or anyone, but they say it's when you're not looking is when you're most likely to find someone.'

Beeez-beeez-beeeezzzz, the buzzer sounded, cutting our chat short. 'I'll A B C you later?' he asked.

I nodded. 'Not if I D E F you first.'

AUGUST 2020

'They're going to send an ambulance,' Dane says urgently. 'You should have told me about your heart. You should have told me everything. I would have come sooner.'

Why would you have come sooner? I reply silently. *Why did you bother to come at all?*

NOVEMBER 2019

'Hello, you,' he said, standing in the dark corridor of my flat.

I'd said goodbye to Francesca earlier, who'd been thrilled with five matches (I'd had two), and he said goodbye to his friend who, it turned out, was matched with Francesca. I could barely remember the taxi ride back to my flat sitting beside him – all I knew was that Dane and I were single at the same time, we were in the same city and we were about to be together.

'Hello, you,' I replied, barely able to speak.

He reached out, cupped my face in his hand, lowered his face to mine. 'Hello, you,' he whispered again, his lips a millimetre from mine.

'Hello—' I breathed as his lips covered mine. My body instantly moved towards his, his body came to find mine.

We undressed each other in my dark bedroom, savouring every moment of revealing ourselves to each other. We kissed again, his skin warm and smooth against mine, our desire heady and intoxicating.

On the bed, he kissed me and I kissed him back, before he broke away and moved down, and down and down until he pressed his lips between my legs. Pleasure pulsed through every part of my body, and I pressed myself back against the bed, weak and whimpering with desire, until he pulled away, moved up and pushed into me, hard, his eyes staring down into mine as he began to thrust and thrust, bringing us closer and closer and closer to ecstasy . . .

AUGUST 2020

Dane is still talking, apologising, telling me what he thinks I want to hear. But all I can think is that he shouldn't be here. He should be in London, exactly where he wanted to be, where he *chose* to be.

NOVEMBER 2019

'I still can't quite believe this has happened,' Dane said to me. We faced each other in bed.

'Neither can I,' I said and immediately bit my lower lip. I kept biting my lower lip to stop myself doing what I did all those years ago and blurting out the L word. I seriously wanted to, though. I wanted to shout, 'I love you!' over and over to get it out of the way. To see, if nothing else, if he'd say it back.

'All those years we wasted,' he said.

'Don't think that. This is when we were supposed to happen. Everything happens when it's supposed to.'

'You believe that?'

'Yes. I have to. If I didn't, it'd drive me crazy to think of all that missed time. And if you don't, that would mean you wouldn't have your son.'

'True,' he stated. His face, relaxed as it had been, was suddenly furrowed and closed in.

'Are you worried about how Leigh will react?' I asked.

'Yes and no,' he replied.

'What does that even mean?'

'It means . . .' he sighed, a bit too dramatically for my liking.

It was going to go wrong. I had let myself relax, I had allowed my heart to beat outside of its boundary, I allowed myself to feel something, and I was going to be punished for it. 'You're going to screw me over, aren't you?' I said to him. 'The sex wasn't all that for you, so you're going to go running off, throwing something about getting back together with your wife over your shoulder.'

'I wouldn't do that to you, I *couldn't* do that to you,' he replied. 'And the sex was amazing.' He paused, and took a deep breath. 'The thing is, there's this thing that could impact on us, in ways I can't quite fathom, yet. But if I tell you, as it sort of involves you, I'll be bringing you into this . . . mess, and that's what—'

'I can't stand this, just tell me.'

'All right,' he replied.

I braced myself again: held my breath, stilled my body, stopped my racing mind.

'Leigh cheated on me. For pretty much the entire time we were together. She said it was because she could tell I was secretly in love with you. She wasn't wrong about me being in love with you, but she was never second best. When I was with her, I was one hundred per cent with her. You never featured. I found out because earlier this year someone sent me a photo of her with the other guy. She flat-out denied it until I showed her the picture.

'A lot of talking and tears later, she told me that Malachi was my son, because she thought I doubted it. I didn't. Not even for a second. But she kept saying I must have a problem with it, and she suggested we did a DNA test to prove he was mine. I said I didn't need a test to prove that. She insisted. Turns out, biologically, he isn't "mine".'

Oh, I thought.

'But like I said to her before, it doesn't make any difference to me. He's my little boy, that's the truth of it. She felt bad about what she'd done, though, and ultimately *she* couldn't deal with it, so we split. I see him every weekend. Every other weekend he stays with me.'

'Sounds like you've got an amicable relationship, so why are you— Ah, I see, you're worried that once she finds out about us, she'll make things difficult for you to see your son because it'll prove her right about you never being committed to her.'

'Got it in one.'

'So are you suggesting we keep this quiet for a while?'

'Well—'

'Because I'm not going to do that,' I ploughed on. 'I'm no one's dirty little secret. You want to be with me, then you tell people, I tell people. You don't tell people, then we're not together. It's really that simple.'

Oh me! I could talk my way out of a relationship much faster than anyone I know, but this was the truth of it: I had lived with a boundary around my heart for so long, that I felt like it had become physical. I was in the process of going for various tests because of potential cardiac problems, and I couldn't put any more strain on myself by letting him hide our relationship away.

I turned my head and Dane was staring at me with a rather impressed look on his face. 'Remember a while back I asked you not to change?'

I nodded.

'Well, I'm glad you have. I like confident, nobody's fool Zari.' He moved to climb on top of me. 'I like her a lot. No secrets. No keeping quiet.' I ran my hand along the full length of his erection, loving the pleasure it created on his face. The other hand I placed on his cheek, keeping his head in the position where he could only look into my eyes, and I could look into his. Slowly I guided him into me again. Both of us sighed loudly as we became one, and both of us stared into each other's eyes as we carefully, luxuriously, made love all over again.

AUGUST 2020

'Why are you here?' I manage to ask him. 'I mean, why now?'

He keeps getting up to look out of the window. Obviously waiting for the ambulance to arrive.

'Randal called me . . . a lot of things. I mean, he rang me, and after a lot of abuse that I think mostly came from Elise, he told me everything. And he said you'd cut yourself off from everyone, that you were all alone and it was all my fault because of how much I'd hurt you.

'He also told me that it was Elise who sent me the evidence of Leigh cheating. Although you never said anything to her, she said that it was so obvious at her wedding how we felt about each other. She couldn't stand by and let Leigh carry on cheating.'

He comes back across the room. 'I'm so sorry. For everything. I'm so very, very sorry.'

I'm going to pass out, I realise. I'm going to pass—

NOVEMBER 2019

'Whose house is that?' Leigh's voice was particularly loud coming out of the speaker of his phone during his video call. He'd just spent twenty minutes talking to Malachi, as they happily updated each other on the latest news in their lives, even though they'd talked for the same amount of time last night. The relationship he had with his son was joyous to listen to: they talked and shared like old friends, and last night, Dane had told Malachi he was staying at his friend Zari's house. I was sure this was what prompted Leigh to ask Dane to hang on the line while she sent Malachi to put on his pyjamas. I was sitting on the other end of the sofa, out of sight, legs curled up underneath me, book in my lap, pretending to read.

We'd kind of settled into a routine of being together after only five days. It didn't feel like five days, of course. It felt like he'd always wake up here, make me a cup of warm water with lemon before he went to work, then, in the evening, we'd practically tear each other's clothes off, we'd eat dinner, he'd call his son and we'd rip each other's clothes off all over again. The other day he'd even taken a few hours off work to come with me to the hospital for my latest heart appointment.

'It's Zari's flat, here in Brighton.'

'What happened to the place where you were staying?' she asked.

'Nothing,' he replied. If he minded his ex questioning him, he didn't show it. 'It's still there.'

'Why are you at *her* flat then?'

I watched him take a deep, courage-giving breath before saying, 'I'm staying here . . . because we're seeing each other.'

Silence. A long, long stretch of silence. 'I knew it,' she eventually stated. 'I knew the second those test results came back you'd go sniffing round her again.'

'I didn't go sniffing round her,' he replied calmly. 'The last time I saw Zari was at Elise and Randal's wedding, four years ago. Then I ran into her last week.'

'And she just happened to be single? Yeah, right, pull the other one, it's got bells on. You two are pathetic if you think anyone's going to believe that.'

'It's the truth,' he said simply. 'And I'd like to remind you that I wanted to stay married. You were the one who was convinced that my feelings towards you and him had changed.'

Leigh paused dramatically. Then a sob, a small, near-silent sob. And then another. 'Did you ever love me?' she asked through the sobs. 'Did our relationship ever mean anything?'

I closed my eyes, wondering what he was going to say. I was sitting right there, and she was 'crying' in his face. What would he say that would make it all right for her and all right for me?

'Yes, Leigh, I did. Of course I did. You know I did. But we're not together any more. You're seeing someone else, you have been for months. We can all move on and be happy now, can't we?'

She continued to sob down the phone. I was immune to Leigh's sobs, having seen them weaponised to get her out of trouble years ago, but I could feel the anxiety coming off Dane as she continued to 'cry'.

How many times had she cried to get what she wanted over the years? How many times had he given in for an easy life? 'Look, Leigh, this isn't helping any of us. I'm going to go.'

'OK, OK,' she said, trying to stem her flow of tears. 'Please don't come down tomorrow.'

'What?' he replied.

'I know you want to see Malachi, but I need time to process this and I can't do that if you're here. I'll tell him something came up and you can video-call him as normal.'

'You're not being fair,' he said.

'This is so huge for me, I need some space to spend time with my son.'

With my eyes closed, I could hear the inflection, the ever so slight but very definite extra emphasis on 'my'. She was warning Dane. By keeping him away this weekend and her use of 'my son', she was warning him what was to come.

Dane sighed. There really was nothing he could do. 'Next week for definite,' he said.

'Yes, yes,' she said, then cut the call.

'It'll be fine,' he said, his words sounding hollow. 'It'll be fine.'

We both knew it wouldn't be fine. We both knew worse was to come.

AUGUST 2020

'I love you,' Dane says as they load me into the ambulance. They won't let him come with me no matter what he says – if he wants to accompany me to the hospital, then he has to get there under his own steam.

Don't bother coming to the hospital now, I try to shout through my oxygen mask. *I've been perfectly fine without you all these months, so don't play the good guy now.*

DECEMBER 2019

'I'm sorry. I love you, and I'm so sorry,' he spoke without pausing on the phone, his old trick of saying things quickly so I wouldn't have a chance to interrupt. 'She wants us to try again. She thinks she gave up on us too quickly, and what she wants more than anything is for us to make it work for Malachi's sake. He's loved having me back these past few days, he's so noticeably happier, so I feel I owe it to him to try.'

Three missed weekends it'd taken – she'd kept Dane away from his son for three weekends, and by the time he was begging her to let him see their child, we all pretty much knew it was over for him and me. Except, I suppose, I thought he might actually come back and tell me in person. But no, a phone call was all I was worth, apparently.

'I'm sorry. I'm so sorry.'

Stop saying that! I wanted to snap. *Stop saying that because it doesn't mean anything.* 'And you couldn't do this to my face, because . . . ?' I asked, sounding far braver than I was feeling.

'Because if I see you, I won't be able to leave. And then I'll have to choose between you and my child. If I don't see you, I can . . . I'm sorry, I'm so sorry.'

'Were you always this weak, Dane? Or is it a new thing you've developed just for me?'

'He's my son,' he stated.

Yes, he was. And that was Leigh's weapon that there was no defence against. 'I hate to say I told you so at such a time,' I said, 'but I totally told you so. I should have known you'd break my faulty heart all over again. When will I ever learn?'

'I'm—'

I cut him off. I had to, for my sanity. To be able to keep going after this latest test result.

AUGUST 2020

'She's so beautiful,' Dane says. 'So beautiful.'

I'm too weak to hold her. The last few hours have been a blur and more than one nurse has hinted that the level my blood pressure got to with my type of heart condition (a specific type of angina), they'd all been surprised I had survived.

'And I'm sure that's not the only thing people will remember her for,' I say.

He looks up at me, suddenly serious. 'I was an idiot. I can't believe I thought . . . I didn't last two weeks living back there. I'm so sorry I put you through all this.'

'So, if you were only in the house two weeks, where've you been all the rest of the time?'

'Living alone, doing lots of thinking. Getting money together for a legal battle because Leigh's told me she's going to fight dirty. But on the plus side, I am on the birth certificate, I have been involved in his upbringing, and, you know, I'm not going to give up.'

'Good for you, Dane. You finally got yourself a backbone.'

A grin spreads slowly across his face. 'I deserve that.' He looks mollified, then upset again. 'The amount of times I wanted to call you but couldn't because what I did was unforgivable.'

'Yes, yes it was.'

'So you're not going to forgive me?'

I stare at him. The man I love. And I do love him. Can't stop myself, even if I did start to hate him. The father of my child. 'Let's not talk about that right now,' I say. I don't know if I can forgive him, but I don't want our daughter's first hours to be marred by such talk.

'Actually, let's talk about it right now. Us not talking about it is what got us into this mess. Let's talk about it. We've seen the world change so much, we've learnt what is important – are we really going to avoid stuff because it's difficult?'

He has a point. 'All right: you hurt me so badly I don't know if I'll ever be able to forgive you.'

Dane looks down at his daughter, smiles at her and then looks up to face me. 'I understand that. And I'm so sorry. There's nothing I can do to undo it, but I *can* remind you that I love you. I *can* let you know I will wait as long as it's necessary for you to believe I love you and that I will never hurt you again. I *can* tell you that I'm going to devote myself to this little one. And I *can* promise you that I will do everything in my power to show you how much I love you from this day until eternity.'

'Eternity is a big word and a big, big time.'

'You're worth it. You're worth every second.' He stares down at his daughter. 'And so is she.'

'Yes, she is.'

'Do you think we're going to make it, Zari?' he asks earnestly.

I look at him holding our daughter, and I flash back to him standing beside a pallet in the warehouse where we worked. He was wearing our awful brown and orange uniform, but his eyes were bright and his face was smiley, and just being around him made me happy, made my joyful heart beat in triple time.

We've wasted so much time. So much time. And haven't I learnt that we need to not squander time? That it is precious, and we need to spend as much of it as we can with the people we love?

'Yes,' I say to him, 'I think we will.'

Author Biographies

Rowan Hisayo Buchanan is a Japanese-British-Chinese-American writer. Her debut novel *Harmless Like You* won the Authors' Club Best First Novel Award and a Betty Trask Award. Her latest novel, *Starling Days*, was short-listed for the Costa Novel Award. She has written for *The Atlantic*, *Granta* magazine and *The White Review* among other publications.

Sara Collins studied law at the London School of Economics before qualifying as a barrister in 1994. She worked as a lawyer for seventeen years before obtaining a master's degree in creative writing with distinction from Cambridge University in 2016, where she was the recipient of the Michael Holroyd Prize. Prior to publication, her debut novel *The Confessions of Frannie Langton* was shortlisted for the Lucy Cavendish Fiction Prize, and was published in 2020 by Penguin in the UK and HarperCollins in the US to critical acclaim. The novel has been sold for translation into more than fourteen languages, as well as being optioned for television, and has made an appearance in the 'best of' lists in *Oprah* magazine, the *Guardian*, the *Observer*, and *Essence*, to name a few, as well as on Apple and Amazon. *Oprah* magazine named her one of the Women of Summer 2019, and the *Sunday Times* called her 'a star in the making'. *The Confessions of Frannie Langton* is the winner of the 2019 Costa First Novel Award.

Daniellé DASH is a scripted comedy and drama development executive at Balloon Entertainment, where she works with under-represented and emerging voices. She writes regularly about race, gender and popular culture on her website DanielleDASH.com, is a columnist at *Trench Magazine* and contributes to *Black Ballad*, the *Guardian*, *Stylist* and *Grazia*.

Sareeta Domingo is the author of *If I Don't Have You* (Jacaranda Books, 2020) and *The Nearness of You* (Piatkus Books, 2016), and is creator, editor and a contributing writer of romantic fiction anthology *Who's Loving You* (Trapeze, 2021). She has also written numerous erotic short stories and an erotic novella with Pavilion Books. Her books for Young Adults are published under S. A. Domingo and include *Love, Secret Santa* (Hachette Children's, 2019). She has contributed to publications including *gal-dem*, *Black Ballad*, *Stylist* and *TOKEN Magazine*, and has taken part in events for Hachette Books, Winchester Writers' Festival, Black Girls Book Club and Bare Lit Festival, among others. She lives in southeast London.

sareetadomingo.com
@SareetaDomingo

Sara Jafari is a British-Iranian author and editor based in London. On the side, she runs *TOKEN Magazine*, a literature and arts print magazine which showcases writing and artwork by under-represented writers and artists. She is a contributor to *'I Will Not Be Erased': Our stories about growing up as people of colour*, and her debut novel, *The Mismatch*, is published in 2021.

Dorothy Koomson is the award-winning author of sixteen books and several short stories. She wrote her first, unpublished novel when she was thirteen and has been making up stories ever since. Her third novel, *My Best Friend's Girl*, was chosen for the Richard & Judy Book Club Summer Reads of 2006 and reached number two on the *Sunday Times* Bestseller List. Her books *The Ice Cream Girls* and *The Rose Petal Beach* were shortlisted for the National Book Awards, and a TV adaptation loosely based on *The Ice Cream Girls* was broadcast in 2013. Dorothy has lived and worked in Leeds, London and Sydney, Australia and is currently residing in Brighton on the South Coast.

dorothykoomson.co.uk

Kuchenga is a writer from north London. She is an avid reader of black women's literature as a matter of survival. She is the child of pan-Africanist parents who encouraged her to cultivate a well-used personal library as a form of protection and an asset of immeasurable value. Her personal mission as a Black transsexual woman is to live a long, healthy life and archive her writing and imagery for the use of Black girls in the future who are in pursuit of yet more evidence that they are worthy. She has been published in many online magazines including *Vogue* and *Harper's Bazaar*.

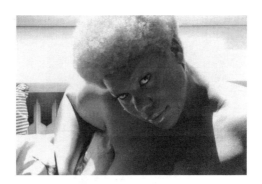

Kelechi Okafor is a writer, presenter, influencer and tour de force in challenging how we think about race and femininity in tandem and is a regular media contributor. Her podcast *Say Your Mind* is centred around social commentary on current affairs and pop culture from a Black-British woman's perspective. Kelechi has appeared on the BBC Three show *Work It*, which draws on her experience as a fitness expert and her work in pole dancing and twerking as a form of enabling women to embrace their bodies without hyper-sexualisation, particularly with victims of abuse.

Amna Saleem is a Scottish Pakistani screenwriter, journalist and broadcaster based in Glasgow with several TV projects in production. In 2020, her script, *Psychic Overload*, was one of just ten chosen from a BBC Writersroom open call which pulled in a record-breaking 6,408 submissions. The resulting short was produced and shot entirely over video chat in keeping with the rules of lockdown. Her very first sitcom, *Beta Female*, can be found on BBC Radio 4. Amna has written for publications such as the *Guardian*, *GQ*, *Glamour* and *HuffPost*. She can often be seen on screen digesting the news or compulsively oversharing online. Making people laugh so hard that they temporarily forget their worries is her favourite thing to do in the whole world

Varaidzo is a writer, editor and artist. She is a contributor to the bestselling anthology *The Good Immigrant*, and her short story *Bus Stop* was shortlisted for the *Guardian* 4th Estate BAME Prize 2018. Her artwork has been featured in the *Metro* and *Vice UK*. She has presented radio shows for BBC Radio 4, Reprezent Radio and Worldwide FM, and is the producer of the podcast 'Search History'. In her personal work, she has a particular interest in documenting stories of the African diaspora in the digital age through film, art, audio and fiction. She currently splits her time between Peckham in London and Liverpool.

Acknowledgements

This anthology was born of my deep desire for plentiful and amplified voices from global-majority backgrounds writing stories of romantic love. It was also born of my love and admiration for writers whose work is not easily categorised. I am still astounded by every single one of the authors in this anthology, who were willing to acknowledge my reaching out to them, and who lent their incredibly literary talents. This project would not exist without them and I am so deeply honoured to have my work among theirs, and that they were open to my editorial insights on their stories. I am unendingly grateful.

I must also extend my deepest thanks to Katie Ellis-Brown, who listened to my idea, responded so enthusiastically, and shepherded this project into life at Trapeze. Huge thanks as well to the fantastic Marleigh Price, who took up the baton and worked tirelessly to support and uphold this anthology – the perfect editorial partner. Thank you so much for all of your insights and help.

ACKNOWLEDGEMENTS

I want to acknowledge the incredible work of Nikesh Shukla and all the contributors to *The Good Immigrant* – truly so many of us move in your wake and were fuelled by the success of your pioneering anthology. I hope others are inspired by this project to collect and amplify short fiction!

All my love to my husband Will, my twin brother Lawrence, my parents Larry, Valda, my sister-in-law Deirdre, and to all of my family all over the world. I feel you constantly buoying me up and egging me on!

To my wonderful friends, Lulu, Micallar and Cicelia, I love you all, ladies – thank you for supporting me and believing in me. Thank you as well to Mel and Nat of Black Girls Book Club, and to all the incredible women I have met through BGBC. More books for us, more power to us!

To Sara Keane, my agent, thank you for helping to usher this book into existence, in particular with all the complexities of working out a deal for an anthology like this! I so appreciate it.

And thank you so much to you, dear reader, for purchasing this book and absorbing each of these stories. May you be loved.

Credits

Sareeta Domingo and Trapeze would like to thank everyone at Orion who worked on the publication of *Who's Loving You*.

Editorial
Marleigh Price
Katie Brown
Lucinda McNeile

Copy editor
Anne O'Brien

Proofreader
Jenny Page

Audio
Paul Stark
Amber Bates

Contracts
Anne Goddard

Paul Bulos
Jake Alderson

Design
Lucie Stericker
Rabab Adams
Joanna Ridley
Nick May

Editorial Management
Jane Hughes

Finance
Jasdip Nandra
Rabale Mustafa
Ibukun Ademefun

Marketing
Lucy Cameron

Publicity
Francesca Pearce
Patricia Deever

Production
Claire Keep

Sales
Jennifer Wilson
Esther Waters
Victoria Laws
Ellie Kyrke-Smith
Frances Doyle
Georgina Cutler

Operations
Jo Jacobs
Lisa Pryde
Lucy Brem